A Thousand Sunsets

KAYLA MARTIN

For all the shy people who were too nervous to take a chance on themselves.

And for my family, you inspired this book and I'm sorry in advance for what you'll have to read. But it's not as bad as that one year when the aunts passed around 50 Shades of Grey.

"My heart... It feels like my chest can barely contain it.
Like it's trying to escape because it doesn't belong to me
anymore. It belongs to you. And if you wanted it, I'd wish
for nothing in exchange, no gifts, no goods, no
demonstrations of devotion. Nothing but knowing you
loved me too. Just your heart, in exchange for mine."

-Yvaine, *Stardust* (2007)

AUTHOR'S NOTE

Dear Reader,

A Thousand Sunsets is very near and dear to my heart. This story is based on my family and our annual summer vacation, where we have had eighty people attend before. This is the place where I practiced driving, flirted with boys, tried smoking weed for the first time, and some people in my family even found love. I am lucky to be so close with my extended family and cousins, which is what I wanted to highlight in this book, and this series.

Being able to showcase these types of relationships was not something I was willing to cut down on. So while there are a lot of characters in this book, know I did my best to keep it as small as I could. There is no need for you to have to remember every single character, as some will come up more in later books, but be prepared that the whole family is around throughout this one. Included in this book is a Murphy Family Tree and camp map for reference, if you get lost.

Please also be aware that this story contains multiple open door romance scenes that have on-page consensual sexual intimacy. If you are interested in knowing which chapters these scenes happen during you can visit the Dicktionary before the acknowledgments.

This story covers the following topics: biphobia, slut-shaming, underage drinking, mentions of parent death (past), strained parent relationships, depression, and therapy. I hope I have done these topics justice based on my own experiences and through the guidance of my alpha and beta readers. As always, your mental health is the most important thing, please take care of yourself first before anything.

All my best,
   Kayla

PLAYLIST

Over the course of writing this book music was used to get in the right headspace. The songs on this playlist represent the overall story and vibes of *A Thousand Sunsets*. If you enjoy book playlists you can find it on Spotify by searching "A Thousand Sunsets"

Saturday Sun by Vance Joy
Electric Feel by MGMT
Talk Too Much by COIN
Electric Love by BØRNS
Cruel Summer by Taylor Swift
blind by ROLE MODEL
Candy Wine by Lostboycrow
Wonder by Shawn Mendes
Are You Bored Yet? by Wallows, Clairo
Watermelon Sugar by Harry Styles
Summer Days by Martin Garrix, Macklemore, Fall Out Boy
Loverboy by A-Wall
River by Miley Cyrus
Latch by Disclosure, Sam Smith
Nonsense by Sabrina Carpenter
Late Night Talking by Harry Styles
Golden Hour by Kacey Musgraves
Come With Me by Surfaces, salem ilese
Strawberry Sunscreen by Lostboycrow
Do It 2 Me by Allstar Weekend
Rose Colored Lenses by Miley Cyrus
Animal by Kesha

Summer Love by One Direction
Fire for You by Cannons
Death By A Thousand Cuts by Taylor Swift
Hold the Sun by Maya Hawke
Summer by Kesha
A Thousand Years by Christina Perri

MURPHY FAMILY TREE

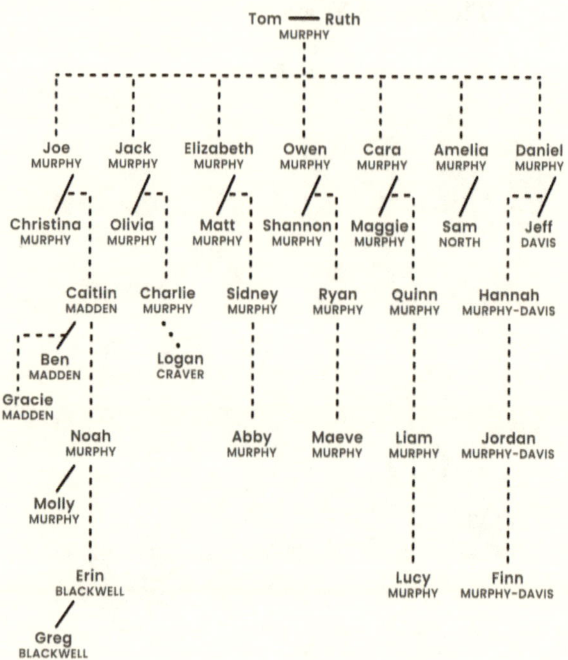

CAMPGROUND MAP

For a full color map visit kaylamartinauthor.com

ONE

SIDNEY

I can smell the morning summer air of fresh cut grass flowing through the open front door as I sit glued to the dining room chair in a staredown with my laptop, while Mom runs in and out of the house packing last minute things. I watch my reflection on the screen, my head resting on top of my knee, with my too-short hair falling out of a messy bun. I've been sitting here for so long the cup of coffee in my hand is now cold.

I tap the touchpad before the screen can lock, the email that's been taunting me since it arrived stares back at me. It's the final step to the next phase in my life, and for such a simple thing, it feels like more than an email.

I check on the other tabs I have opened, including the security deposit form and Google Maps with the route from my new apartment to my new job mapped out. I don't understand how a thirteen mile drive in upstate New York can take me twenty minutes, but in Los Angeles it's going to take an hour. I'm due to start an entry-level position at one of the best marketing agencies in LA next month and I know it's going to be an adjustment.

Once I submit the deposit, there's no going back. I will officially be moving across the country by myself. It doesn't sound too bad, but considering I've never lived anywhere alone, it's a bit intimidating. There's also the fact that I don't know anyone out there, but that's what I want, I think.

"Sidney! Hurry up, we have to leave," my mom calls from the kitchen, pulling me out of my thoughts.

"Five minutes," I shout, taking the last sip of my cold coffee, hoping to find some courage through the caffeine to hit submit. I distract myself from my laptop and stand up to grab my mini floral backpack, double-checking to make sure I have last-minute items like my phone charger, deodorant, and my glasses case. I pivot back around and stare at the large submit button. Did it get bigger? Taking a deep breath I do a quick click of my touchpad, and it's done.

I send a short email to the landlord, rereading to confirm I didn't embarrass myself with any mistakes or misspellings of her name. One of my biggest pet peeves is when someone's name is in the email and the recipient spells it wrong. If someone's name is in their email you should be able to spell it right. It's 'Sidney' not 'Sydney', people, it's not hard. After confirming three times that her name is spelled right, I hit send and power down my laptop, slamming it closed. No turning back now. Grabbing my backpack and sunglasses, I head toward the kitchen.

"Good, there you are," my mom says as she comes whipping around the corner, forcing me to step back into the dining room so she doesn't knock me over. Her blonde curly hair, sprinkled with gray, bounces as she comes to a stop. I'm essentially a mirror of my mother with my blonde curls, blue eyes, pale Irish skin, and short height but my face is slightly rounder like my dad's.

"Jeez, Mom, slow down."

"Sorry honey, I'm running around making sure we have everything. Here, take this." She shoves a basket of food into my arms. "This needs to go into the camper. Your dad is out there now."

I grab the basket from her and adjust my backpack, making sure I don't drop it or the food. "You've been going on this trip every year since you were born. You don't have to worry about forgetting anything."

"You say that now until we get there and have to drive to town right away to get bread." She glares at me.

"Okay, that happened one time. And no one told me I was in charge of packing the bread," I shout the last bit in my defense as she disappears back into the kitchen. I remember they wouldn't stop bringing up my mistake that year. I got embarrassed every time and hated all the attention on me. Slipping on my Crocs, I head out the front door to pass off the food to my dad.

My younger sister, Abby, is already in the backseat of the truck. Her brown hair is tied up on top of her head in a more successful bun than my own. She always looks effortlessly pretty, compared to my bun that's falling out. At least her sweatpants and crewneck are covered in fur. She's on puppy duty this morning, making sure our six-month-old yellow Lab, Sammy, doesn't get in our parents' way.

"Thanks, Sid. Got everything taken care of?" my dad asks, taking the basket from my hands and placing it in the camper. Dad's been up for a few hours now, no doubt tinkering with last-minute things in the camper. His brown salt-and-pepper hair looks like he's been running his hands through it, and there's some oil or grease on his cheek right above his beard.

"Did it a minute ago." I give him a salute, pointing to his face and rubbing my cheek.

"Awesome. That's a big step, kiddo. We're going to miss you out here." He wipes his cheek with the back of his hand and squeezes my shoulder. Meanwhile, I'm on the brink of tears. He's right, this is a big step. I've graduated college, and I'm moving into the next phase of life. I'm excited but also scared shitless.

I'm normally the quiet one while Abby is the social butterfly. When I first applied to the job, I confided in her how scared the idea of leaving home and making such a big change made me. She said it was "typical Taurus behavior," which didn't comfort me as much as she meant it to. I'm aware I have to come out of my perfectly cozy shell, and I need to do it soon. This trip is the perfect excuse for me to see what Cali Sidney could be like. Hopefully she can find the strength to order pizza over the phone.

On top of moving to a new place, this is probably going to be my last camping trip for a while. Every summer, my family spends ten days camping at Sutter State Park in the Thousand Islands on the St. Lawrence River—or the River. When I say family, I mean everyone on my mom's side. Grandparents, aunts, uncles, partners, spouses, second cousins, you name it. If you're a part of the Murphy family, you go to the Islands for the annual family trip. Sometimes I think my dad enjoys it more than my mom, since he was the one to insist that he take the Murphy name when they got married.

In the past, I've never had a problem taking time off from my part-time jobs to go for the full trip before, but now I'm beginning to think I might not be able to attend for a few years.

With starting a new job, I'm nervous to ask for too

much time off, and I would rather fly home for the holidays, weddings, or other future events. I don't see how taking off ten days for the camping trip would pan out, and I'm afraid to admit that to my family. No one ever misses this trip without a good reason, opening them up to loving but passive-aggressive jokes about not being there. My parents and Abby know about my move, but the rest of my family has no idea. I've asked them all to keep quiet about it until I'm ready to tell everyone. Abby and I have cried a few times over the past two months, but she promised to FaceTime me during any family functions that I'll miss.

This year, I plan to soak up all the Islands will give me. If I could bottle up the feeling of being up there, I would guard it with my life.

TWO

SIDNEY

I jolt awake as my sister pokes me in the side with her dagger of a finger.

"Sid, look, we're almost there," she shouts, pointing out the window at a roadside rainbow-themed motel. "I'm so excited! I want to get down to the beach so bad."

I stretch and re-adjust myself in the backseat of the truck to the best of my ability. It's cramped back here with me, Abby, and Sammy, but I still fell asleep about half an hour into the three hour trip. Abby always wakes me up when we pass the motel, since that means we're almost at the campground.

My family has been doing this camping trip for over fifty years. It started with my grandparents, and everyone quickly fell in love with the Islands—it's our special place. Some of my aunts and uncles even met their partners up here. At almost every family function throughout the year I hear people saying, "Are you going to the Islands this year?" Without fail, that will start the second we leave this trip.

I'm really hoping no one asks me about next year,

because I don't have the heart to tell them the truth. We might be a bit codependent as a family, and I'm certain I'm going to get shit for it. I don't want this trip to be any different, and I don't want to be the center of everyone's jokes for ten days. I know I should tell them—but maybe toward the end of the trip.

I roll down the window and inhale the smell of the Islands. We might be a few miles away from the River, but I swear I can smell the water already.

I turn to Abby. "Same plan as usual once we get there?"

"Of course, but let's aim to beat our time from last year. I bet we can get our tent set up in under half an hour," she says confidently.

"Definitely. Do you think Ryan and Maeve are there already? If they're done, we could rope them into helping us." I open my phone tracking app to see where they are. I have almost all of my cousins in this app, which is helpful for times like this when we want to see where everyone is while traveling. "Bingo. They're there." I show her their bubbles on the map.

"Perfect," she claps and starts to collect her things around her, putting on her Crocs and adjusting her sunglasses. "They'll want to go to the beach, too. I'm sure they would be willing to help us."

It's the same routine every time we get there, give or take a few fights from setting up. Everyone sets up their campers and tents as fast as they can so we can head to the beach. My beach bag is already packed, with my swimsuit on the top for easy access.

Dad pulls into the campground, and my heart starts to pound. I've never felt anxious about this trip before but knowing it will potentially be the last one for a while makes everything feel different. He pulls the camper over to the side of the road and gets out to check us in at the registration booth. From here, I can see some family members are already setting up. Everyone has "their sites," similar to when you have a favorite seat in college, but there are no actual assigned seats. Booking sites can get intense when we have to compete with other campers—it's like The Hunger Games: The Islands edition.

I can see the majority of the twelve sites reserved are already in various stages of set up. Campers are being backed in, dogs are being corralled, and some family members are finished with their set-up and are helping others with drinks in their hands.

Aunt Shan's site is set up like she's been here for a week, even though they got here this morning. Their site is always the central hub for our family, home to the nightly campfire and makeshift kitchen where we cook breakfast and dinner. Their two kids, Ryan and Maeve, look like they're finishing setting up a tent.

We're still missing a few people, but I'm sure they will all trickle in as the day goes on. By this afternoon, the Murphy family will be in full vacation mode.

Abby and I hop out of the truck, with Sammy following close behind. I attach his leash to his matching collar, and we head toward our campsite. Mom and Dad are in charge of backing the camper in, so we are tasked with keeping Sammy out of the way and mingling until it's time to unpack. The two rows of campsites create a circle of campers with space in the center for tents and extra picnic tables. It creates the perfect space for everyone to eat together.

"Fucking finally," Maeve shouts as soon as she sees us, throwing the bag she's carrying toward her older brother, who catches it and drops it into the grass. She's already in shorts and a hot pink tank top, her swimsuit strands peeking out around her neck. Her summer-tanned skin is the perfect complement to her long brown hair and deep brown eyes. There's a glow to her skin—no doubt from sweating—that makes her look like a model and not like she just finished setting up a tent. She almost crashes into Abby as she hugs her, and Abby's hair still manages to come out unharmed and beautiful. There's a tinge of jealousy that tugs inside of me. I know I look like a mess right now and the humidity is making my hair frizzier by the second.

"Shit, what time did your parents get you up this morning?" I ask her as she breaks her hug with Abby, giving me a side hug. She bends down to say hi to Sammy, scratching behind his ears.

"Honestly, I have no idea, I blacked out and did whatever they told me to do. Ry and I finished my tent a minute ago. He's got to do his next." She stands back up and adjusts her pink sunglasses, popping her gum right as her brother arrives with a handful of drinks. They could almost be mistaken for twins, even though he's two years older. He's also dressed for the beach, with a pair of green flamingo trunks and a matching tank top.

"Oh my gosh, you're the best." She grabs the drinks from his hands and passes one to each of us before opening one for herself. Abby and Maeve are underage, but in the Islands, everyone drinks since the family always watches out for each other. We all have plastic Mason jar drink cups that we carry around, filled with our drink of choice. Everyone's cups have different colored lids, and it's the safest way to carry drinks around the campground, especially at night when the park rangers are on patrol.

"No problem, gotta start the vacation off right. I'm going to set up my tent. Beach in an hour?" he asks, holding up his drink toward us and taking a sip as he skips away.

"Thirty minutes if we can do it," Abby shouts.

"Let me hook Sammy up to the tree and grab him some water, then we are setting up this tent," I say, downing half of my drink.

"Perfect, I'm dying to get in the water. Cy told me there's a new lifeguard. I guess Luke got fired at the end of last year for getting drunk and trying to steal a boat from the marina. It was a shit show." Maeve sips her drink, cocking her hip with a raise of her eyebrows.

"Wait, have you been down there already? When did you see him?" I ask her, confused as to when she talked to the head lifeguard for Sutter State Park's small beach.

"He saw us setting up when he pulled in this morning. He drove by and said hi and filled us in on the gossip." She takes a quick look around before she leans in and whispers, "You should have seen how flustered Ry got when he came over. I swear it was the cutest thing I've ever seen."

It's been known for a few years that Ryan has a major crush on our favorite lifeguard, but he's too scared to do anything about it. It seems like Cyrus is oblivious to this fact, and somehow Ryan's lack of coherent speech whenever he is around hasn't clued him in.

"I wonder if Ryan will finally make a move this year? It's been a while since anyone has kissed one of the lifeguards," I ask, finishing my drink.

"If he doesn't, I might have to do it for him," Maeve chuckles, heading toward our site.

"Did Cy tell you anything else? I've been DMing him on Instagram since last week and he said we missed a ton," Abby asks. Both she and Maeve are great at making friends and keeping in contact with them, whereas I tend to keep to myself and let them take charge when it comes to social events.

"OMG YES! I can't believe I forgot the best part. They distracted me." She stops and throws her hands up in the air. "I guess Luke did everything because he was upset his boyfriend broke up with him. Then his ex-boyfriend ended up taking the open lifeguard position. I swear this place could have its own reality show."

"No way," we shout at the same time.

"Way," Maeve laughs, tossing her head back to finish her drink.

Over the next thirty minutes, the three of us each have two more drinks and manage to get the tent completely done, air mattresses and all. Which is impressive considering how buzzed we all are. I can't tell if my cheeks are getting sunburned already or if it's the alcohol. My parents didn't end up needing much help since we packed light this year, and Sammy slept in the shade under one of the trees the whole time.

Abby is already in her suit, and I can see her sunscreen lip balm sticking out of the strap of her suit on her shoulder. She has fair skin like I do, but her lips always seem to burn the second she steps into the sun. For Christmas this past year, I bought her a whole makeup bag full of sunscreen lip balms because she's always losing them. She's currently mixing us drinks for the beach—vodka cranberries for both of us.

Grabbing my maroon one-piece out of the top of my bag, I get dressed quickly. This suit is my favorite for family events because the neckline doesn't expose too much of my cleavage, and there are two sheer horizontal stripes across the center, making it the perfect amount of sexy while staying modest enough for family. After double-checking my beach bag for my towel, sunscreen, and a book, I step out of the tent and zip it up.

"Cheers, bitch," she hands me my cup, lifting hers up and taking a sip.

"Cheers to another memorable Murphy trip," I lift my cup toward hers and sip. "How many of the cousins are ready?"

"Well, what do you mean by 'ready?'" she asks, making an air quotes gesture with one hand and rolling her eyes.

No matter how ready they are, add twenty more minutes. Someone is always running around making a drink, going to the bathroom, finding a towel, or deciding they want a different suit—basically anything to hold us back. We've learned over the years if you stop waiting and leave camp, eventually people will catch up. If they end up having to sit on the grass instead of the beach, that's on them.

"Let's head out, I need to get into the water." I can feel the sweat dripping down my back as I swing my bag over my shoulder. Grabbing a small bowl of strawberries for the walk, my feet automatically start heading toward the beach. The water's calling me like a moth to a flame.

"Agreed. Maeve had her suit on when we got here, and I have no idea where she disappeared to." Abby follows close behind me shouting across to Aunt Shan's site, "Hey Ryan, tell Maeve we are going to the beach. Meet us down there." He waves a hand at us, but he's distracted with making multiple drinks.

The road down to the beach is all downhill, perfect for going there and awful for hiking back up. I remember when we were kids we always biked down, and I would never peddle down this hill, letting gravity guide me. I can't imagine riding back up it today, and I'm not sure how we did that multiple times a day back then.

We stay silent on our way down, and the closer we get the cooler the air feels as the water grows nearer. The River is still pretty cold in the summer, which is refreshing when it's over eighty degrees. Rounding the corner at the end of the road, the area opens to a parking lot for the camp marina. Memories of fishing off the dock and boat rides flood my thoughts.

The newly renovated bathroom and shower building is right next to the marina and blocks most of the view of the River.

I stop Abby right as we approach the corner of the building. "Hold on, I want a moment to savor this."

She hooks her arm in mine. "This is always my favorite part, too." We step around the corner together.

We're standing at the top of a small hill with a man-made beach—no more than 150 feet wide—at the bottom. On the other side of the beach is another small hill and rec hall where you can play board games, paint, or do other crafts. When we were younger, we would spend all day in the rec hall making friendship bracelets and boondoggles —or lanyards, as the incorrect people would call them. We've gotten into plenty of fights in the past with other families about the correct term for them. One time it came dangerously close to turning into a physical fight.

There's a volleyball net near the rec hall and the land comes to a point with a rocky shore where it meets the River. We've always called it the Point, but I don't know if other campers do, too. The River is wide and goes on for miles, and if you stand on the shore you can see Canada on the other side. Our phones never work up here because the service is never any good. If we bring them too close to the Point, we get "Welcome to Canada" texts. Now we leave our phones at our campsites, going full vacation mode. Liam is the only one who constantly complains because he can't text his long-term, long distance, low-commitment, casual girlfriend who we all think is made up.

The sight of the water is truly breathtaking, I glance over at Abby who's smiling from ear to ear, as happy as I am. Suddenly, we hear footsteps fast approaching and flip-flops getting closer, until our cousins are running past us down the hill. They run down and start throwing down their towels and kicking off their flip-flops, running straight into the water. Maeve comes up next to me and hooks my other arm.

"Holy shit, I see him," Maeve says, pointing with her free arm to the lifeguard sitting in the middle of the beach. "That's the new lifeguard."

All of our eyes go straight to the lifeguard chair, the view partially blocked by the umbrella that sits to the right. I can't see much of the new lifeguard, but I can tell from his shoulders that he's probably tall and muscular—and shirtless. He lifts his left arm to the back of the chair, revealing a full sleeve of tattoos.

"Oh fuck me." The sentence is out of my mouth before my brain can stop me. My face heats, and they both stare at me before we break out into laughter and run down to the beach.

THREE

This morning I woke up and could tell there was something different in the air, and it wasn't the fresh smell of fish coming from the River. Fridays are usually pretty busy for the beach at Sutter State Park. It's always the start of new families coming to camp for the weekend, which I don't usually care about. However, Cy has been talking about this specific Friday all month. Apparently his favorite family, The Volleyball Kids, arrive today for ten days. The regular camp staff has nicknames for the yearly campers that everyone knows. This family has a tradition of playing volleyball against the lifeguards to start their trip, hence the nickname.

I've heard some stories about them over the last two years when I would hang out with Cy, but this year it's like he talks about them more than usual. It might be because I see him more since he helped me get the lifeguard gig.

I've been up on the River now for two years. We met in college, and he would never shut up about living here. When I dropped out of college sophomore year, and my dad kicked me out of the house, Cy graciously offered to help me find a place I could afford on my own.

Ever since then, I've been saving up my money and picking up odd jobs around town to go to The Culinary Institute of America this coming fall. A year ago, I got a line cook job at an Italian restaurant in town, but I usually work the dinner shift, which is why the park makes perfect sense. With all the additional income, I finally have everything saved for school in the fall, and it's so satisfying to not be constantly stressed about money anymore.

I enjoy working at the park. All the other lifeguards are already part of my social circle, and the quick turnover of campers always makes each weekend different. I've already been roped into different activities not in the lifeguard job description.

The Volleyball Kids' game is one example. Connor can't do it tonight, which means the game will have to be tomorrow after work. It seems like Cy has a special liking for this family, and I can't figure out why. They sound like your average middle-class family that comes up here every year, but he keeps telling me, "You'll see, they're one of the most fun annual families." He won't give me much more to go on.

Right after noon, a loud group runs onto the beach, dropping their stuff and heading right into the water. I get a better look at them as they emerge from the water, and it looks like they're a mix of older teenagers, and some in their early twenties. These must be the ones Cy keeps talking about because the second I look down from the guard chair at him he's grinning from ear to ear at me. It's honestly unsettling. With his dark hair and brown eyes peering over his sunglasses, he resembles a mad villain.

Four lifeguards are working today, and we rotate between the three positions every half-hour. Allison is currently out on the raft, I'm in the chair, and Taylor and Cy are on the beach, ready to handle anything quickly. They're both sitting on the picnic table to the right of the lifeguard chair, which he stands on to talk to me.

"This is them." He points toward the water at the group. I notice his cheeks suddenly turn pink, standing out against his light skin. I have a suspicion he's interested in this family for other reasons he failed to mention.

"They're not a bad-looking family," I nod toward the ones in the water, keeping an eye on my best friend. His blush deepens, confirming my suspicions, and now I need to figure out which Volleyball Kid he's crushing on.

"I—I mean yeah, I guess so, I never noticed before. Anyways, it doesn't matter, they're just cool." He waves his hand at me, brushing me off.

"Sure, man, whatever you say. How many are there?"

"There are fourteen cousins, but the oldest ones are all partnered up, and I mainly hang out with the ten around our age. The youngest ones are eighteen now." He points with two fingers toward the group, then toward another group walking onto the beach. I turn to see a group of three setting down their towels and bags. I can't get a good look at most of them because the girl in front runs toward us in a blinding bright pink bikini. I swear you could probably see her at night in that thing.

Cy jumps off the picnic table, the girl jumps into his arms, and he spins her before setting her down. She's brushing her long brown hair out of her face when she looks up at me and gives him a hip bump.

"Aren't you going to introduce me to the newest Sutter State Park lifeguard?" She puts her hand on her hip and blows a bubble with her gum.

"Right, right. Maeve, this is Zach Moretti, my good

friend and newest lifeguard," he gestures up toward me, still in the chair.

She waves up at me, the sun bouncing off her hot pink sunglasses. "Hiya, Zach, it's so nice to meet you."

I wave back. "Nice to meet you. I've heard great things."

"You better not be gossiping about me," she shouts, hitting Cy on the shoulder.

"I swear, I was only saying good things." He puts his hands up in defense.

I'm quick to defend him. "He really did. I heard there are a lot of you?"

She slaps her palm to her forehead. "Duh, you need to meet them too." She spins toward her family on the beach. "Hey ladies, come over here."

Since I'm in the chair, I can't talk to them too much. I'm supposed to be watching the water for any sign of danger, but Cy is the head lifeguard, so he won't yell at me for being a bit distracted. I do a quick scan of the water before turning back to them as the other two girls come up next to her.

Seeing the three of them lined up, you can tell they're related. They could be mistaken for sisters with the same fair skin, similar small rounded noses, and soft cheekbones. My eyes move down the line, taking them all in, until my heart stops at the instant draw I feel toward the last girl. She has her sunglasses on, and I can't see her eyes, but her blonde curly hair barely falls past her shoulders. I have the urge to run my fingers through it. She's wearing a maroon one-piece, and now maroon is my new favorite color. Her full lips are wrapped around a strawberry, and I can't take my eyes off of her. My heart doesn't start beating again until Maeve starts to introduce them.

"Ladies, this is Zach Moretti, the newest lifeguard."

She gestures up toward me and back down toward them. "Zach, meet Abby and Sidney."

A unison "hi" rings out between them, both giving a wave, but I'm only looking at Sidney.

"Nice to meet you both, I'm looking forward to this volleyball game I keep hearing about," I say, hoping to keep them talking longer.

"We're looking forward to kicking your butts," Abby quips, giving Sidney a hip bump. Sidney nods and directs her gaze anywhere but at me. I can see a faint flush on her chest, disappearing under her suit. I crave to find out how far her body flushes, what color her eyes are, what her voice sounds like. I don't know why, but I'm being pulled to her like I've never experienced before.

"We'd love to stay and chat, but we just set up our whole camp and need to get in this river ASAP," Maeve chimes in, pointing to the water.

"Of course. Enjoy the water," I say with a wave. They head to the water to join their other family members. Lucky for me, it's my job to watch the water, and you can't tell where my gaze is with my aviator sunglasses on.

Cy glances down at his watch and then up at me. "Allison is coming in from the raft soon, then she's going on break. Do you need anything before heading out there for the next rotation?"

"No, I'm all set. Do you want me to come down and head out there now?" I ask, gesturing toward the raft where Allison sits on the guard chair. There isn't anyone out there with her, so switching over will be easy. Maybe I'll get lucky, and Sidney will swim out while I'm there.

"Yeah, let's do that," he nods, as I climb down from the chair and head toward the water.

FOUR

ZACH

When I reach the raft, Allison looks relieved. It's a good thing this chair has an umbrella too, otherwise her freckled skin would be burned by now.

It's nice being out here. Everybody refers to it as the raft, but really it's a year-round small dock-like structure anchored to the floor of the river. There's a ladder to climb up onto it and a lifeguard chair. I love it because you're right on the water, and the people who swim out are usually fun. My favorites are always the kids who want to do nothing but jump off a million times, always telling me to watch their different trick jumps. You aren't supposed to do flips off the raft, but if Cy isn't watching, I'll let it slide occasionally.

"I saw The Volleyball Kids, right?" Allison asks me, hopping down from the chair and nodding toward the group still in the water.

"Yeah, I got introduced to some of them. Sidney and maybe a Maeve," I say, bringing the surfboard up to the side of the raft. Climbing up the ladder, I hold the board with my foot to keep it close for Allison.

"That sounds right. You'll get it quick. They say each other's names a lot. Although, I still mix them up sometimes."

We switch positions, and I climb up into the chair as she climbs down the ladder onto the surfboard.

"I'm pretty good with names, but they all look so similar I guarantee I'll mix them up," I say, shrugging and adjusting on the chair. These wooden guard chairs aren't super comfortable, but they hold up in all types of weather.

Before Allison pushes off the raft, she turns back my way. "Did you notice if Cy got flustered when they showed up?"

"He did. He blushed a little. What's up with that?" I lean forward and whisper like someone might to hear us, despite no one being around in the water.

She leans forward and raises her eyebrow. "He for sure has a crush on Ryan, and according to Maeve, Ryan almost one hundred percent has a crush on Cy. The problem is neither of them realize the other's crushing, and it's exhausting waiting for them to figure it out," she explains, rolling her eyes and pushing off the raft.

"No way, I love that. He needs someone good in his life." I smirk and lean back in the chair.

"I agree. You'll like Ryan." She starts to drift away from the raft before pointing toward the beach. "Here he comes now." Then she's off, paddling toward shore, and my gaze shifts to the water to find Sidney and the rest of her family swimming my way. My goals for this shift are now to figure out what color Sidney's eyes are and to remember who is who in this family.

I watch them swim out, and I see everyone has a different method. Some of them are clearly racing out here, while others, like Sidney, are taking their time.

The first pair of guys reach the raft, fighting each other

to climb up the ladder first. Followed by a girl who is clearly out of breath from racing. Unlike the brown hair of the guys, hers is blonde like Sidney's.

One runs his fingers through his hair and gives me a nod. "Hey man, I'm Ryan." He steps closer, reaching a hand out to me.

"Hey man, I'm Zach. I love the trunks." I shake his hand and nod toward his flamingo-covered trunks.

"Aren't they great? Liam here is so jealous he can't pull them off," he gestures toward the other guy who is now standing next to the girl.

"No way, you're jealous you can't pull off these sun shorts." Liam does a small spin before facing me. "Hey, I'm Liam."

I shake his hand and introduce myself, then nod toward the girl who is laying on the raft, panting, with her arm draped over her face. "She okay?"

"I'm good, I'm good." She throws her hand up and waves me off, keeping her eyes closed. "I haven't exercised in months and thought I could beat these two."

"She's never beat me in a race, and I plan to keep it that way." Liam gestures toward her, and she pops up on her elbows immediately at that last comment.

"Fuck you, Liam. I'll win one day when you least expect it." She points his way and moves over on the raft, getting out of the way of the next few coming up the ladder.

Quickly, the last one I don't know comes up, with similar pale skin and facial features to the others I've already forgotten the names of because I'm searching for Sidney. With all the physical similarities, I'm going to need to find memorable things about them to remember their names.

She quickly moves to the other side of the raft, sitting

down with her feet hanging off the edge next to Lucy. Then, the last three girls I met on the beach climb up, Sidney at the back of the group. I'm disappointed she kept her sunglasses on while swimming, and I still haven't found out what color her eyes are.

Abby lies down on the raft, and Maeve, who seems to be the loudest among the group, stands next to the chair with Sidney next to her. "Hey Zach, long time no see. Guess it's time for you to meet more of the Murphy fam." She gestures toward everyone on the raft.

"Pleasure to meet everyone. So who is who?" I ask. Allison's right, this might take me a while to master.

Maeve turns toward Sidney. "Sid, why don't you do the honors since you're the oldest here?"

"Only by a few months," the girl next to Lucy shouts.

Sidney seems to stand up taller as everyone's attention turns to her. I can tell she's anxious, shifting back and forth on her feet and playing with the hair tie around her wrist. Now that I'm more level, I notice she's short, I would guess around a foot shorter than my six-two.

"Zach, take notes." She nods at me, and I almost fall out of my chair at the sound of her voice. I don't know what I was expecting, but her voice has a certain command in it that I'm eager to learn more about. To potentially find out if she's commanding in all aspects of her life. I feel like a magnet being drawn to her, and I don't understand it.

"I'll do my best," I say, tapping my pointer finger to my forehead, and leaning forward on my knees, trying not to get caught up in my thoughts. I have the urge to reach out and touch her to make sure she's real, but she's too far away and probably doesn't need a stranger touching her.

"Okay, so as you know, I'm Sidney." She points to herself. "You've met some of us, but I'll repeat to be safe. Abby's my younger sister." She points to Abby who gives a small wave, applying some lip balm. "Next we have Ryan and Maeve, the loudest pair of siblings," she says, pointing toward the two of them who give identical waves. "Then we have Quinn and twins, Liam and Lucy." Quinn nods, and Liam and Lucy wave at the same time, accidentally hitting each other's arms, then hitting each other on purpose. Sidney leans over Maeve and whispers, "They're always fighting, feel free to ignore them."

I get the faint smell of something floral and give her a small nod and wink, which causes her to blush and pull her bottom lip between her teeth. If one wink can get her this flustered, I can only imagine how much she would blush if I reached out and pulled her lip free with my thumb.

She takes a deep breath and continues with the introductions. "Lastly we have the triplets, but they aren't here yet. Will you be able to remember that or do we need to write it down?" Sidney turns toward me with one hand on her hip and the other over her sunglasses, and I tell myself it's so she can see me better.

"You'll be quizzed until you get it right," Liam calls from where he's still sitting on the edge.

"I think I'm pretty good with names, but don't quiz me right now," I say with a chuckle, sitting back in the chair and repeating all their names to myself.

"Tell us more about yourself, Zach," Quinn calls.

"Okay, let's see. I've been friends with Cy for about four years now, moved up here about two years ago, and now I'm working here, thanks to him." I gesture toward the beach.

"How old are you?" Maeve crosses her arms with a tilt of her head.

"Turned twenty-two in March," I reply.

Maeve nods, and I see her give Sidney a small nudge with the hand under her crossed arm, no doubt trying to hide it from me. If I was a betting man, I would guess Sidney is my age.

"Okay fam, let's get this vacation started," Ryan says, moving to the back of the raft rubbing his hands together. "Everyone in the water!"

Then he is off at full speed, jumping into the water and executing a perfect corkscrew, making a splash large enough to hit all of us. Almost everyone screams before running and joining him in the water, but a few stay on the raft.

The shift goes by fast after that. I spend the next thirty minutes listening to them tell me stories about previous years and the plans they have for this year. I learn Sidney and Quinn are the two oldest and the most prepared out of the bunch when it comes to planning for events. Ryan and Maeve are definitely the loudest and keep talking over their cousins and each other. Abby, Liam, and Lucy fall somewhere in the middle of loud and quiet, and I caught Abby raising her eyebrows and rolling her eyes at Sidney multiple times.

Seeing all of them joke and reminisce about the past leaves a sting in my chest. I'm an only child and don't have any cousins, so I've never had a family dynamic like they have. I didn't know my grandparents either, and after my mom passed, my dad and I were the only ones left. I've always wondered what it would be like to be a part of a family where people know and accept you for who you are. Where you don't have to do everything on your own, and there is always someone willing to help you out.

Cy did a great job at welcoming me into his circle when I moved up here, but it has always been his circle. I like all his friends, and I'm grateful for them, but I can't help but feel like the new guy when they talk about any time before I moved up here. I never feel like I can be myself around them, always changing depending on who is around.

I've gotten to know a ton of people from all the jobs I've had over the past two years, and while everyone is friendly, none of them are home to me. I can't help but think that what the Murphys have is what I've been missing.

Sidney hasn't said much, only the occasional comment here and there, but I can't seem to take my eyes off of her. She hasn't jumped into the water yet either, which means she hasn't taken off her sunglasses. The next rotation is coming up soon, and I'll get a short break before beach duty. Cy is next out here, which is annoying because I'm itching to ask him about Sidney. I see him hop off the guard chair and wander over to the surfboard, while Abby stands up and faces me.

"Well, Zach, it was nice meeting you, but if I spend another ten minutes out here, I'm going to be a lobster the rest of the trip, and we need lunch." She turns to her family. "Ready to head back up to camp?"

Quinn stands up with Sidney, and Maeve following suit. "Yeah, I need another drink." She stretches and moves to the edge of the raft.

They all jump into the water, except for Sidney, and a small part of me hopes she'll stay even though I know she won't. She walks to the edge of the raft and stops, removing her sunglasses first so she won't lose them in the River. Then, she turns toward me. It's a good thing this chair has a back, or else I would have fallen into the water. Her eyes are a piercing blue, the perfect reflection of the sky and river. Whatever shade of blue they are is my new favorite color. Forget the maroon of her suit. I need that blue everywhere.

"It was nice to meet you, Zach. We'll see you around," she says.

Then she's in the water, swimming away from me, and I'm stuck in this damn chair. I can't move anyway, because I'm still taken aback by how one glance from her took my breath away. I'm not going to have enough time to get back to the shore before they leave, and I hope they'll come back down after lunch so I can see her again.

I *need* to see her again.

FIVE

SIDNEY

oly. Fucking. Shit.
The last half hour just became the best half hour I've ever spent at the Islands. Over the years, everyone has had crushes on the lifeguards, and we always discuss which ones we would date or hook up with, but it's always been hypothetical. No one's ever actually done it. One time, Quinn kissed one of them on a dare, and things got super awkward. We all agreed not to mess up our favorite vacation spot with awkward breakups or the aftermath of a hookup. But it doesn't stop us from looking, and it doesn't hurt to look at Zach.

He's tall and tan, dark brown hair that's longer on top and shorter near his neck. His facial hair is scruffy, a few days past a five o'clock shadow. I got a better view of his tattoo sleeve on the raft and saw it was mostly roses with vines mixed in connecting them.

I did my best to not stare at him, but I couldn't help myself from thinking about what his facial hair would feel grazing against my thighs or how his tattoos would feel under my fingertips. My sunglasses helped hide it, but I kept glancing over at him, and I think he kept looking at me, too. At least, I hope so. I'm not usually the one to talk to people. Compared to Maeve and Abby's extroversion, I'm content to gaze from afar.

When we get back to the beach, we dry off, pack up our things, and start hiking up the hill. Not everyone comes with us, some choosing to stay at the beach or return to the raft since Cyrus's shift out there starts next. We all notice that Ryan decides to stay.

We stop at the water spigot on the hill to get the sand off our feet. Maeve glances around and whispers, "Okay, we're far enough away now."

Then the four of us erupt, all talking over each other.

"Did you see his tattoos?" Abby asks.

"His laugh was the cutest thing I've ever heard." Quinn sticks her feet under the water to clean them.

"I swear, he's straight out of a romance book." Abby nudges me.

"This week is going to be so much fun." Maeve crosses her arms and grins wickedly.

"I stand by when I said 'oh fuck me,' because oh my god he could fuck me," I say out loud, because apparently, I have no filter when it comes to my thoughts about him. Heat rushes through my entire body, and I'm sure I turn red as they all turn my way, mouths wide open. I never say anything that forward, usually keeping my thoughts to myself.

"Okay, Sid gets dibs." Abby points at me, sticking her feet under the water. "If she's saying shit like that out loud, I want to see what else she'll do."

I cover my face with my hands. "Shit, why did I say that?"

Maeve squeals and hugs me, shaking me back and forth. "Yes! Let your freak flag fly!"

"Sidney, I didn't know you even had that sentence in you," Quinn says, turning off the spigot as Maeve lets me go.

"I knew this week was going to be fun. Let's go make more drinks and plot how to get Sidney plowed by the new lifeguard," Maeve shouts and starts skipping away.

"Maeve, don't yell that." I chase after her, the others following. "We will not be plotting anything." Abby comes up next to me and hooks her arm in mine.

"We might not plot directly, but we won't *not* plot." She winks and nudges my hip. I'm never going to hear the end of this. I never should have said anything. I don't like the attention on me, and I know they aren't going to drop this, no matter what I do.

Thankfully, the rest of the hike up to camp they don't talk about Zach, instead we discuss what our next move will be. Lunch first and maybe a quick nap. Since it's the first day, we're all tired from driving and setting up. Plus, spending so much time in the sun makes all of us want to relax.

We all go to our respective campsites, agreeing to meet up in our makeshift dining area with our lunches. I mix a new drink and notice the rest of the cousins have arrived and are almost done setting up. Caitlin and Ben are here with their five-year-old daughter, Gracie, the first and only great grandchild. We're all obsessed with her. Seeing everyone here, together, gives me a sense of completion and belonging only my family can give me.

The next few hours pass quickly. We eat lunch, lay our towels on the grass, put some music on, and fall asleep in the sun. The background noise of everyone catching up, making drinks, and playing lawn games is like my own version of ASMR. It could put me to sleep anytime.

Since we always have so many people, different families take turns being in charge of dinner each night. It's always a fight for whoever gets to do pizza night since no one has to cook, so we've started rotating to keep it fair. Tonight's dinner is provided by Aunt Shan and Uncle Owen, which means Ryan and Maeve are on cooking duty. Maeve ended up roping me and Abby into helping since she helped us put up our tent when we got here.

Now I'm sitting at a picnic table cutting up vegetables for salad with them and Maeve has been talking for the past ten minutes about some drama between her sorority sisters and something to do with Instagram. I'm not listening to her though, because all I can do is think about Zach, which is frustrating. I don't want to be thinking about him and his square jaw, his pecs with the perfect amount of chest hair, or his tattooed arm and how it would feel wrapped around my waist as I—

"Hello? Earth to Sid. Are you there?" Abby waves her hand in front of my face from across the table, knife in hand.

"Shit, sorry, what's up?"

"Maeve wants to know if you brought the stuff for tonight?" Abby picks up a piece of cucumber and pops it into her mouth.

"Yeah, it's all in the tent." I point to the tent with my knife and go back to cutting. It's a first night tradition to go down to the Point when it gets dark. As a kid, Caitlin and the older cousins would always leave the campfire and disappear for hours. They told me they were "adult walks," and I never understood what that meant. When I turned sixteen, I finally got the coveted invitation. It turns out these walks I had always wondered about were everyone going to the Point—smoking weed and drinking. The younger me had never been so disappointed until that moment. At one point, I had a theory there were mermaids in the River, and they could only visit at night or risk being caught. Sometimes, I still tell myself it's true if I hear a suspicious splash at night.

Now, I'm the oldest one who still goes on night walks. The park has quiet hours starting at 10 p.m., which means we only hang out down there for about an hour, so we don't get kicked out by the park rangers. This year, I got tasked with supplying the first night joints for everyone, which are tucked away nicely in the side pocket of my duffle bag.

Over the years, the lifeguards have caught on to our annual tradition and sometimes stay after volleyball to hang out with us. I can't help the small tinge of hope that Cyrus will show up with Zach since we had to move the volleyball game to tomorrow.

"Do we think the lifeguards are coming tonight?" I ask, keeping my eyes on cutting so the question doesn't sound suspicious. "You know, because I don't have enough joints for us plus them, so you might want to DM them." I think that sounded cool, cool as a cucumber. I chuckle to myself at my joke and pop a cucumber into my mouth.

Ryan is all too quick to answer, "Cy said he was planning on it and he might bring some of the other lifeguards, too. I told him to make sure to bring anything they would want to smoke or drink."

"Perfect." I nod quickly. "He didn't say who he was going to bring?"

"Nah, he only said that he didn't know about Zach, because I guess he works at some restaurant at night? It's the Italian place we've gone to a few times right on the

River," Ryan says, completely oblivious to the way my shoulders drop when he mentions Zach won't be there.

I'm about to ask him more questions, but Aunt Shan calls over to us, "How long is it going to take the four of you to cut up some vegetables? We need help over here."

Ryan and Abby get up to go help, while Maeve and I take the vegetables to the buffet. Aunt Shan has set up two tables in an L shape in front of her camper to create a buffet, where everyone will line up once the dinner bell is rung.

Right as I'm mixing the vegetables into the salad, someone grabs my leg.

"Auntie Sid!"

I look down to see Gracie, Caitlin's daughter, attached to me. She's looking up at me with her bright blue eyes. Her pin-straight light brown hair is falling out of a braid, her green shirt and jean shorts are covered in dirt, and her shoes are nonexistent.

"Hey Gracie, did you have fun today?" I ask her, moving away from the buffet so she doesn't knock me into it.

"Tons of it! I saw six butterflies and found a ton of worms. Plus, Aunt Shan told me I'm on dinner bell duty." She's jumping up and down now, and I understand her excitement.

The dinner bell is a rusty cowbell Uncle Joe found one year at an antique shop. He brought it to the Islands to act as a dinner bell after his kids kept missing dinner because they were too far away to know it was time to eat. Ringing the bell has now become one of the top-tier dinner jobs, and for the past two years, Gracie has held to it tightly.

"That's so cool, Gracie. Why don't you go find Mom and clean up those dirty hands before dinner?" I say, crouching down in front of her so I'm not shouting down at her.

"Okay! Be right back." She runs in the direction of her site.

She returns twenty minutes later, complete with a total wardrobe change, now sporting a butterfly-covered romper. Dinner goes by in a blur as people get their plates and head over to the center of camp to the picnic tables we've set up. Leftovers are packaged away and stored in camper fridges for lunch tomorrow and late-night snacks around the fire. Dishes are left around the back of Aunt Shan's camper, where she has a dishwashing station set up, our Mason jar mugs from this afternoon on the drying rack.

The campfire has been started, and there are folding chairs circling it. Tonight we'll make s'mores and tell stories we all know by heart but love to hear retold. Gracie doesn't remember them fully yet, and she always acts like it's the first time she's heard them.

The campfire is one of my favorite aspects of the entire trip, every night always ends with us around it well past quiet hours. Laughs are shared, snacks are passed, drinks are often spilled, and there are countless memories made. When we were kids, we would play telephone for hours, and no phrase ever made it around the circle without at least one change.

Now, most of the cousins only stay at the fire for a little bit to start before we break away for drinking and playing card games before going to the Point. Similar to getting ready for the beach, getting ready for the night walk always takes half an hour as people make new drinks and gather anything else they might need.

I've got my small backpack on, stocked with joints, lighters, bug spray, and a bag of pretzels I grabbed from my parents' camper. I switched my Crocs and shorts for a pair of black Vans, sweatpants, and my favorite bookish crewneck. I can already smell the scent of the campfire clinging to my hair, so I pull it back the best I can with a claw clip.

Abby finishes making our drinks—Arnold Palmer with whiskey—before heading down to the Point.

We do our best to stay quiet, so we don't disturb any of the other campers, but the Point is far enough away from other campsites that we usually don't get in trouble for being too loud.

The River is calm tonight, and the moon is almost full, lighting up the Point perfectly. Everything is so peaceful. I can hear crickets and the faint crash of water on the rocky shore.

We go to our usual spot—a bench and picnic table that sit as close to the edge as possible without being in the water. The triplets start skipping rocks, the ripples creating mesmerizing circles in the glass-like water. Abby helps me get the joints and lighters out, putting them on the picnic table so everyone who wants to smoke can grab one.

Once everyone has either a lit joint or a drink in their hand, Ryan clears his throat and stands up on the picnic table bench. "My fellow cousins, it is with great honor that I toast to our first full day of the Islands. May this trip bring us new memories, great laughs, no sunburns"—he looks right at me and Abby—"And hopefully no one passes out and locks themselves in the bathrooms"—then he looks right at Liam who chuckles—"To the Islands!" He raises his drink and takes a sip.

"To the Islands!" we all ring back at him, toasting each other.

Everyone breaks off into conversations after that, but I head over to the empty bench a few feet away and set my backpack down. Leaning back on the bench, I close my eyes. I let the sounds of the water and the laughter of my cousins surround me. I know I need to tell them about my move, but I'm not ready yet. I don't want to lose the vacation relaxation and replace it with the sadness of not returning next year.

The bench dips next to me, and I open my eyes to see my sister sipping her drink. "You okay over here?" She reaches up and wipes a tear from the corner of my eye. I didn't realize I'd begun to cry.

"Yeah, I'm okay," I sniffle, wiping my face with the sleeve of my crewneck. "Just thinking is all."

"Do you want to tell them?" she leans in and whispers.

"Not yet, I want a few days without thinking about it first."

She simply nods and faces the water. She grabs my hand and gives it a small squeeze to let me know she's right there with me.

Cyrus ends up showing up with Allison a bit later, and I can't help the disappointment that washes over me when Zach doesn't show.

SIX

ZACH

I pull my boat into the campground marina, adjusting my navy ball cap sitting backward on my head, and take a sip of my coffee from my travel mug.

Friday nights always kick my ass at the restaurant, but I'm grateful Mario is flexible with my schedule, allowing me to work both at the camp during the day and at the restaurant at night. Usually, I'm done by 11 p.m., but last night I was there until midnight. I worked about thirteen hours yesterday, and this coffee is my lifeline this morning.

Cy's pickup truck is parked in the lot already. Allison is the only one off duty today, and I don't know how she got so lucky to have the entire weekend off. Lifeguards get two days off throughout the week to ensure we have the right amount of coverage on the beach, and my wild weekend falls on Tuesdays and Wednesdays. I usually spend them running to the farmer's market to get fresh ingredients for the restaurant or picking up an odd job for someone around town.

I secure my boat to the dock and hop out, grabbing my backpack with my uniform. I wave hi to George, the dock attendant, and Sally, the shop clerk, as I pass them on my way to the guard shack.

When I swing the old creaking screen door open, I see Cy has propped the big wooden door open and is rummaging through the folded towels next to the lockers.

I make my way around him to my locker and try to create some noise before speaking so I don't scare him. "What are you looking for?"

He jumps as he sighs, standing to face me, pushing the heels of his hands into his eyes. "I can't find my damn whistle. I've looked everywhere."

I quickly scan the small front room of the shack. Next to the front door is a bench topped high with extra rescue buoys, shelves full of first aid materials adjacent to it. The lockers are against the far wall, next to shelves filled with towels. I peer around the corner down the hall into the bathroom, showers, and storage room where we store the surfboard and a kayak, but I don't see his whistle anywhere. I come back into the front room and bend down to check under the bench, catching sight of something shiny behind one of the posts. I reach and pull out his now super-dirty whistle.

"Here it is," I say as I stand up and hand it to him. I catch a glimpse of his bloodshot eyes and disheveled hair. "You okay, man? You're looking rough."

He goes into the bathroom to rinse his whistle and shouts, "Yeah, I'm hungover. I came back here last night to hang with The Volleyball Kids."

I do a quick change out of my shorts and briefs and into my suit. "How did it go? Did I miss anything?" I need to ask him about Sidney since I never got the chance to yesterday. I was disappointed when she didn't end up coming back down to the beach after they went up for lunch.

"Nah, not much. Same old stuff." He comes out of the bathroom and slips his whistle over his head.

I decide to go for it. "Hey, are any of them single?" I face my locker, put away my bag and grab my whistle. I play with the bracelets on my wrist, hoping he hasn't picked up on this nervous habit of mine.

"The ones you met yesterday are all single. I guess Quinn recently broke up with her boyfriend, so I believe that makes them all available." I turn to face him. His arms are crossed, and he's smirking at me with a raised eyebrow. "Why? Has someone caught your eye?"

I let out a small huff. "Nah, I wanted to know if it left Ryan open for you." I wink at him, throwing a towel his way.

He barely catches it and starts mumbling, "No, no—I'm not—me and Ryan aren't—"

I put my hand on his shoulder. "Let me know if you need a wingman." I back away toward the storage room giving him finger guns as he fumbles with the towel.

I pull the surfboard out of the shack and head down the hill to the beach, where I see Connor shoveling sand into a pile in front of the guard chair. If we ever have to jump down off the chair, it's safer to have a cushioned landing. Connor always likes to see how high he can get the pile, swearing he can get it to his height of six-three. I highly doubt this, plus we don't need the pile that high.

I run back up the hill to grab an extra bottle of sunscreen before I forget. Connor always forgets to bring some down to the beach, and he's the one who needs it the most. I'm not sure why he thought mixing a job where you spend the day in the sun with his skin would be a good idea. He's Irish through and through with his red shaggy hair and pale skin. Looking at him practically gives me a sunburn.

I almost run into Taylor as they're coming out of the shack, already dressed in a yellow tank top, swim trunks, and one-piece under them. "Woah, Zach, what's the rush? You're never this bouncy in the morning." Taylor lets me slip by, holding the screen door open.

"Ready to get the day started, I guess." I shrug as I grab the sunscreen and head back down the hill, picking up the surfboard from where I had abandoned it. I didn't think I had been any more energetic than usual this morning. Maybe making my coffee extra strong was the cause. It definitely has nothing to do with the idea of seeing Sidney today and again later tonight for the volleyball game.

The four of us spend the next ten minutes getting things ready for the day. We have to bring everything in at night because things often get stolen if we leave them out. Cy told me this was the third surfboard within the last few years, and he swears he brought the last one back up to the shack before it was stolen.

The guard chair has a shelf under the seat for all our extra stuff, including first aid supplies, sunscreen, and a small cooler to keep our water bottles cold. Taylor heads out to the raft, the umbrella tucked between their legs as they paddle out. Cy adjusts the umbrella on the chair since he's up there first. And Connor flips the beach sign to read "OPEN" and I see a huge group of people come around the bathroom building. I know it's The Volleyball Kids because I see Maeve in hot pink running down the hill, her brown messy bun bobbing from side to side. Behind her, Sidney's hand in hand with a little girl in a unicorn-themed one-piece with a small tutu around the waist. Sidney's in the same maroon one-piece as yesterday, and I can hear her laugh from here. I watch them come down the hill with so much joy that my chest tightens, and I can't help the grin that spreads across my face.

"What's got you so happy, man?" Connor steps into my line of view.

"It's Saturday. What's not to love about Saturdays?" I lie, hoping Connor buys my bullshit excuse. "Can you hand me the sunscreen?"

He reaches under the seat and tosses me the bottle before heading over to the sand pile to tinker with it, resetting the parts that fell during our set up.

I start applying sunscreen to my arms and chest, paying extra attention to my tattooed left arm. I hope keeping my hands busy for a few minutes will help me not stare at Sidney as she sets up on the beach, but I can't help sneaking glances at her. My eyes automatically go to her each time I lift my head, and I'm grateful for my sunglasses.

The whole family takes up a spot to the right, close to the picnic table I'm sitting on next to the guard chair. It seems like everyone's here, the younger people spreading out towels while their parents set up beach chairs. Almost everyone in a beach chair has a book with them. I spot Sidney pull one out of her bag and set it on her towel, followed by a bottle of sunscreen and a bag of strawberries.

It's good she's using sunscreen. Not everyone does, and she should be using it if she has any tattoos. Does she have any tattoos? She would probably have something small, maybe on her legs? That's when I realize I'm staring at her legs as she applies sunscreen. Is she moving in slow motion? It feels that way.

Dammit, Zach, pull it together and stop staring at her applying sunscreen.

I reluctantly tear my gaze away from her, adjusting myself in my swim trunks.

"You good down there?"

I almost jump off the picnic table as Cy yells down at me from the chair.

"Yeah, yeah, I'm all set."

"Okay, do you know you've been rubbing sunscreen on the same spot for the past five minutes?" Cy laughs and leans back in the chair, resting both arms on the back.

"I had a long night at the restaurant." It's not a lie, but it's not the reason I was distracted, and I'm starting to suspect I might not survive today.

SEVEN

ZACH

half-hour goes by of me sneaking glances Sidney's way until I see her and the little girl she was with earlier approaching out of the corner of my eye. I do a quick scan of everyone in the water and onshore, making sure I'll be able to talk to them without endangering anyone here. It's Connor's shift in the chair now, but I'm still on the picnic table and don't have to rotate spots for another thirty minutes.

I run my hands through my hair and turn right as Sidney and the girl reach the table.

"Um, hi Zach," Sidney gives a small wave, her voice timid. I don't know if I make her nervous, or if she's always like this around new people. "Hey Connor," she gives him a much more enthusiastic greeting, and I can't help the jealousy that fills me as he waves back before returning to watch the water.

"Hey Sidney, good to see you again," I say with a wave and direct my focus to the little girl holding a box filled with nail polish. "What do you have there?"

"Zach, this is my cousin's daughter, Gracie. She has a

question for you." Sidney gives Gracie a push, and she hops forward on the sand.

"Actually, my real name is Grace, but everyone calls me Gracie," she corrects with a quick nod of her head.

"Hi Gracie, I'm Zach, real name Zachary. It's lovely to meet another member of the Murphy family. What can I do for you today?"

"I was wondering if I could paint your toenails?" Gracie shouts at a decibel loud enough for the whole camp to hear, and I chuckle.

I glance at Sidney's toes and notice they're painted bright orange, with the nail polish making it far past the toenail. She must have gotten them done last night because I would have noticed that yesterday. My eyes move up her body to where her hands are clasped in front of her, and I see her fingernails are painted the same. She's playing with the hair tie around her wrist again, and I want to reach out and wrap her hand in mine, to find out what's causing her to fidget so much and learn how her skin feels under my fingertips. My pause causes Sidney to jump in before I can reply to Gracie.

"It's a family tradition. The youngest members paint the nails of the whole family, and for the last few years we've gotten the lifeguards involved," she explains, brushing her hair behind her ear and adjusting her sunglasses. I wish they weren't on her face so I could look into her eyes. "Since you're the newest lifeguard, I thought it was fitting for you to go first. Isn't that right?" She glances at Gracie with a smile that's brighter than today's sun, and I can't help but notice that it was her idea to come to me.

"Correct," Gracie shouts, smiling at me. "I have plenty of colors to pick from, and I can do—oh my gosh!" She gasps midway through her pitch and points right at my navy blue nails. "You already have your nails painted."

I grin as she keeps her fingers pointed at my hands with a look of pure wonder in her eyes. I always love that look when little kids realize my nails are painted, especially the boys. I love being able to show them nail polish isn't only for girls. I would always paint my nails with my mom and having them painted always makes me more confident.

I wiggle my fingers in Gracie's direction. "I do. But you know what?" I whisper and lean closer to Gracie. "I don't have my toes done." I stick out my leg and wiggle my toes so she can see them.

"Right," Gracie nods once and sets the box down on the bench, quickly opening it up and sifting through her colors. She huffs and glares at me with one of the most serious looks I've ever been given, and I think I might be in trouble. "Zachary, I do not have that color." She points to my nails and frowns.

"That's okay, they don't have to match. I love the color that Sidney has. Did you do those, too?" I point at Sidney's toes and smile at Gracie. I glance back at Sidney, whose cheeks are now a brighter shade of red. I can't help but find some joy in the fact I make her blush, and I need to find out what else makes her blush.

Woah, focus. There's a little kid right there who wants to paint your toes.

"The orange? That one's my favorite!" Gracie jumps up and down as she retrieves it from her box.

"It's settled then. Orange it is." I lay my feet flat out on the bench, and Gracie steps in front of me to start painting them. She's so short she doesn't have to bend to reach them. I hear Sidney let out a sigh like she had been holding her breath for longer than she bargained for. I can't get distracted by her right now, so I focus my attention back on

Gracie as she puts more than enough nail polish on my big toe, some of it running down the side.

"Gracie, remember to wipe the brush off on the sides of the bottle first," Sidney says, mouthing "sorry" at me, and I regret having to look up at her lips to understand it. She isn't making this whole "don't-get-distracted-by-Sidney" thing easy.

"Oops, sorry," Gracie says, wiping the brush against the bottle.

"Don't worry about it, kid. A little nail polish on the skin never hurt anyone." I wave my hand nonchalantly at her.

She glances up at me before continuing to the next toe. Sidney silently watches at the edge of the table, and her hovering makes me nervous.

"Sidney, why don't you have a seat?" I pat the table next to me.

She jumps, like she wasn't paying attention, and gives me a small smirk with a quick upturn of the corners of her mouth.

"Oh right, thanks, but um, I'll sit here." She points to the bench of the table and sits as far away from me as she can. Gracie is now in her groove. I don't want to distract her and risk getting nail polish on my entire foot. So instead, I take this opportunity to learn about Sidney.

"Did you do this when you were a kid?" I gesture from her to Gracie. I realize my sunglasses are still on, so I take them off and place them on my head. I'm hoping she'll mimic my move so I can see her eyes. I heard once that if someone likes you, they copy your movements and gestures.

"No, I'm not gifted at it," she sighs and places her arm on the table, resting her cheek into her hand. With her other hand, she takes her sunglasses and places them on her head. I don't know if there is any scientific proof in this theory, but now I'm saying there is. "My little sister was usually the one to do it, her and Lucy. I acted more like their business manager, collecting the money from anyone who got their nails painted." She's playing with her hair ties again, looking back up at me. I finally get to look at her eyes for the first time today, the blue as vibrant as I remember. The water and sky are being soaked up in them, and I swear I could drown in them.

"Oh yeah? And what did you do with the money?"

Gracie quickly chimes in, shouting, "Ice cream and candy!"

Damn, does this kid ever say anything at a regular volume?

"Well, of course." I throw my hands up in the air.

"Hey! Don't move." Gracie glares at me and points the nail polish brush toward me like a weapon.

I freeze with my hands in the air, my eyes locking with hers in a standoff. She holds her position, and I hold mine until she seems satisfied enough to go back to painting. I slowly lower my hands back down to my knees and turn my head toward Sidney. "Well, that sounds like a pretty successful business model."

She lets out a small laugh. "It was. We were fueled by sugar and sunshine." She nods toward my bracelets. "We made plenty of those too at the rec hall."

I lift my arm and give my wrist a slight shake. "That's where all these are from." I glance down at Gracie to make sure she isn't going to yell at me again for moving, but she's completely focused on painting my toes.

"Did you make all of them?" Sidney asks me.

"No, they're from campers."

"And you keep them on? Even after they leave?"

"Yeah, I love them. I've never had anyone make me a bracelet before, and now all these campers come up and give us bracelets, I can't toss them." I remember the first time a group of kids came up to me and Cy with a handful of bracelets they had made and had us pick our favorites. I ended up with a blue, green, and white one. That one sits at the top of the bunch and hasn't left my wrist since that day.

"Hm, maybe I'll have to head back up there and see if I remember how to make one," Sidney says, gesturing behind her up at the rec hall.

I'm about to ask her more questions, but Taylor comes back from the guard shack and sits on the other side of the picnic table.

"I see toenail painting has commenced. Can I go next?" Taylor takes a sip of their water and points at the box of nail polish.

"Yes! Pick out a color," Gracie shouts, popping her head up, and getting a few drops of nail polish on my toes. I hear Sidney sigh and move forward like she wants to tell Gracie to be careful, but she stops herself knowing it won't help.

Instead, she turns to Taylor. "How was your year, Taylor?"

"Oh, you know, same old boring college stuff. I'm glad it's summer." Taylor takes another sip of their water before continuing, "I HAVE to tell you about what happened at my birthday party last month."

Sidney instantly smiles, Taylor has that effect on people so I'm not surprised. They start telling stories about the past year, and Sidney comes alive. She talks with her hands, laughing. It's nice to see she's comfortable with Taylor, and I hope we'll be able to work up to the same level of friendship, if not more. I know it's not ideal to form new friendships when I'm leaving this fall, but that doesn't stop me from daydreaming.

Gracie is in the process of finishing my pinkie toe, and when she finishes, she steps back and puts the nail polish brush away.

"Done. That will be a dollar, please." Gracie sticks her hand toward me, palm up.

I laugh at her. I could see her running a great business one day. "First, they look fantastic. Thank you, Gracie." She nods, hand still extended. "Second, these are still wet and my wallet is up in the shack. Can I pay you later?"

Gracie huffs and puts the orange bottle back in the box and stomps over to Taylor. "Fine, Zachary. But if you wait until tomorrow it's another dollar."

"Deal." I reach my hand behind me and across the table to shake hers. She has to climb up on the picnic table bench to reach me, then she's back to digging around in the nail polish box.

"Taylor, did you pick a color?" she asks looking around the table to see if Taylor pulled one out.

"Not yet, I got distracted." They look at Sidney with wide eyes like Gracie might yell at them. "How about this green, to match my hair?"

Gracie simply nods and takes the bottle from Taylor's hands and starts on their toes. I'm stuck here for a few more minutes, waiting for my toes to dry, but we should be getting close to rotating soon.

Taylor and Sidney's conversation has died down now, so I decide to jump in. "Tonight is the volleyball game, right?"

Sidney nods. "Yeah, right at sunset. Last year we kicked your as—sorry, butts," she corrects herself, glancing toward Gracie. "That's the maddest I've ever seen Cyrus."

"This year will be much easier," Taylor chimes in. "Zach is like a professional athlete."

Sidney raises an eyebrow at me. "Oh really?"

"Not quite, I played hockey most of my life until I left college, but I haven't played much volleyball." I notice Sidney's cheeks flush as I tell her this, and she puts her sunglasses back over her eyes, but I can feel them all over me. I reach up and run my hand through my hair, going slower than normal for her benefit. She pulls her full bottom lip between her teeth, and I'm glad there isn't a kid at my feet anymore.

"Whatever, you play sports, close enough," Taylor says, waving their hand nonchalantly at me. They're watching Gracie paint their nails and don't notice me and Sidney still staring at each other. There's no way I'm going to be the first to look away.

The angel on my shoulder tells me to look away and let her be, while the devil tells me to do so much more and to find out how far that blush on her body spreads. I meet them in the middle and forfeit the stare down by winking at her. Her blush instantly deepens, and I swear I see her shiver. I smirk, happy for my small victory in making her squirm.

"Why did you stop playing?" Sidney breaks the silence first, cracking her neck and reaching behind her to stretch. The movement causes her breasts to push forward and all my blood rushes to my dick. Sidney smirks, and I know she's doing it on purpose.

"I never wanted to play," I tell her and run my tongue along my top lip, raising my eyebrow at her, waiting for her next move.

"Why didn't you want to play?" she asks, moving her hand to rub her neck and shoulder, slowly slipping her fingers under her bathing suit strap and pulling it down.

"I played to appease my dad. It was his thing, not mine," I answer, watching her move her hand along her skin. She parts her mouth slightly, and I have to adjust my position as my cock thickens, imagining slipping my tongue between her lips.

Sidney puts her strap back into place and rests her hands on the table. She looks like she's about to follow up with another question when Gracie pops up.

"All done!" she announces to the table and, let's be honest, the whole beach.

I turn around and peek at Taylor's toes because Gracie did that much faster than mine, which means they must be a mess. My suspicions are confirmed as I peer over the table and see they have green nail polish on almost the entirety of their toes.

"They look great. Here's a dollar." Taylor grabs a dollar out of their pocket and hands it over to Gracie.

"Thank you, it has been a pleasure doing business with both of you." With that, Gracie puts the bottle away, grabs her box, and starts skipping back toward her family.

Sidney stands up and starts to follow her before turning back and putting one hand on the picnic table. She leans in so closely to me that I get the faint smell of the floral scent from yesterday.

"Looking forward to our win this year, and don't forget to pay the kid." She nods back toward Gracie and winks at me before spinning around and returning to her family, leaving me the one blushing.

EIGHT

SIDNEY

I'm tying my favorite black sneakers, foot propped up on the picnic table bench, when one of the triplets, Finn, comes up behind me and plants his hands on my shoulders.

"You ready to kick some lifeguard ass?" he yells in my ear, even though he's less than a foot away. I have to put my hands on the table to keep myself from falling face-first into it.

"Finn, can you fuck off?" I snap at him too quickly.

Ever since I talked to Zach this morning, I've been on edge. When I rejoined my family on the beach I could see everyone's eyes on me. Maeve had raised her eyebrows like she knew why I took Gracie over to the lifeguards. It felt like I had a big tattoo on my forehead that read *"I THINK ZACH IS ATTRACTIVE."*

Then, all afternoon and through dinner, my aunts and uncles kept making comments about my singleness, about the new cute lifeguard, about how I looked nice in my swimsuit, and I wanted it all to stop. I understand they mean well and want me to be happy, but I don't need them commenting on my appearance or relationship status. This is one of the reasons I keep to myself most of the time. This volleyball game should help me release some of this frustration without harming anyone.

"Sorry, Sid. I forget I'm taller than you now." He takes his hands off my shoulders and backs up, giving me room to finish tying my sneakers. The triplets were the shortest cousins for the longest time, and I could easily pick them up and give them piggyback rides. Now, Finn is almost a full foot taller than me and often forgets his own size.

"It's okay. Sorry I snapped." I spin around to face him. "I'm having an annoying day, and you almost knocked me over. But, to answer your question, yes. I'm ready to kick some lifeguard ass."

"Oh, hell yeah! Let's do this." Jordan, the second triplet, suddenly pops up out of nowhere and picks me up and spins me.

"Jordan, put me down," I yell hitting him as he continues to spin me once more before setting me back down. "Where's Hannah?" I ask, checking behind me. "I don't need another surprise triplet attack right now."

"She's down at our site," he points behind him.

"Ry sent us to get you. Everyone is ready to head down to the court," Finn pivots and starts skipping away, followed by Jordan, and I grab my water bottle and head toward their site.

Ten minutes later, we're hiking up the hill, passing the rec hall on the way to the volleyball court, though I wouldn't really call it a court. It's more like a volleyball net in the middle of an open patch of grass. It's right next to the edge of the hill, and we've hit countless balls in the water over the years. Our rule is if you hit it in the water, you have to get it, which always causes arguments over whose fault it actually was. No one wants to go in the water this close to sunset and become a magnet for the bugs. I've already got four bites on my ankles from the first night, and I don't need any more.

Ryan heads to the far side of the net and drops his duffle bag on the ground before pulling out an old volleyball. Maeve and Quinn open the camp chairs they brought down, and Maeve pulls out her speaker to give our game a soundtrack. The two of them never play since they don't want to and have been perfecting being our cheer squad over the last few years. Maeve has a special touch for finding the perfect song or movie score to match the mood of the game.

We discuss who is going to play first for us, since we always play four versus four, and switch out every few serves. Right as we decide that Ryan, Abby, Liam, and Lucy will start, Maeve starts playing the *Jaws* theme song. I turn to her and raise my eyebrow. She smirks and pops her bubblegum, pointing behind me.

I turn around to see the five lifeguards coming up the hill in matching red tie-dye shirts that say "Team Lifeguard." They're adorable, and I can't help it as I break into a wide grin as I picture them making the shirts together.

"Wait, what the fuck? Why didn't we get matching shirts?" Finn throws his hands up in the air, some of his drink splashing out of his straw.

"We don't need matching shirts to beat them. We've got enough talent to do that blindfolded." Ryan puffs his chest and saunters toward the lifeguards, stopping right in front of Cyrus.

"You want to put your money where your mouth is, Murphy?" Cyrus bites back at him.

"Nothing would bring me more joy than taking your money, Cy," Ryan says, stepping closer to him, fully invading his space. I don't know what's going on between them, but their energy is more confrontational than in past years.

"How about we play the normal way with no blind-folds or betting?" Zach leans around Cyrus and throws one arm over his shoulder. He glances my way, flashing me a quick smile. I'm sure I'm about to throw up. Then it hits me how bad of an idea this really is.

I'm not the most athletic person, per se. I mean, I'm better than Maeve or Quinn, but I'm nowhere near "play-for-an-actual-team" good. I can serve pretty well, but when it comes to spiking or saving a ball, my cousins know to cover me. Usually I play less, and we've established a good balance. Now, I realize I'm going to have to play in front of and against Zach, and he's probably going to be right across from me with my luck. Looking at me. Spiking the ball with his much taller frame. I'm so screwed.

I don't know why I'm so nervous all of a sudden. I'm not here to impress him, I'm here to have fun with my family and my Islands friends that I only see once a year. However, I'm not *not* trying to impress him. Usually, if I get this nervous about potentially embarrassing myself, I would sit on the sidelines, but Cali Sidney wouldn't. No, she would play and continue to flirt with Zach like she did this afternoon. I'm going to play.

"I don't know, making this interesting sounds fun."

Wait, did I say that? What the hell? Everyone is staring at me, so it must have been me.

Zach instantly takes my bait. "Oh yeah?" Then he gives me a small wink, and I try not to react to the effect he has on my body. My body feels like it's on fire from one interaction with him. I can't imagine what would happen if he reached out and touched me.

"In your dreams, Moretti." I cross my arms and glare at him. "I was talking about the bet."

What bet? What am I doing? I don't have a bet in mind, but I'm not about to let anyone know that.

I don't break eye contact with Zach, but I'm aware of everyone watching me, and I'm pretty sure Maeve pulled out popcorn a second ago.

Zach steps away from Ryan and Cyrus and throws his backpack on the ground next to Ryan's duffle. "What kind of bet?"

Now Zach is right in front of me, and I have to tilt my head to keep eye contact. His scent washes over me, and it's masculine, with a hint of lavender and sunscreen. His green eyes are challenging, an invitation for my mischievous side to come out and play.

I run through the options in my head. First, skinny dipping sounds fun and very on-brand for a bet, but I don't want to skinny dip with my cousins if we lose, so that's out. Second, a money bet is boring. Third, I can't pick anything in the style of seven minutes in heaven because we aren't fifteen. Then I've got it.

I lean around Zach to meet Cyrus' eyes. "Are you still planning to throw a party later this week?" Usually, Cyrus throws at least one party at his place when we are here, and I assume he plans to do the same this year.

"Of course," he nods.

"Perfect. How about if Team Lifeguard wins, the Murphys will buy all the alcohol for the party." I hear multiple protests behind me, and without breaking eye contact with Zach, I flip them all off over my shoulder. "But, if we win, all five of you have to be our designated drivers for the evening and make sure we have drinks all night long."

"I don't know—" Ryan starts to say.

"Oh shut up, Ry. You started this. The girl is doing

business," Maeve shouts from behind me. Everyone goes silent after that, and all eyes are on Zach now.

I hold my breath waiting for his answer. Sure, it's kind of a dumb bet, but it's the best I could come up with that didn't cause too much harm and is still beneficial to the winner. Plus, none of us are ever excited about driving to Cyrus's house and back.

Zach does a quick glance behind him, and I see the other lifeguards give him a nod before he faces me and sticks out his hand. "You're on. First one to eleven wins."

"Deal. Prepare to make drinks for ten all night, Moretti." I reach out to shake his hand, and my skin tingles the second he closes his fingers over mine. The calluses of his fingers against my skin are rough, and I wonder what they would feel like running down my bare back. I realize we've been shaking hands for too long and drop his hand, pivoting and returning to the sidelines to wait for my turn. Maeve and Quinn stare at me with knowing glances, and Hannah comes up next to me, giving me a small hip bump.

"Feeling competitive tonight?" Hannah asks.

"I guess so. I thought I'd make things more interesting this year," I say, shrugging my shoulders.

"I can't *wait* to see how this plays out." Maeve readjusts in her chair and starts to play "Bad Blood" by Taylor Swift right as Ryan gets ready to serve.

NINE

SIDNEY

Forty-five minutes later, the game is tied 10-10, the sun has set, the camp lights are on, and I haven't embarrassed myself yet. Taylor is the only lifeguard not playing right now, but they are loud enough on their own to cheer for their team. Meanwhile, Maeve and Quinn have abandoned their chairs and are standing up holding hands, and Maeve has started playing the *Pitch Perfect* version of "The Final Countdown". Abby, Ryan, Hannah, and Jordan have their arms linked since their fate is now in the hands of Finn, Lucy, Liam, and me.

It's Zach's serve, and my heart rate has never been higher. Of course, his serve is annoyingly perfect and goes right to Liam who bumps it to Finn, setting Lucy up for a perfect spike to the other side. Zach manages to get to the ball before it hits the ground, bumping it to Allison. Cyrus sets it in time for Zach to come and spike it over the net. His spike flies like it's going to land in the middle of the four of us, and I see my opportunity.

"Got it," I yell before I realize I've miscalculated the landing spot of the ball, and in order to get it I'm going to have to dive. With all this adrenaline running through me, I dive right for the ball and into the grass. The dirt and rocks scrape against my arms, and a cloud of dirt blocks my vision, but the ball connects with my hands, and I pray it goes over the net.

I hear screams, and I can't tell if they are cheering for us or them until Abby is at my side. "Sid, are you okay?"

I push myself off of the ground. There's nothing but pain in my forearms, and I can't breathe. I let out a groan because there is no way I'm going to cry right now.

"Slow, don't get up too fast," Abby says, putting her hands on my shoulders and helping me sit down on the ground.

"Wait, what happened?" I look up, and I see everyone has stopped playing. Zach is headed our way with his backpack. "Did we win?"

Abby lets out a small laugh. "Yeah, we did. Your save was awesome, and Lucy managed to send it back over the net in time. Allison was so shocked you dove for the ball that she couldn't react fast enough to save it."

Zach reaches us and crouches down, setting his backpack between his legs and unzipping it. "Hey Sid, killer save. You okay?"

I do my best not to notice how his shorts move up his thighs and expose some of the paler skin underneath. He's so close that I can smell him again, and it makes me dizzy.

Heat rushes to my face, and I look over at Abby wide-eyed, having trouble breathing at the moment.

"She'll be okay, she kind of knocked the wind out of herself with that dive," Abby chimes in for me. "She got scraped up, too."

"I did?" I inspect my arms and don't see anything.

She sighs and lifts my arms. "Yeah, I would say so."

Zach winces and starts digging around in his backpack.

I tilt my head to see that the other side of my arms are red. Both of my arms are bleeding, and I can't tell how long the cuts are because the blood is mixing with the dirt, smearing it all over. Luckily I'm wearing athletic leggings, so my knees and legs are fine but might suffer some bruising later.

"Oh, oops. That's my bad," I say, chuckling.

"I think it's my fault since you were trying to block my spike." Zach pulls multiple things out of his backpack. "Do you mind if I take a look?" He nods toward my arm.

"No, go ahead." I stretch my arms toward him, and he wraps one hand around my wrist, turning my arm over. I don't know if I'm still winded or if it's because Zach's touching me, but my breathing has not improved since sitting up.

"Abby, could you get me some water?" he asks without taking his eyes away from my arm.

"Sure thing."

"You know you don't have to do this. I can take care of it." I go to pull my arm away, needing the physical contact with him to end before I do something dramatic. He squeezes my wrist and furrows his brows at me, a deep line forming between them.

"I know, but I feel responsible for this." He turns my arm toward me. "Please let me help you?"

"Okay," I say, barely a whisper. And I almost faint right there from the twinkle in his green eyes as I tell him yes.

Abby comes back and hands Zach a water bottle. He takes it from her with a quick thanks and uncaps the lid before stretching my arm out and pouring water over it. He reaches down to his pile of stuff and grabs a small towel and wipes both of my arms. I flinch at the sting of it.

"Sorry, you've got a few small rocks in there. I'm going to need to take those out," he says, inspecting my arms.

"Lifeguard training worked well, huh?" I nod to his bag. "You had all that stuff in your bag?"

"Yeah well, I say it's always better to be prepared." He leans to whisper to me, "I was a Boy Scout, plus you never know when a pretty girl is going to need assistance."

"I'm not some damsel in distress, Moretti," I reply, channeling some of the feminism back into me before I fall into some kind of hero trance and give myself over to him.

"My apologies, prin—"

"Is she good, Zach?" Cyrus calls over. I'm pretty sure he almost called me princess, and I don't know why that gives me butterflies.

"Yeah, it's only a few small scrapes. It looks worse than it is. I'm going to make sure it's cleaned out," he replies over his shoulder before returning to my arm.

I flinch again as he pulls out the final rocks stuck in my skin and wipes my arm one last time.

"Sorry, almost done."

I stay silent, watching him apply some Neosporin and put two Band-Aids on each of my arms. He gathers everything up and puts it away, and I haven't stopped staring at him, mesmerized by the movement of his hands. He zips his bag and lifts his head to look at me.

"Do you need another minute?" he asks, standing up and holding out a hand toward me.

"No, I'm good now." I reach up, grabbing his hand, and he helps me stand up. His hand is around mine like it was always supposed to be there, and I miss the warmth when he drops it. I wipe the dirt off my knees and ass, and I realize everyone has moved over to the Point. "I'm embarrassed, is all. Thank you for helping me."

Zach adjusts his backpack and pulls his ball cap from the side pocket. He brushes back his hair before placing it backward on his head, and it's like he's trying to kill me.

"You shouldn't be embarrassed—that was impressive. The cuts aren't bad, but we don't want you getting an infection on vacation, right?"

"Right. Well, shall we join the others?" I nod toward the Point.

"I gotta head out, but I'll be back in the morning," Zach sounds disappointed as he tells me this and reaches out to tuck a piece of hair behind my ear that must have come out of my ponytail during the game. His hands keep finding their way to my skin, and I desperately need them to find their way to other places on my body.

"You can't stay for one drink?" I can't help but push. I want him to stay, I want to hang out with him more when he isn't working.

Zach steps closer to me, and I can feel his body heat. I have to tilt my head to look up at him, and his lips look impossibly soft, illuminated by the moonlight. If I step forward I bet I could—

"Sid, did you hear what I said?"

I'm pulled back from my train of thought and look down. "Sorry, no I didn't."

He reaches up and places his finger and thumb under my chin to tilt my head back up. "I said, I really wish I could. But I'm worried that if I stay, I won't be able to leave, and I *really* should get some rest tonight."

The look in his eyes tells me he isn't lying, and the dilation of his pupils gives me an idea as to why he wouldn't be able to leave. He moves his thumb up to brush the corner of my mouth, and my mouth parts slightly with a small gasp. He leans down so our lips are a breath apart, so close I can feel the heat of his breath on my lips. I'm about to close my eyes when Zach says, "Trust me, the best thing for me to do is leave right now." Then he releases my chin and jogs toward the marina.

I'm speechless, watching him leave. Right before he disappears around the marina building, he turns around and looks right at me. He's lit by moonlight and the camp lights, and I can see a smile stretch across his face. He lifts his arm up and waves at me. Unable to look anywhere but at him, I give him a small wave before he's gone. And I'm left wondering why he almost kissed me but didn't.

TEN

SIDNEY

Mornings at the Islands are usually one of my favorite times. Sleeping in a tent means when the sun is up I'm either up or sweating because I slept in sweatpants and a hoodie since it's freezing at night. Basically, it means I get up early, even if we were up until 2 a.m. the night before.

Everyone gathers at Aunt Shan's, coffee is brewed, and it seems like breakfast starts earlier each year. Multiple flat-top grills sizzle as bacon and sausage are cooked to perfection. Sammy and the other dogs are currently hiding under the tables and waiting for people to drop food, while Gracie bounces around asking who is going to the beach. The conversation is quiet and revolves around everyone's plans for the day. You can be your worst morning self and no one says anything. I love it.

I'm almost done with my breakfast when Lucy falls onto the picnic table bench and sips her coffee like it will bring her back to life. "Ahh sweet nectar, my savior," she hums as she sips.

"You okay over there?" Maeve throws a piece of bacon

right at her, which she hits out of the air and right toward Sammy, who is grateful for another piece.

"Remind me why I thought it was a good idea to put my tent between Finn, Jordan, Ryan, and Liam?" Lucy throws her hand up in the air, waiting for an answer. "All night they were shouting at each other. Finn and Jordan would say something, then Ryan and Liam would shout back, then"—she sits forward with her elbows on the table—"*Then*, they woke me and Quinn up this morning by shaking our tent! I'm so done with them." She drops her head to the table, defeated.

Hannah, mouth full of eggs, points her fork toward Lucy. "I told you that you would regret that."

"Hannah seriously, swallow first," I say rolling my eyes at her as some of the eggs fall out of her mouth.

"Don't worry, Hannah's really good at swallowi—" Abby doesn't get to finish her sentence before a handful of eggs hits her in the face. A collection of gasps followed by laughter breaks out among our small group.

"Hey, no throwing food," Aunt Shan yells at us from a few tables over. "If you attract seagulls, I'm going to have Uncle Owen capture one and put it in your tent."

A mixture of "Yes, Aunt Shan," and "Sorry, Aunt Shan," ring out.

Once breakfast is done, everyone scatters. Some people do the dishes while others go to their sites to take showers and get ready. I don't need long to get ready, and I use the extra time to read and eat some strawberries to keep my hands busy while I wait for everyone. It's relaxing, and I usually love it.

Today, I don't.

Today, I'm anxious.

The beach doesn't open until ten, and being up since seven has been pure torture. All I want to do is go down to the beach and see Zach, but time has decided to move slower than usual. I need to test this growing crush to see how I really feel about him, while Cali Sidney is interested in testing different boundaries.

I grab my phone from the camper and try to distract myself with social media, but nothing will load. I keep it close anyways, checking the time since that's all it's useful for, and the damn thing never changes. I swear once I looked at it and time went backward.

I can't focus on my book, I can't pay attention to any conversation, I can't get ready any slower, and I can't start drinking because it's only 9 a.m. I'm sitting here bouncing my leg under the picnic table, staring down at my book, pretending to read while eating strawberries.

Abby is headed back from the public showers, towel still wrapped around her head, shower basket in hand. "Are you all ready?"

"Yeah, I've been ready for thirty minutes," I grumble under my breath, biting into my strawberry like it wronged me.

She stops right before she's about to go in the camper and turns around. "Sorry, are you okay?"

I glare up at her. "Fine." I really need to get better about hiding my emotions because she reads my face in an instant.

"Okay, hold that thought." She throws her stuff into the camper, including her towel, and runs over to me with her hairbrush in hand. She sits down across the table from me and starts to run the brush through her brown hair. "Alright spill, that wasn't a good 'fine.'"

I drop my head to the table and reach down to pet Sammy, who is still in a food coma from breakfast. "Why do you have to be so observant?"

"Listen, if I wasn't so *observant*, I wouldn't have left you alone with Zach yesterday while he played doctor with you." She waves her hairbrush toward my bandaged arms, grabbing one of my strawberries in the process.

"Ughhhhhhhh," I let out a groan that startles Sammy, who pops his head up before falling back asleep.

"Use your words. Come on, talk to me," she says as she gently hits the top of my head with her hairbrush.

I lift my head back up and rest my chin in my palms. "I don't know how to do this. Be all cool and collected when I'm losing my shit."

She nods. "Cryptic, but continue."

"When everyone left for the Point last night, before Zach left, we kind of had a moment, and it seemed like we might kiss, but we didn't. He said he would see me today, and we still have like forty-five minutes until we can go down to the beach. I'm dying to understand why he didn't kiss me, and I don't know why I wanted him to. This stuff never happens to me," I say ending my rambling to take a deep breath.

"Okay, I need some back-up," she stands up and starts to run toward Aunt Shan's site.

I drop my head back to the table, waiting for her to return. Soon she's back, hairbrush still in hand, with too many people. I've never told this many people in my family about my love life—or potential love life—but being braver means doing things I'm not used to. Maeve's beach-ready, with her cover-up tied around her waist. Hannah's still in her pajamas, and I know I will not be waiting for her to get ready to go down to the beach. Lucy also carries a hair-brush and wears an annoyed expression, like she's mad she had to stop getting ready for the day.

Abby sits, motioning to everyone to do the same. "Okay, I filled them in on what you told me. I couldn't find Quinn, but we have some thoughts."

Lucy sits next to me and starts to rub my back. "First, I would like to say how excited we are for you. I've never heard you talk about someone."

"Second," Hannah chimes in, "we have ALL been there, crushing on a lifeguard. This is different though. They are usually only crushes, and nothing ever comes of them. It's just fun to look while we're on vacation, and now that we've become friends with them, it's harder to mess around."

"Third," Abby goes next, and I'm starting to suspect they planned this, "it's okay for you to like him. We've all noticed him staring at you when you aren't looking, and he's really sweet. I asked Cy about him, and he said nothing but good things."

Their words are starting to calm me down, but I didn't realize everyone had been talking about us already. I also didn't realize he's been staring at me, probably as much as I've been staring at him. My stomach flips, and I can't tell if it's from Zach or thinking about my family talking about the possibility of me and him.

"And fourth," Maeve starts right as she pops her bubblegum, "if he isn't going to kiss you first, take matters into your own hands and do it yourself. You've already spoken up more on this trip than in the last five years, and I have to say, I'm loving this new side of you. She's feisty, and she's my new best friend."

I sniffle and wipe my eyes. These bitches made me cry, goddamn them. "Thanks, I needed that. I've been anxious all morning."

"Well yeah I'd be anxious if a hot guy was waiting for me and I couldn't see him yet," Hannah says.

"And what helps nerves?" Maeve raises her eyebrow as she gets up and goes to my parents' outdoor drink area, pulling out a bottle of whiskey from under the table. "Shots."

"I'm in," Lucy and Abby pipe in.

"It's not even ten yet, we can't take shots," I say, trying to be responsible.

"Actually"—Maeve grabs shot glasses and starts pouring—"you got yourself so worked up and distracted by talking to us that it's now past ten."

"It's what?" I grab my phone off the table and confirm Maeve's right. "Oh my god, we need to go. Give me that." I grab a shot from Maeve's hands and face the group. "Cheers!"

"Cheers," they all shout, and we down our shots.

"Okay, I'm leaving now. I'm sure Caitlin and Gracie are already headed down there so I'm going to go find them. I'll meet the rest of you down there. Abby, bring me a drink, please." I scoop up my beach bag, and the rest of them scatter to finish getting ready and collect the rest of their belongings as I run to Caitlin's site, hoping I don't seem too eager to get down to the beach.

ELEVEN

ZACH

Last night, I fell asleep the second I hit my pillow. The whole boat ride back to Black Willow Bay, I replayed those last few moments with Sidney. The way her eyes darkened when I touched her face, the small gasp she made when I touched her mouth, the way her breath stopped when I got closer to her.

I wanted nothing more than to kiss her last night, but I couldn't when all of her cousins surrounded us. I also didn't want to kiss her when I wasn't at my best.

Waking up this morning, I realized how bad that decision had been because I had a dream about what could have happened, and naturally I woke up rock-hard. I decide to take the coldest shower I can manage, but it doesn't help too much because my mind keeps going back to her. I don't know what it is about her that makes me feel this way. I only know she makes me smile, and she isn't here for long, so there's no time to waste.

In my past relationships, I never experienced a pull to be around the other person so strongly before. Not that Sidney and I are in a relationship, at all.

Jeez, if she could hear you now, she would pack up and leave, and her family would probably change campgrounds so they didn't risk running into you again.

That had always been a complaint I got from people when they broke up with me: *"You fall too fast," "You come on too strong," "You're really clingy."* I've heard it all, and it always hurts. I'm trying to get better and work on it, to slow down when I get excited about someone.

Things had been going well with Luke. Since he had the lifeguard job, I kept running into him at parties Cy would throw. We flirted for a few months when I first moved here before we started dating. I didn't rush into it, and it worked well for a while. Being with Luke had been fun in the beginning, but then it felt like work.

I started changing myself to match what he liked, and he started demanding to know where I was all the time, becoming angry when I wasn't able to see him because I always worked odd jobs around town. Working nights at the restaurant never lined up with his lifeguard schedule, either. He assumed I was cheating on him when all I was doing was trying to be someone he'd like. Whenever we went to parties at Cy's, he'd get jealous if someone happened to look my way. I finally stopped adjusting myself and ended up confronting him about his attitude three months ago.

He told me I changed, and he was frustrated that he had to be "on guard" because I was bisexual. He said he had to make sure he held my attention because I was interested in twice as many people as him. I wasn't sure if he was projecting his own insecurities on me, or if he really was that biphobic, but I can't change my sexuality to make him comfortable. I had done that enough, trying to mold into something my dad wanted, hiding my true self from him. Needless to say, I broke up with Luke right there and went home, leaving him yelling behind me.

After I broke up with him, he drove back to the campground and got drunk with campers. He took one of the boats out of the marina and crashed it into the dock. It wasn't bad enough to harm anyone, but it was bad enough to be noticed by the park ranger. He got fired the next morning.

A week later, Cy convinced me to take the open lifeguard spot instead of relying on the odd jobs. I felt guilty about taking Luke's spot, but the lifeguard spot paid better than the odd jobs and helped me reach my savings goal at the beginning of this month.

I turn off the shower and shake it off, attempting to snap out of the mood I've put myself in. Thinking about Luke always gets me in a funk, which doesn't help my mental health. I do my best to shake it off as I go through my morning routine of getting ready, reminding myself to take my antidepressants, eating something, and making coffee.

I'm brushing my teeth, repeating some of the mantras my therapist taught me, when I realize the perfect plan. I still have just enough time before work to do this. Pulling the nail polish remover out of my medicine cabinet, I start taking off the nail polish on my fingers.

The beach has now been open for forty-five minutes, and there's no sign of the Murphys. Yesterday, they were here right at ten, and every minute that they're not here feels like an hour. I'm almost jumping out of my skin waiting for them. To make things worse, I'm in the chair, and I can't distract myself with busy work. I'm left to sit here and spin my bracelets on my wrist until the skin feels raw.

Since it's Sunday, there are only three of us working today, and the raft is closed because we won't have beach coverage during shift switches. Connor's still trying to perfect the sand pile, and Taylor's sitting at the picnic table reading a paperback that has no business being that thick. A lot of campers leave on Sunday mornings, so the beach is pretty empty besides a few families and their kids. There's not nearly enough to distract me right now.

I'm about to give up hope and spill all my feelings to Connor and Taylor to fill the time when I hear laughter coming from the top of the hill. I may have only heard her laugh a few times, but I already know I could find her in a crowded room with my eyes closed by listening for the sound of her laughter.

Fuck. I'm so screwed.

I resist the urge to spin around in the chair like a cartoon character and lean back instead, stretching one arm across the back and running my fingers through my hair, hoping that it's as casual as I think. I keep my eyes on the water, but I can see them setting up out of the corner of my eye. Luckily, I'm wearing sunglasses, and I'm able to glance to my right without moving my head. Unluckily, all the blood rushes to my cock, and I have to adjust myself. If one glance at Sidney can do that to me, I'm going to be in trouble the rest of the day.

I compose myself and take a deep breath before turning my head slightly to take in the sight of her. She has a different suit on today, a plum floral print bikini with high-waisted bottoms that perfectly fit her hourglass figure. I can see the smallest sliver of pale skin above them and I imagine how soft her skin would feel there. I'm sure her top is a nightmare to put on, with a million straps crisscrossing in the back. My gaze travels up to her shoulders where I see a small tattoo on the left. It's a small butterfly with book pages replacing one of the wings, and I have the sudden urge to bite it. Her curls are half tied up and some fall past her shoulders while the others perfectly frame her face.

Sidney turns around and her eyes lock with mine. Instead of averting my gaze, I lift my hand off the back of the chair and give her a wave. She waves back before turning back to Gracie to help her unpack her beach toys. My shift in the chair should be over soon, and then I'll be able to do what I've been waiting for all morning.

"Hey Taylor, ready to switch? I really could stretch my legs," I ask, stretching my legs out in front of me, overplaying it.

They instantly put up one finger. "One second, I'm almost done with this chapter."

I start to climb down from the chair and notice Connor rubbing his eyes, glaring up toward the hill. "What's wrong with you?" I ask him.

"I'm hungover and could do without listening to Maeve all day." Connor rolls his eyes and sits down on top of the picnic table.

"Woah, what's your issue there?" I ask, sitting down next to him.

"She's always so loud—it's obnoxious. I don't understand how someone can be that bubbly all the time."

"I don't know, it's nice to see people happy on vacation," I say, coming to Maeve's defense.

"It's…forget it, it doesn't matter. I'm going to go to the bathroom, I'll be right back," Connor stands up and heads up the hill to the lifeguard shack.

I look up at Taylor and mouth *"What the fuck?"* gesturing toward Connor.

"Dude, don't get me started." They lean forward on their legs. "They've never gotten along, and it has caused such a headache since he started. Do your best to ignore them."

"Noted." I give them a small salute and turn back toward the water.

I instantly find Sidney in the shallow end with Gracie. She's squatting and holding a bucket as Gracie reaches into the water and pulls out various rocks, selecting a few from her hand and dropping them into the bucket before reaching for more.

"Finding any good rocks over there?" I call over to them, since they aren't far away.

Gracie pops up like a jack-in-the-box, her bun flopping around her head. "Zachary," she yells, dropping the rocks in her hands and starts to head my way. Sidney hurries behind her, bucket in hand.

Gracie stops right in front of me and spins around, reaching inside the bucket. "I found this one." She holds out her hand and shows me a multicolored rock about the size of her palm.

"That's such a cool one. Got any more?"

Gracie's eyes light up as she dives into telling me all about the rocks she's found. Sidney helps by dumping the bucket out on the table and sitting across from me. I resist the childish urge to stick my foot out and "accidentally" kick her. Although that might be better than reaching out and grabbing her hand, which is what I would much rather do. My hands feel like they're missing something now that I know what her skin feels like.

I'm picking up the rocks and inspecting them when Gracie stops talking. I freeze, thinking maybe I wasn't supposed to touch them, and look at Sidney.

She shrugs and looks at Gracie. "You okay kiddo?"

Gracie snaps her head to Sidney. "Didn't Zach have blue nails?" She turns back to me confused.

I drop the rock in my hand, laying my hands out on the table so she can see all of my fingers. "You know what? You're right, my nails look weird now don't you think?"

She tilts her head up at me, confused.

"I might need them painted," I say, leaning in.

"Oh!" She bounces in place before running toward the Murphys sitting on the beach. I see her talking to a woman in a beach chair, who I assume is her mom.

"Hmmm," Sidney hums, moving her sunglasses to her head.

"What?" I ask her, copying her move and moving my sunglasses to my head, now looking her straight in those blue eyes that I can't get enough of.

"Nothing, it's just interesting that you suddenly have clean nails today." She links her fingers and rests her chin on top of her hands. She points at me with her pinkie finger. "Don't think I don't see what you're doing here, Moretti."

I feign innocence. "Whatever do you mean, princess?" I stretch my hand toward her and tap her pinkie. The single second of contact isn't enough, and I crave more.

Sidney jumps, like I shocked her, and I wonder if she feels what I do. Before she can reply, Gracie is back, nail polish in hand.

"Okay, now that I have my tools I can paint your nails," Gracie opens the lid and pushes the box my way. "Which color would you like?"

"How about orange to match my toes?"

"Perfect," Gracie yells and grabs the bright orange bottle from the box.

I lay my hands out on the table so Gracie can paint them easily. Sidney watches her do it, and I watch Sidney.

"How are your arms today?" I ask, nodding toward Sidney. Gracie doesn't lose focus, zeroed in on my nails.

"Much better." She stretches her arms out and lifts them up to show me the now uncovered scratches. "It felt worse than they actually are, which is good."

I nod. "Looks like they'll be healed up soon. How about your knees?"

She huffs and pops her leg up on the bench, pointing to a bruise right on her knee cap that is turning to dark purple. "You tell me."

"Ouch, that looks painful, princess," I wince and try not to picture all the different ways I could help get rid of her pain.

"All thanks to you, *Moretti*," she says my last name with more emphasis, like she doesn't like my chosen nickname for her. It only makes me want to say it again.

"I said I was sorry," I say defensively, glaring at her and sticking out my tongue.

She sticks her tongue out at me and laughs. I want so badly to reach across this table and pull her to me and find out what sounds she would make if I took that tongue between my teeth. I must have my thoughts written on my face because Sidney's eyes are locked with mine, her pupils dilated. She blushes, and my chest tightens.

Gracie picks that moment to finish my nails. I pay her a dollar and she skips back to join her family. Sidney gets up and follows her with a goodbye, and I realize that's all I had in my master plan to be around her. Without any more ideas, I watch her get further from my reach, not wanting to draw any attention to us in the middle of the beach. I watch her as she laughs with her family and reads on the beach, only to pack up and head back to her campsite.

Sidney doesn't return to the beach at all, and by the time we are locking away everything for the night, I find

I'm disappointed to have to work tonight. Usually, I'm excited to get to the restaurant and start my shift, since cooking is one of the few things that makes me truly happy. Tonight, I resent that I have to work because it means I won't be able to come back after dinner if Cy returns to hang out. I know I've made progress not rushing into things, but time doesn't count when you only have a week, right? I need to figure out a better plan. I need to figure out a way to see as much of Sidney Murphy as I can.

TWELVE

SIDNEY

I roll over on my air mattress and reach for my phone to check the time. Two in the morning; I can't seem to fall asleep tonight. Usually, I read until I fall asleep, but I don't want to wake Abby up by turning on the lantern, and my Kindle is in the camper charging. I could lay here and suffer or I could get up and wander around the camp. I don't want to risk tossing and turning too loudly, so I guess wandering will have to do. I unzip the tent as quietly as I can, opening the smallest amount of space for me to slip out.

I slip on my sandals and notice the fire at Aunt Shan's is out, meaning everyone is in bed and probably asleep. Lucky them. The night air is cooling down, but it's not freezing, and the full moon is in full swing. It's the perfect summer night for a midnight—2 a.m.—stroll. I grab a strawberry hard seltzer from the cooler and toss it in the pocket of my sweatpants.

Heading down the road toward the River, it's so quiet I can hear the popping of dying fires and the chirp of crickets. There might be a few people still up, but with quiet hours starting at ten, most people are in for the night by midnight. Plus, the park rangers are always driving around telling people they're being too loud.

I'm pretty sure I'm not technically supposed to be wandering around right now, but if they drive by, I'll hide behind someone's car. I'm too far away from our campsite to go back now, so I might as well commit. I get down to the River and the water is so still, it looks like glass. In the distance, I can see the bridge to Canada. It's soothing.

Usually, I would sit on a bench at the Point, but the guard chair is calling to me tonight. Kicking off my sandals, I cross the beach to the picnic table next to the chair. Climbing up the side of this chair used to be much easier a few years ago.

Adjusting myself so I'm comfortable, I take out the seltzer and open it. I get about halfway done with my drink before I hear footsteps behind me. Panicking, I toss my seltzer off the front of the guard chair into the sand pile below, hoping it goes straight down, and get into the fetal position in the chair. If this park ranger wants to come yell at me he's going to have to find me first.

The footsteps get closer and I hear a familiar voice. "Sidney?"

No. Fucking. Way.

I stretch out enough so my eyes peer out from behind the guard chair to see no other than Zachary Fucking Moretti.

"Oh, hey Zach." I stick my arm up over the back of the chair and give him a small wave. I can only imagine what I look like right now, only the top of my head and a hand visible.

Meanwhile, Zach looks like an angel with a glow surrounding him thanks to the camp lights. He's wearing dark sweatpants with an equally dark "Black Willow Bay, NY" hoodie paired with slip-ons and a backward hat. I'm starting to hate that fucking hat because it's a weakness of mine.

"You up for some company?" He nods toward me and takes one hand out of his hoodie pocket to point my way.

"Sure, why not? You're already here." I sit up in the chair and brush some sand off my hoodie.

Zach shuffles over to the picnic table, leaving his shoes behind in the sand. He shows no signs of stopping and every intention of coming up here with me. I'm suddenly aware I'm not wearing any underwear, since I never sleep in them.

I move over so he will have room to sit next to me, but there isn't much room since the guard chair is barely wide enough for two people. My heart rate speeds up thinking about how close he will end up being to me. We haven't been that close since he almost kissed me, and I have so much built up energy that I'm not going to survive tonight. He scales the side of the chair like some kind of spider monkey, and it's a good thing he didn't see me struggle to get on it a few minutes ago.

Then Zach's sitting right next to me, and I can't breathe. I know I must be breathing, though, because my heartbeat is loud in my ears. I don't understand what it is about him that causes my heart to almost jump out of my chest. I barely know him.

"Did I see you ditch a drink into the sand?" He peers down to the sand pile and the clearly drink-sized hole in the middle of it.

My face floods with warmth. "You definitely did. I kind of panicked and thought you were that mean park ranger," I say, shrugging with a small laugh.

"You know drinking isn't actually against any rules,

right?" he laughs as he leans back in the chair and shifts toward me, his arm resting on the back of the chair.

"I do. Like I said, I panicked, so it was more of a hiding reflex." I don't shift my body toward him. I'm going to sit facing forward and not stare at him. I only came down here to try and tire myself out so I could fall asleep and looking at him will have the opposite effect.

"Well, if I see him come back around, I'll be sure to hide you. We wouldn't want your family getting in trouble again now would we, princess?" He leans in and smirks at me, his lavender scent invading my space.

"Hey! I'm not a princess." I hit his arm that's not resting on the chair, and I'm fucked. I forgot how good he felt under my fingertips, and that's just through his hoodie. I need to find out what his bicep would feel like under my grip as I hold on to him as he thrusts into me. My face-forward plan is ruined because now I'm facing him, and every part of my body has a mind of its own, telling me to never turn away. "Just because my family doesn't bury our poop in the woods and lives comfortably back home does not mean I'm a princess. My family has only almost gotten kicked out once, but I guess Cyrus exaggerated everything about us. Didn't he?" I'm crossing my arms now, still facing Zach, but at least I'm not touching him. I need to get my heart rate under control before I jump him in this chair.

"No, not everything." Zach smirks again and I swear, I'm dying to kiss that smirk off his damn mouth.

"What do you mean 'not everything?'" I raise my eyebrow. "That cryptic sentence could mean anything."

"Guess you'll have to wait and find out, won't you, princess?" He smirks a-fucking-gain. "What are you doing out here anyways?"

"I could ask you the same thing," I shoot back. If he's

not going to give me any information, I'm not going to give him any either.

"True. Okay, when I'm having a hard time sleeping, I like to be on the water. It's relaxing, so I'll take my boat out, go slow, and stick to the shoreline. I like to have a destination, so I'll boat here and back. Plus the view isn't bad at night." He gestures to the water. "The bridge kind of looks like Christmas lights."

"Hm. I could see that. I couldn't sleep either." I offer up some of my truth, seeing as he gave me some of his. But I can tell he's not telling me everything. "Any reason for you?"

"Not sure yet, but I might have an idea. Gotta figure out some stuff first." He shrugs and rests his head on his arm, looking out over the water. "What about you?"

"I don't know you well enough to tell you that."

"Well, how about a game of twenty questions? Maybe you'll be ready to tell me by the end."

"Seriously? You want to play twenty questions right now?" I huff, but it's not a bad idea. I could use something to distract me from my thoughts.

"Yeah, why not? You got somewhere else to be?"

He has shifted closer to me, so I move to face him more, my legs coming up over the edge and tucked in. "Nope, let's do it. Ten questions each. What's your favorite color?"

"Easy, blue. What's your favorite food?"

"Pizza. Yours?"

"Meatballs. What do you do for a living?" he asks.

"Marketing. Tell me what happened with Luke."

Zach tilts his head and glares at me. "That's not a question."

"Fine." I roll my eyes. "Would you please tell me what

happened with Luke? Cyrus told us something happened, but he wasn't specific." I know I should have waited longer before diving into the bigger questions, but I want to know what happened from his side.

He sits up straighter, and his hands come to his lap, playing with his bracelets. "There's not much to tell. We dated for a while, but he's the jealous type, and I didn't want to deal with it anymore. He kept acting like I was going to leave him for the next person that walked by because I'm bi, and it got exhausting trying to appease him." He looks back up at me and shrugs, like it's no big deal, but I know that's not the case. I understand how critical people can be when they find out you're bisexual. They either think it's an open invitation for a threesome or that you're interested in everyone.

"I never liked him anyway," I whisper, like it's a secret. "I'm bi, too, so I get it. I'm sorry you had to deal with that."

"I knew you were a good one." He smiles at me, and my stomach does a flip from his praise. "What about your exes?"

"They're nothing significant," I tell him. "A few dumb high school relationships that didn't last long. Then two college relationships. One girlfriend who ended up transferring. One boyfriend who I wasn't compatible with. Now I'm single as a pringle," I finish up, laughing to myself.

"Makes sense." Zach nods, taking in the information. "How about your favorite flower?"

"Roses," I say, and he raises his eyebrow at me. I know he's thinking about his tattoo sleeve because I'm thinking about his tattoo sleeve. It's almost burned into my brain at this point. Most people have a reason behind their tattoos, so there must be a story there.

"Why do you have a rose tattoo sleeve?" I ask, before I can chicken out.

A smile flashes across Zach's face as he shifts forward. "They're—" he starts and stops, shifting again. He doesn't continue for what feels like hours, then he sniffles and wipes his eyes and I realize he's crying.

THIRTEEN

If you had told me earlier this week I would be sitting in this chair at 2 a.m. crying with one of the most beautiful people I've ever seen, I wouldn't have believed you.

"Oh my gosh, I'm so sorry," Sidney shuffles closer. Her knees brush against my leg and send a chill through my whole body. I turn my head toward her as she reaches up to cup my face. Her palm is so warm, I close my eyes and lean into it just the slightest. Her thumb brushes a tear from the corner of my eye. It feels so good to have her next to me, near me, that I don't care that I'm crying in front of her. "I didn't mean to make you cry. You don't have to tell me anything. I know we barely know each other."

She starts to pull her hand away, but I reach up and grab her wrist. She lets out a small gasp but lets me move her hand to my opposite one. Wrapping both of my hands around hers, I flip her palm up as I trace the lines in her skin down to the hair tie around her wrist.

"Sorry, I like to keep my hands busy when I'm anxious," I apologize and start to move her hand back toward her to reach for my bracelets instead, but she squeezes mine and pushes back.

"I get like that too. You really don't need to tell me anything," she says with the warmest, reassuring smile.

I look at the water before continuing, "We do barely know each other. But I want to tell you. No one ever actually asks why I picked roses, I don't talk about the reason a lot in general because sometimes it's too painful." I take a deep breath, and Sidney gives my hand another squeeze, encouraging me to continue.

"They're for my mom. She passed away when I was twelve. Her name was Rosa, and she always had flowers in the house, but she especially loved roses. After she died, the flowers stopped because my dad didn't see a point in buying something that was just going to die. But I wanted a reminder of her. When I turned eighteen, I started with one rose by my wrist, and these roses won't ever die. After about five additional appointments adding a new one each time, my artist finally asked if I wanted them to mock up a whole sleeve for me. The whole thing has been finished for about two years now."

I glance back up at her, and I see she's using her free hand to wipe her eyes.

"Shit, Sidney. I'm sorry." I release her hand to bring mine to both sides of her face, wiping away the rest of her tears like she did for me.

"Zachary, don't you dare apologize. That was the sweetest thing I've ever heard." She points her finger my way, my hands still around her face as I look into her eyes. I really don't want to kiss a girl right after I told her about my dead mom, but I also really want to kiss a girl right after I told her about my dead mom. I decide it's probably not the best time and return my hands to my lap. She reaches out and places her hand back into mine, resuming the position we were in a minute ago. "I can't tell you how much I appreciate you telling me about your mom. It must be so hard. I hope you'll tell me more when you're ready."

"I miss her. All the time." I sniffle again. It's good to tell someone about my mom, even if I only shared the smallest thing. I can't talk about her without risking a full sob fest, little pieces revealed will have to do. "Anyway, I believe it's my turn? If you still want to play?"

"Correct, ask away." She gives me a curt nod of permission.

I clear my throat before asking her the obvious question, "Why can't you sleep tonight?"

"Oof, I'm beginning to think we got too deep too soon." She gives a small laugh, then she's the one playing with my hands, tracing my fingers all the way down to my bracelets. "I'm scared," she says in a whisper so low I almost miss it.

"About what?" I don't glance up at her, continuing to watch her play with my hands and bracelets.

"I'm scared to be on my own. After vacation, I'm moving to LA for work. It'll be my first time in a new city where I don't know anyone. I know I'll have my family if I need them, but I really don't *want* to need them. It's not that I don't love them, I just want to know I can do it on my own."

I feel her gaze on me so I lift my head, and I can see her eyes brimming with tears again. "I think that's really brave." I give her hand a light reassuring squeeze.

"You do?"

"I do. It's really hard to make such a big life change like that, and it's even harder to admit you're scared. I was scared shitless when I moved here, but at least I had Cy." I release her hand so she can wipe away tears and rest my arm back against the chair.

"Thanks, I needed to hear that." She tucks a flyaway piece of hair behind her ear, and I watch her, so mesmerized by the move that I miss her next sentence.

"Huh?" I ask, and she laughs at me as I take my hat off and run my fingers through my hair before putting it back on.

"I said how about some lighter questions?"

I nod and gesture my hand toward her since she would be next.

"Okay, let me think." She brings her hand up to her face to think and places her pointer finger on her lips. My dick notices her full lips lit by the moonlight, and I adjust my position to make sure my sweatpants don't give me away. She smirks underneath her finger and points to my hat. "Why are you wearing a hat this late?"

"That's easy. I wear it when I boat. It keeps my hair in place. Who's your favorite lifeguard?" I smirk at her and lean in, close enough to see a light blush flood her cheeks.

"That's easy. Allison." She bites her bottom lip and crosses her arms across her chest.

I throw my head back and place my hand over my heart. "Ouch, princess. You couldn't even pretend to think about it?"

"Sorry to burst your bubble," she says with a shrug. "Are you more of a cat or dog person?"

"Cat. I spend way too much time on Reddit cat subs. Did you know there's one for almost anything cats do?"

"No way, seriously?" She laughs and moves closer, mirroring my position with her arm now draped along the back of the chair. Our hands are almost touching, and my heart rate picks up.

"Yeah, endless hours have been lost to the Reddit rabbit hole. What about you? Cat or dogs?"

"If you met my puppy, you would know I'm a dog

person. However, I suppose I could always be persuaded into liking cats." She waves her hand nonchalantly before setting it back on the chair.

"I'm great with dogs," I tease. "I bet I would be his favorite if he met me."

"Oh right, of *course* you would," she teases back, dragging out her words for dramatic effect. "Because everyone always loves Zach the lifeguard after meeting him once." She rolls her eyes at me and puts up one finger. I take my hand and tap her finger in the air with my own, surprising her.

"What can I say? I'm irresistible," I tell her, resting my hand back against the chair. "Now I believe it's your turn again, princess."

She stares at me, a twinkle of mischief in her eyes. She looks around, no doubt checking for the park ranger, then leans in so both of her knees are touching my leg. Our hands are an inch apart. Every nerve in my body goes off as she whispers, "Zach, do you want to kiss me?"

I'm speechless, but I manage to whisper, "Yes."

She wastes no time bringing her lips to mine. Leaning up on her knees to match my height, she pushes me backward. I catch myself from falling off the guard chair with one hand as the other cups her face. I've kissed plenty of people before, but no kiss has ever felt like this. My body is on fire, and I haven't even fully kissed her yet. Pushing back, I part her lips with my tongue, slipping it into her mouth right as she lets out a soft moan that shoots straight to my dick. I can feel her hand digging into my thigh, keeping herself steady as she kisses me back. She tastes like strawberries with a hint of sunscreen.

Sidney pulls away from me, taking off her glasses and putting them in her hoodie pocket before jumping off the guard chair into the sand pile. She smirks up at me, hand on her hip. "Next question, are you brave enough to follow me?"

Then she's off toward the water, throwing her hoodie over her head exposing her bare back, and stripping off her sweatpants. Before she dives into the water I get a sight of her white ass, almost brighter than the moon. I watch her start to swim toward the raft before my brain catches up and tells my body to start moving.

I jump into the sand pile and undress, throwing my clothes in the same pile as Sidney's. Thankfully, she's focused on swimming and doesn't see my full-fledged erection before I get in the water. I'm a pretty fast swimmer, so I go slow with my strokes as I swim out to the raft, letting her get there first.

Once I reach the raft, I see her hanging onto the ladder, still in the water, and appearing to regret her sudden choice to swim out this far completely naked. There's nowhere for us to go, and you can bet there's no way I'm getting up on that wooden raft naked. I tread water a few feet away from her, and her eyes are anywhere but on me.

"Didn't think that one through, huh princess?" I laugh.

She shoots me a death glare that makes me laugh more.

"I don't think you are supposed to swim once the beach is closed either. And wasn't it my turn to ask a question? I don't appreciate you taking my turn." I start to swim closer to her, still far enough away that I can't reach out and touch her. Her shoulders are below the water, and her curly hair is wet and stuck to her head.

"Well, it's a good thing there's a lifeguard here. Now, ask your question." She rolls her eyes and waves her hand, splashing me in the process and letting out a small giggle.

"Can I come closer?"

She holds her breath before answering, "Yes."

I swim a few feet closer, before stopping with a raise of my eyebrow as I look at her. She simply nods and shifts herself on the ladder so she's completely facing me now, one hand holding onto the ladder behind her. I close the last bit of distance between us, still treading water and keeping my hands to myself. I can see the rise and fall of her chest now, the top of her boobs coming out of the water with every quick inhale. I would give everything to see them right now, but she's the one who ran away. I'm going to let her lead.

Her gaze doesn't break from mine as she says, "Go again, I-I can't think of anything."

I love to see her flustered like this—her chest and face are bright red and her blue eyes are almost black, piercing my soul. "Can I touch you?"

I lift my hands out of the water to show my intention, and she grabs both of them, coming off the ladder fully now, almost crashing into me. She puts my hands on her waist, and her skin feels so smooth under the water, but I can't hold both of us here and tread water. I lift her back to the ladder and set her on the second rung, her breasts now exposed, water dripping from her perfectly taut nipples. She arches her back to avoid the first rung, and I place my foot on the bottom of the ladder to give myself some leverage, not taking my eyes off of her breasts.

"Zach, please," she whispers as she reaches up behind my head and curls her fingers in my hair, pulling me to her breast. I suck one nipple into my mouth. She's cold from the water, and she shivers, moaning loudly as I suck.

I let go of one of her hips to cover her mouth and look up at her. "You're going to have to keep quiet, princess, unless you want the park ranger to come over here," I say before sucking her other nipple and taking my hand off her mouth.

"Oh fuck, *fuck Zach*, that feels so good, holy shi—" she gasps as I cup her other breast and pinch her nipple between my fingers. Her grip on my hair tightens, as she pulls me closer, moaning again while I suck and lick.

I release her nipple, and she lets out a small whimper. "I told you, you have to be quiet."

Then I'm capturing her mouth with mine. My hands move to hold the ladder behind her, caging her in. She wraps her legs around my waist under the water, pulling me flush against her. We line up so perfectly, even awkwardly floating in the water. She moans as our centers connect, my erection fitting perfectly between her legs. She moves her hips seeking friction, our tongues fighting for control. I pull her bottom lip into my mouth and tug enough for her head to fall backward and hit the side of the raft. The loud bang of her head against the wood snaps me out of what we are doing, what we were probably about to do in this river.

"You okay?" I cup the back of her head making sure she didn't hurt herself.

"Yeah, Zach, I'm really *really* okay right now," she laughs and squeezes her legs together around me.

"Right, okay, well," I'm mumbling now, staring at this magnificent siren wrapped around me, fully ready to let her lead me to my death with her song of gasps and moans. I take a deep breath, letting my heart catch up with my brain. "We should swim back before someone sees us?"

She nods. "Right, good idea. Don't want to get caught in the water with our pants down." She laughs at her joke, releasing her legs from around my hips. I instantly miss the heat of her around me, and I'm left with nothing but the cold of the water.

"Damn, princess, you've got some serious jokes," I laugh, swimming backward and giving her room to get off of the ladder.

"Why thank you, I always save my best for my favorite lifeguard." She smirks at me, starting to swim away.

"Wait, you said Allison was your favorite," I yell too loud as she swims ahead of me before she goes under the water.

She emerges a few seconds later and turns around. "I lied," she yells, before dunking under again to swim.

Sidney beats me to the shore, and she's out of the water in an instant. I almost forgot she's completely naked until I see her lit in the moonlight, skin shining from the water. I stop swimming and let my feet hit the sand, taking in the sight of her. Then I realize she's running up the hill to the guard shack.

I move quickly, reaching the shore and chasing after her. I grab our clothes and shoes from the beach before running up the hill. She's standing outside of the door, one hand covering her breasts and one between her legs, like my mouth wasn't suctioned to her a minute ago.

I search the pile of clothes for my pants and pull my keys from the pocket to unlock the door. "You know I would have brought you a towel?"

"I know," she whispers. "But I didn't want to wait in the water, and I thought this would be faster."

I shake my head, unlock the door, and let her in first, giving me the perfect view of her ass. I deliberately don't turn on the lights in the guard shack as I enter. If there's a park ranger still out, I don't want them to come knocking on the shack door wondering why someone's here so late. The small rectangular windows near the ceiling let plenty of moonlight shine through. I set down our clothes and reach for towels. When I turn around, I see her leg disappear around the corner into the showers.

"Sidney, what are you doing?" I whisper yell in her direction.

"Washing off. I've got sand and dirt all over my feet now," she whispers back as the shower turns on.

Let it be known that Sidney Murphy is going to be the death of me.

FOURTEEN

I hit the water pump on the wall and jump back as the shower comes to life. I pump it a few more times so it stays on long enough to get warm, sticking my feet under to rinse off the sand and dirt that clung to my feet when I ran up the hill. Completely naked.

Holy shit. I can't believe I ran around the campground naked.

I chuckle to myself, ducking my head under the water to rinse my hair. This is the summer of Cali Sidney, who's apparently very brave, and so far, she's made some amazing choices. I wipe the water off of my face, and I open my eyes to the most beautiful thing I've ever seen, thankful my nearsightedness isn't too bad.

"You're going to catch flies like that, princess," Zach chuckles and points at me. I snap my mouth shut so fast I can both hear and feel my teeth chatter.

"I mean, your upper body is built like a sculpture, but damn, your cock is perfect too? It's almost unfair," I say, Cali Sidney taking over completely. I see his dick twitch and grow harder. I'm glad to see the cold water and chilly air hasn't affected him too much. I could feel his cock between my legs in the water, but seeing it is something else. I need to wrap my mouth around it, get my hands on it, have it inside me, literally anything. He could fuck my tits, and I would say thank you. At that moment, I decide to be the one to make this man come apart, *now*.

"Like what you see?" His eyebrow arches and he twirls, ending by popping his hip.

I let out a small laugh. I can't believe he has me so turned on, and he's making me laugh in the same breath.

"Fuck it. I hope you're strong, Moretti," I challenge, launching myself at him and jumping into his arms to kiss him.

Thankfully, he catches me with one arm around my waist while stumbling back a step, never breaking the kiss. Once he has his balance, his other arm comes right under my ass to keep me steady, squeezing my ass cheek. He leads us back to the shower wall and presses me into his body, the tip of his cock right below my center. If I slid down lower he would have no problem slipping in.

Our kisses quicken as the water pours over us and slowly turns off. Zach puts all his power into our kisses, holding me up against him. Our kisses are frantic, but sensual as he explores my mouth with his tongue. I moan when he bites my lower lip, and I can feel him smile. He bites down harder, causing me to moan louder. He captures my mouth again, stifling my noises. The slickness between us has my heart beating faster knowing it's from more than the water. I need more, and my hips have a mind of their own, starting to move between us, causing me to slide down his body more.

"Fuck, princess." He tightens his grip around my waist and helps guide my hips by moving my ass. "I need to put you down before you slide down any further."

I let out a whimper and pout, despite knowing he's

right. I don't want this to stop, but I'm horny, not stupid. There are plenty of other ways I can satisfy this ache between my legs. I unlock my ankles from behind him, letting him slowly lower me to the floor. He keeps me pinned up against the shower wall, standing over me, both of his hands next to my head. He peers down at me like he wants to devour me.

I tilt my head to meet his gaze as we both take a second to take in the sight of each other, our heavy breaths the only sound I can hear. "Now what?"

He chuckles and leans down to whisper in my ear. "What do you want to do?" He nips the side of my neck, making me gasp.

"I want to watch you fall apart for me," I say as I reach up and curl my fingers through his hair, bringing his mouth to mine in a fierce kiss. Pulling away from his mouth, I kiss the skin above his facial hair and make my way to his ear to whisper, "And I want you to make me come." I can't believe I'm the one doing and saying these things. I've never been this forward before, but the idea of being with Zach makes me feel brave and confident.

He reaches down to lift one of my legs up, holding me in a firm grip. "You sure?"

I nod and reach between us to take him into my hand as I bring him back down to my mouth for another kiss. I feel him gasp into my mouth as I squeeze him from root to tip, my thumb gliding over the head where I can feel a bit of precum. I spread it around and stroke him again, my fingers barely able to meet around him.

"I need you to touch me, Zach. I need it now."

His hand moves from the wall to reach down between us to find where I'm smooth and wet for him. I gasp as he parts me, running his fingers back and forth before returning to my clit. I move into his touch, seeking more friction.

"God, princess, look how you're riding my fingers, and I haven't even put them inside you yet." His voice sounds husky and determined as he smirks down at me.

I let go of his length to reach down to cup his balls, which causes his smirk to turn into a moan. "I could say you're equally needy."

Wrapping my hand back around him, I continue to move into his touch. He puts pressure on my clit with his thumb, sliding two fingers down my center. One pushes into me, and I arch my back, encouraging him. He pushes all the way in, and I cry out.

He drops my leg suddenly and moves his hand to my chin, cupping my jaw and tilting my head up. "Sweetie, you have to stay quiet. How many times do I have to tell you that?"

"At least one more time," I smirk, reaching up to grab his hand, moving it down to my neck, and squeezing gently.

Zach gets the hint and squeezes harder, causing the right amount of pain and leaving me with just enough air to moan. He grins like the devil, kissing me and thrusting his finger in and out of me. I do my best to keep stroking him, but the pleasure is too much with his hands lighting small fires anywhere they touch. He adds a second finger inside me, and I can't help but get louder. I can hear my muffled moans, as much as he tries to quiet them with his mouth.

He breaks our kiss and moves down to suck on my neck, biting it and making me gasp. "I need to watch you come, princess, but I really can't have that park ranger finding us." He releases my neck and puts his hand over my mouth. "If you need to scream, bite down."

I nod and nip at his hand as he picks up his pace, curling his fingers in the perfect way to make me squirm against him. Through a pleasure-induced haze, I bring my hand back to his dick and work him faster. His head drops to watch while he works me with his fingers, removing one from inside me to join his thumb at my clit, pinching it in the most delicious way that has me biting down on his hand. I can feel the orgasm quickly approaching, biting down harder. He brings his finger back inside me with his other, and keeps his thumb on my clit, going faster now. Then he hits that spot right inside me like a detonator and I come around his fingers, biting down hard enough to draw blood. It tastes like pennies mixed with pleasure.

He takes his hand off my mouth and grabs my jaw to tilt my head up. "Fucking beautiful, princess." He kisses the top of my head. "Now clean up." He takes his fingers out of me, bringing them to my mouth. I suck his fingers and taste the sweetness of myself on him, and he stares at me through hooded eyes.

I take his cock, still in my hand, and tilt my hips up to rub the tip along my center, coating it in my come. He groans, moving his hips. I start to stroke him faster with the added lubricant, squeezing the head of his cock and running my finger along the underside. I reach down with my other hand to cup his balls, and he almost falls into me.

Zach lifts his head to meet my gaze before kissing me again. He mutters into my mouth, "I'm clos—" then his release hits, coating my belly.

I slow my strokes and release his balls, giving him a chance to catch his breath. Running my finger along my belly and his come, I lift my finger between us. "Now you clean up."

Instantly he takes my finger in his mouth, licking his come off and nipping at the tip of my finger. Then he turns me around and hits the shower pump, making water rain down on me.

I fall back into the warmth of his chest, my knees weak from my orgasm. He wraps his arms around me and starts slowly rubbing his hand up and down my belly, helping me clean up. My head falls back against his shoulder as one of his hands comes up to cup my breast, bringing his mouth to my neck. I let out a moan when his hand slips between my legs to rinse me off.

"Fuck, Sidney, you're so fucking soft," he mumbles against my neck. My body jolts as his fingers swipe over my clit, still sensitive from my orgasm. "Can you give me one more, princess?" he whispers in my ear.

"Yes, please," I gasp. With Zach, I feel so safe wrapped in his arms. I trust him more than some of the people I've been in relationships with. I don't know if that says more about him or me, but I'm not going to try to dissect that right now. I focus back on the way his fingers are moving over me and bite my lip to keep from moaning.

He pinches my nipple at the same time he pinches my clit, and I arch back into him, his mouth still on my neck. I can already feel the orgasm building, rocking my hips into his hand as he picks up his pace.

"That's it, Sid. Let go for me, I'll catch you," he whispers and nips my earlobe.

I turn my head to kiss him right as my climax crashes into me, letting his mouth muffle my screams. He holds me tight to keep me standing, my knees giving out. His other hand keeps rubbing my clit, guiding me through the aftershocks of my second orgasm. He kisses me slowly as I come down, reaching to turn the water back on.

"Sorry," he says, taking the water and carefully wiping between my legs, avoiding my clit this time. "I couldn't help myself when I saw how beautiful you were when you came."

I laugh and give him a small peck on his lips. "Hey, you don't hear me complaining, do you?"

He laughs and slowly moves me into an upright position, turning me to face him. He cups my jaw and runs a thumb across my cheek. "This blush is going to kill me, Sidney." More heat spreads across my face, not sure how much more red it can get after that.

"Stay here, I'm going to grab us some towels. The bathroom's right over there if you need it." He points behind him, then disappears around the corner.

I quickly run over to the bathroom to pee, since I don't feel comfortable peeing in the lifeguard's shower. Hooking up? Sure that's fine, but I draw the line at peeing in here. Right as I'm coming out, he is back with two towels, one wrapped around his waist. I take the other one from him and start to dry off. When I lift my head, I see him watching me, pupils still blown.

"What?" I chuckle nervously as I wrap the towel around my body.

"I'm thinking about how bummed I am that we hooked up here, and how I can't fuck you properly." He smirks at me, leaning against the wall and crossing his arms. The way his arms flex and the moonlight hits his tattoos is also making me thoroughly bummed it didn't happen either.

"Well, Moretti, maybe we can try again, but please don't ask me to bring you back to my tent." I move past him to see he's gotten the sand off my clothes and laid them out on a bench, my glasses folded on top of my hoodie.

"No, that sounds awful," he agrees. "Plus you're way too loud for that."

"I'm not," I whisper-yell and point a finger at him, getting dressed.

"Um, you sure about that?" He waves his hand in the air, teeth marks clearly visible on his palm.

"Point taken. My apologies if I hurt you." I pull my hoodie over my head, and by the time I put my glasses back on, he's dressed, too.

"You didn't." He steps closer to me and leans down, hands in his pockets. "I very much enjoyed every second of that."

I take his face in my hands and bring his mouth to mine for a quick kiss. "Thank you, Zach. I'm definitely going to be able to fall asleep now."

"No problem, princess. Glad I could be of assistance."

He locks the door as we leave, and I'm looking around to check for any signs of the park ranger anywhere. "We're all clear, I don't see him."

"Perfect," he says, grabbing my arm and pulling me into a hug. He relaxes in my arms and I could fall asleep standing here if he would let me.

"You're working tomorrow?" I ask.

"I am, I'll see you then?" His big hopeful eyes pierce me, and I don't know how anyone would ever be able to say no to that.

"Of course, my tan isn't perfected yet." I move to my tiptoes to kiss him.

This kiss isn't like our previous ones. It's slow and calm, and it goes on for what feels like minutes, slowing down to let us have this perfect moment. We finally pull apart and say goodbye, him heading toward the marina and me back to camp, still unsure if tonight had been a wildly vivid dream or reality. By the time I crawl back into the tent and my head hits my pillow, I'm still not sure.

FIFTEEN

SIDNEY

S omething soft hits me in the face with enough force to wake me up.

"What the fuck, Abby?" I put my arms up over my face in time to block something else from hitting me. I sit up and see she's thrown two pairs of rolled-up socks at me from across the tent. "Can't you ever wake me up nicely?"

"*Sidney,*" she whisper-yells, throwing another pair of socks at me. "*Marie.*" Socks. "*Murphy.*"

"What?" I hiss back at her, searching for my glasses and moving socks away from me. I turn back toward Abby and she's sitting up on her air mattress pointing at me.

"What's on your *neck?*"

I panic and start swatting at my neck. "What, is there a spider? Is it a bug? Why wouldn't you get it instead of throwing socks at me?"

"Oh, that's no bug." Her demeanor is calmer as she tosses me a compact mirror. "Take a look." She's smirking now, and I still have no idea what she's talking about, but I assume I'm in no immediate danger since she's in no rush to save me.

I open the mirror, inspect my neck, and gasp. Right at the base of my neck on the left side is a small hickey. Zachary. Fucking. Moretti. Gave me a goddamn hickey. He's a dead man.

"It wasn't a dream," I whisper to myself, and I rub my fingers over the hickey. On top of me never talking to my family about my relationships, I'm pretty good about making sure there are no visible marks leftover from sexual encounters. This one is small, and hopefully I'll be able to cover it up.

If my family sees it, the floodgates for questions and comments will be opened. I bruise pretty easily so I'm not surprised I have one. Usually my boobs will end up with bruises if the person is rough enough. I drop the mirror and lift up my hoodie to check my boobs, and sure enough, there's some bruising right around my nipples.

"Sidney! Maybe a warning before you flash me?" Abby shouts and throws another pair of socks at me. "What the hell happened to you?"

I stare at her. "I—uh—last night—"

"Please put your boobs away," she sighs.

"Oh, right. Sorry." I pull my hoodie back down. "Okay so…" I trail off. I've never been on this end of the conversation with Abby. Usually, she's calling to tell me all about her hookups or the situations her and her friends have gotten into. But Cali Sidney desperately wants to share everything about Zach. I take a deep breath. "I hooked up with Zach last night."

This time a pillow hits me in the face.

I fill Abby in on everything that happened last night, leaving out the specific details of what we did in the shower. By the time we emerged from our tent, breakfast was ready and everyone was already itching to get down to the beach.

Now everyone is relaxing on the beach, reading and enjoying vacation. Meanwhile, I'm a live wire. The second we got down here, Zach's eyes were on me. I saw him and instantly blushed. I know I can't let my eyes wander his way, or I'll completely give myself away. Abby's no help, widening her eyes every time I glance her way. I'm trying to mind my own business and these two are making things increasingly difficult.

My body temperature rises, and I know my blush is only going to get worse if he keeps staring at me. I need to cool down and fast.

I set my book down and stand up. "Anyone want to go for a dip?" The River water will have to do since I don't want to run to the showers.

"I'll come." Maeve sets her book aside, followed by Quinn and Lucy. We head into the water, and it's the perfect temperature to cool me down, but I still jump at how cold it is. I try to focus on the sand and how squishy it is between my toes, but I can still feel his damn eyes on me, even more now.

I swim out far enough so my shoulders stay underwater, and my fear is confirmed when I turn around toward my cousins, and Zach's gaze is on me.

"Hey Sid, you might need some more sunscreen, your face is really red," Maeve says, swimming up next to me and pointing at my face.

"Maeve, I don't think that's a sunburn," Lucy giggles, nodding behind her toward Zach.

Maeve, subtle as ever, whips her head to look right at him. Of course, fearless and friendly Zach smiles and waves, not breaking eye contact with me.

"Care to share with the class?" Maeve turns back toward me and my face gets warmer.

"Ugh, no, please stop looking at me," I groan, and I dunk underwater to cool my face down. I know I can't survive under the water unless I miraculously grow gills and will eventually have to face my cousins. When I resurface, all three of them are staring at me.

"Well? Are you going to spill?" Quinn cocks her eyebrow, glaring at me.

"We kind of kissed..." I whisper all I'm willing to reveal. They don't get the full story like Abby, but I know I have to tell them something or they won't leave me alone.

Quinn floats there, mouth agape. Meanwhile, Maeve and Lucy shriek and splash water at me. I glance up at Zach and can tell he's trying not to laugh. I know I'm in some serious trouble.

"Wait, does Abby know?" Quinn asks, glancing back as Abby makes her way into the water toward us, no doubt coming to see why we were all shrieking.

"She knows, I told her about it this morning." I still can't believe I told her everything, but it also felt thrilling to tell her, because I wasn't going to believe it happened if I didn't tell someone. It wasn't the first time I told her about hookups, but the first time I went into detail about one. It felt freeing to tell her everything and watch her reactions, and it makes me want to tell them more so I can see those same surprised faces.

I've unlocked this new and spontaneous side of Sidney that's been buried deep down, and is finally deciding to surface after meeting Zach. I should have been more prepared that they'd ask me questions, especially since they're always sharing with me. Being on the other end of things for once is starting to be something exciting instead of something scary.

Abby swims up between Maeve and Lucy, her hair tied up as high as it can go, and her blue sunglasses match her blue scrunchie. She doesn't say hi or acknowledge anyone but me and says, "Do they know?"

"They know," I reply.

"Do they know I know?"

"They know you know," I nod and sink deeper into the water, my heart pounds at the excitement, but I'm sure I'm as red as a tomato and giving away all my emotions with my face.

"Is he looking at us?"

I nod.

"Has he been looking at you all morning?"

I nod.

"Do you want to go back up to camp?"

After a small hesitation, I shake my head.

All four of them shriek this time as I fully submerge myself underwater. Coming back up I don't dare glance his way, but I don't feel his eyes on me anymore, and I don't want to find out why. "You have to keep this between us, I don't want all the parents knowing about this and making him feel uncomfortable," I plead at them and they all nod in unison. The last thing I need is my uncles pulling some overprotective bullshit or my aunts asking him about his hopes and dreams.

Quinn speaks first, "You know we wouldn't want that either. But this is going to be really hard to keep secret if you two don't stop giving each other 'fuck me' eyes."

"Plus you are never the one to make a big commotion. People have already noticed the little pep in your step this morning," Maeve chimes in next. I groan at the fact that everyone seems to be talking about me behind my back.

"But we can do this, as long as you need us to. Scouts honor," Lucy says, holding up three fingers.

"You got kicked out of Girl Scouts for fighting," Abby points out.

"Whatever, those girls were bullies, they deserved to be hit." Lucy shrugs, floating next to Abby.

"Abs?" I glare her way, if anyone would spill it's going to be her.

"Hey, I haven't said anything all day. Not even to Mom. I can keep a secret if I need to. Did you know that—oh wait I probably shouldn't tell you."

"Abby," I splash her, and she backs up, giggling.

"No, but really I won't say anything, this is your summer. The summer of Sid," she says, lifting her hands out of the water and spreading them across the sky like a movie theater marquee. "But also, don't get any more hickeys or everyone will find out."

"A hickey?" Maeve shrieks. "I thought that was a scratch mark or something."

I smirk and shrug at her before Quinn says, "Fuck, he's coming." She nods behind me, and I turn my head so fast I pull a muscle in my neck.

"Ouch, fuck," I rub my neck and turn back toward them. Of course he picks this moment to switch shifts, and I can't tell if I'm annoyed or excited about it.

"Smooth move dude, no one will question that at all." Lucy rolls her eyes at me. Zach comes up behind us on the surfboard. He slows down as he starts to pass our group, staying on the other side of the buoys and ropes.

"Everyone doing okay over here? I heard some screaming." He flashes us a smile and my face gets ten degrees hotter.

"Actually, Sidney's having a rough morning, she might need some mouth-to-mo—"

The last portion of Maeve's sentence is unintelligible as I dunk her underwater and quickly talk over her splashing, "All good here, you just keep up the good work."

The good work. Really, Sidney? Like I didn't let this man do unspeakable things to me last night?

Thankfully, he ignores me trying to drown my cousin and nods. "Sure thing, scream again if you need anything." Then he has the audacity to wink at me. He knows exactly what he's doing, and I might have to drown him instead.

Quinn gasps as I release Maeve from under the water. "I'm sorry, did he just wink at you?" she whispers as he paddles away.

"I missed a wink?" Maeve throws her arms up in the air, clearly disappointed.

"That was definitely a wink. Sid's not very good at keeping quiet." Abby gives me a side-eye.

"Oh, hell. I'm not going to survive the rest of this trip," I mutter. I wish the current would take this opportunity to drag me away.

"Yeah, sorry, babe. You're pretty much doomed. But, I also need more details, and for that, I need a drink." Lucy smirks at me, placing her hand on my shoulder before starting to swim back to shore.

SIXTEEN

ZACH

S itting on the raft, I have a good view of Sidney and her cousins over by the Point. If I lean back enough in the chair, I can see all of them clearly. They got out of the water and moved over there right after I checked in on them.

I could tell by the redness of Sidney's cheeks the conversation was probably focused on her, and I also had a good guess as to what they had been talking about. They're far enough away now that I can't hear them, but I can tell by the drinks being spilled and the arms waving the conversation is interesting.

All five of them whip their heads my way, and I'm caught staring. No point in hiding it, I've been staring at her all day. I can't help myself—everything about her draws me in. When I'm not staring at her, I'm wondering when the next time I can see her is. And if I'm staring at her, I'm thinking about the next time I'll be able to touch her and make her moan like last night. I wave, and they break out into laughter, all four of them hitting Sidney at the same time.

There's a bit of envy bubbling inside me that they went all the way over there, instead of swimming out to the raft. Really, I want Sidney closer to me. I don't know how I'm going to last another fifteen minutes out here, it feels an eternity away. Once I'm done out here I get a small break, and I need to find her during that break.

When I return to the beach, I don't see her anywhere. Her family is still here, and her cousins are back in the water. I curse under my breath, frustrated I lost sight of her.

It's been a while since I had some food, so I head up to the guard shack for a protein bar to kill some time in the hopes that she reappears. The protein bar helps, and I end up eating three of them before I push open the screen door of the shack to head back down.

Right as I step out of the door, I run into someone. I hear the loud creak of the door shutting behind me, my hands flying up to the person's arms to keep them from falling over. My hands register who they're touching before my brain does, and I take a deep breath when I find Sidney looking up at me.

"Fuck, Sidney. I'm so sorry. Are you okay?" The words rush out of me as I inspect all her limbs, making sure I didn't hurt her.

She swings her arms up and rests her hands on my forearms, my hand below her shoulders. "Breathe, Moretti. I'm fine. You need to watch where you're going," she laughs, rubbing her thumbs over my bare skin.

Her blue eyes are so warm and welcoming, I can't help myself, and I pull her toward me into a hug. She fits so perfectly into my arms as I reach and cup her head with my hand, and she reaches around my back to squeeze me tight. All my worry washes away with her arms wrapped around me.

"Hey, Zach?" she whispers, and I can feel the heat of her breath against my chest, reminding me of the heat of our breath mixed together last night.

"Yeah, princess?" I ask with a content sigh, holding her closer and resting my chin against the top of her head.

"Maybe you should let me go, because everyone can see us." She lifts her head, and her gaze is cautious.

I peer around her and see her entire family is looking up here. "Fuck, sorry," I mutter as I let go of her and step away a few paces.

She laughs, "I mean you don't have to jump away like I'm poisonous." She reaches her hand out and grabs mine, pulling me closer to her. She doesn't realize she is, and it's an intoxicating kind of poison. She's slowly infecting me with those blue eyes and soft lips, and I want nothing more than to have her in my veins.

"Right, sorry, you scared me." I rub my thumb over her hand. "I'm actually glad I ran into you. Well, not glad I ran into you, 'cause I wouldn't want to hurt you. But glad I figured out where you were, because I lost you for a second there, princess, and I thought, 'well if Sidney went back up to her site, I might just have to go up there—'"

"Zach," she cuts off my rambling and squeezes my hand. "Did you—"

"Will you go on a date with me?" I say before I lose the nerve to ask her.

"Wait, what?" She drops my hand and her eyes are wide like I asked her a complex math problem.

"I was hoping to propose a date to you." I play with my bracelets to help me get through this speech I've run through for the past few hours. "I have the next two days off, and I wanted to know if you would be interested in going on a date with me?" After last night, I realized letting her in a little bit wasn't going to be enough. I want her to know more about me than we get out of a game of twenty questions.

She's still staring at me and saying nothing, and I'm pretty sure she's frozen.

"Sidney?"

"You want to hang out with me?" she asks, pointing to herself.

"I do," I say with a smile.

"Oh wow, that's um. Wow. You know I'm only here for like a week, right? Then I'm moving across the country. You didn't miss that last night?"

"I don't care. Say yes, princess," I whisper, leaning down toward her.

"Yes," she whispers, barely audible. "But one question." She holds up one of her fingers in front of my face and closes one eye, her nose wrinkling in the most adorable way.

"Shoot." I tap her finger with mine.

"If you have the next two days off, why not do two dates?"

"We could do that," I agree, trying to hide how giddy I am that she was the one to suggest it. I originally had two dates planned but didn't want her to think I was clingy.

"Perfect, two dates it is," she says, stepping closer to me.

"Seal it with a kiss?" I ask, one hand coming to her hip as my heartbeat skyrockets.

She glances behind her, down toward her family, and back at me. "Maybe not right here, but…" She reaches behind me and pulls open the screen door of the shack, pushing me backward with her other hand until we're inside.

My hands grip her hips, and I push her against the wall. "Looking for a repeat, huh?"

"No!" She smacks my arm. "Do you see this?" She points to a small hickey on her neck, and a sudden rush of pride makes my dick swell in my shorts. "You have to be *careful.* I bruise easily."

I dip my head and lick the side of her neck, right over the hickey, before giving it a kiss. "Sorry about that. I'll make sure to keep them out of sight next time," I whisper into her ear.

"I thought you were going to kiss me, Moretti?" she challenges, reaching behind my neck and pulling me closer, flush against her. She moans when she feels my length press against her through our suits.

"I've thought about nothing but your moans all morning." I cup her jaw and tilt her head up toward me before I crash my mouth to hers. The kiss is anything but soft, and as we frantically devour each other, she starts moving her hips, and I reach down to pick her up. She wraps her legs around my waist and continues to grind against me, never breaking the kiss. I run my fingers along the edge of her swimsuit, right down to where I know she's soaked for me. She moans, anticipating what's coming next, and I swallow it so no one will hear her.

Suddenly, the door flies open. "Zach what are you—oh shit! Sorry," Allison yells, turning around and slamming the door shut, leaning against the outside of it.

Sidney peers at me through her lashes, chest heaving and lips swollen from mine. I rest my forehead against hers.

"Do you really have to do that when he's working?" Allison groans through the door.

"Sorry, Al, we kind of got carried away," Sidney calls back, laughing. She gives me a quick peck on my lips before releasing her legs from around my waist and dropping to the floor. "Zach will be right out, but he needs a minute."

Allison mumbles something like *"Oh for fuck's sake"* before she goes back down to the beach.

Sidney slips out from between the wall and me, leaving me to rest my head against it.

"Okay, well, you take a minute and come back out when you can. I'm going to go jump in the River," she giggles and starts to open the door and step out before turning around. "What's the plan for tomorrow?"

I turn my head toward her, still connected to the wall. Considering I'm trying to get rid of my current hard-on, seeing her skin flushed because of me isn't helping. "Spend the morning with your family. Meet me at the marina office at three and wear something sporty, a swimsuit under would be ideal." I turn my head back at the ground and give her a thumbs up.

"Sounds good. I can do that," she says through a laugh, clearly enjoying my ridiculous state. "And I'm looking forward to it." Then, she's out the door and back down to the beach.

SEVENTEEN

SIDNEY

I'm ten minutes early arriving at the marina the next day. I probably would've been here twenty minutes ago, but my cousins wouldn't let me leave camp without packing potential outfit changes, since I don't know what Zach has planned. Quinn French braided my hair in two braids while Abby shoved clothes into my backpack and Maeve told me how to "play it cool."

I'm wearing a red bikini I initially brought as a backup, but it was one of those *if-I-feel-confident-enough-I-can-wear-it* types of bikinis. With the triangle top and strappy back, it shows off way too much cleavage for a family vacation, and the high-waisted bottoms are more cheeky than my other ones. Currently, my black paper-bag shorts and red crop top cover the suit to hide it.

I move my backpack to my other shoulder and crack my neck. Thanks to Abby I have a pair of underwear, a bra, a pair of sweatpants, and a long-sleeve shirt. She tried to throw in the only sundress I brought and a hoodie, but I told her I didn't want to carry all that stuff around.

As I get closer to the marina office, I can hear Zach's

laugh coming from inside. My stomach feels like it's hosting the Summer Olympics, tumbling and tense, and I take a deep breath before stepping into the office.

It's a small building right next to the docks, with an L-shaped counter and room for a few people around it, with a small office in the back. I stop to take in the sight of Zach resting his elbows on top of the counter talking with the clerk, Sally. His tall frame barely fits in here, and seeing his tattooed bicep lean against the counter makes my mouth water. He's wearing a pair of swim trunks that have the appearance of regular shorts with the pockets and stitch, a lanyard sticking out of the side pocket, and a "Black Willow Bay, NY" T-shirt. He's topped the whole thing off with his backwards navy cap, and I feel like I should check my face for drool.

"Hi, dear," Sally calls over to me, interrupting her conversation with Zach. She's one of my favorite people here, with her short gray hair and glasses on a cord around her neck. I've known her for as long as I can remember. I would spend hours here finding the best piece of candy with my cousins. I don't see her much nowadays, since I haven't had a reason to come here in years.

"Hey, Sally, it's good to see you." I slip around the edge of the counter and give her a quick side hug.

She squeezes me and I expect her to say the classic "look how big you've gotten" line that every older person tells you after not seeing them for a while. Instead, she surprises me when she says, "Zach here was telling me all about his plans for you two. It sounds like you are really going to have some fun."

I look over at him and raise an eyebrow, coming back around the front of the counter and leaning against it. "Oh really? Like what?" I turn back toward Sally and rest my chin in my hand.

"Nope! Good try, but Sally here is sworn to secrecy," Zach chimes in, pointing to Sally. She mimes zipping her mouth shut and throwing away the key.

"Well, fine then. Are we going to head to our first activity?" I ask, pushing off the counter and adjusting my backpack.

"As it turns out, we are at our first activity." He stands and gestures to the candy counter, filled with all kinds of old and new candy.

"The candy?" I ask, slightly confused.

"The candy." He drums on the counter and points at me. "Since you said you always used to get some from here, I wanted to treat you to your pick before we head out."

Sally's eyes are gleaming, more than happy to be watching this whole interaction unfold. Trying to play it cool like Maeve said, I don't scream and swoon like I want to. Instead, I nod my head and move next to him to consider the candy options. Seeing them from the top is strange, so I squat down to eye level, recreating my view from childhood.

After thinking through my options, I settle on the perfect pick. "Sally, I will have my usual, please."

Sally smiles and laughs, reaching for a Sour Blue Raspberry Lollipop Paint Shop candy and handing it to me. "You kids used to clear me out of these years ago. I haven't seen so many colorful tongues since."

"I can't wait to see that," Zach laughs, turning to Sally. "How about I buy all of them now?"

I gasp and hit him in the shoulder. "What? Zach, no!"

He sighs, and swings his head my way. "Yes, Sidney, yes. You can give them to your cousins when you get back tonight. Sally, bag 'em up."

She dumps the whole box into a small plastic bag, and

there must be ten left in various flavors. Abby and Maeve are going to absolutely love this.

He grabs the bag from Sally and gestures toward the door. "Shall we?"

We say goodbye to Sally and head out of the marina office where he leads us down the docks to a small open bow boat with room for six. I can tell it's older, based on the wear of the red exterior and the tears on some of the seats. The open bow section is covered in a triangle cush-ion, creating one large seating area. He moves around the side of the boat and steps in using the back seat, and I notice the boat is named *My Ladybug.* I can't help the small tinge of jealousy, wondering who in Zach's life holds that title.

He reaches his hand out to help me get into the boat, and I take it, slowly stepping on the seat and then down in front of him. He doesn't let go of my hand the entire time, and once I'm standing in front of him he pulls me closer and wraps one arm around my waist as the other comes to the back of my head. My hands reach up to his chest, twisting in his shirt when he leans down to kiss me. I move to my tiptoes and open my mouth to him, our tongues tangling in a slow kiss. He tastes minty like toothpaste, and he still smells like sunscreen and lavender. I'm dizzy when he finally breaks the kiss and peers down at me.

"Hi, princess, you look exquisite this afternoon," he says, kissing the top of my forehead.

"Hi, Moretti, you smell really good," I reply, letting out a small laugh.

"Do I? Good thing I showered for this." He smirks back at me before he bends to sniff my hair. "You smell like flowers." He bends further to sniff my neck and gives it a small kiss. "And sunscreen. That's good, we wouldn't want this perfect skin to get burned." He rubs his thumbs over my cheeks, which are burning at his touch. "This is the only part of your face that should be turning red."

I stand there staring at him, trying to figure out how he can make me feel so nervous and safe at the same time. We're standing in a boat in the middle of a full marina and it's like we're the only two people on Earth. Before I can find words that won't scare him off, he starts talking again.

"You don't say much, do you?" He tilts his head.

"Not particularly," I admit.

"That's fine," he shrugs and moves to start untying the boat from the dock. "I can do enough talking for the both of us."

"Do you need help?" I ask and point to the ropes.

"Nope, have a seat, grab a life jacket if you would like one, and relax. We have about a thirty minute ride, then we can really kick things off." He moves to the wheel, resting one knee on the seat and pulling the key from his pocket while I sit down at the back of the boat, my backpack in my lap.

I'm mesmerized by the way he seems so at home here, the way he makes things look so effortless. If I ever tried to drive a boat, there's no way I would get out of the marina without hitting something, but Zach was made for it. I should be taking in the view of the different islands on the River, but I can't take my eyes off of him.

We don't talk during the ride, since it's noisy with the sound of the wind and waves. I'm glad Quinn insisted on braiding my hair so I don't have to worry about it resembling a bird's nest after this. Zach looks back at me every so often, and I give him a thumbs-up each time.

Soon we're pulling into another small marina. The docks are filled with fishing boats and paddle boats. The shore is lined with racks of kayaks next to a building with a sign for 'Fred's Boat & Kayak Rentals.'

An older man wearing a bucket hat with salt and pepper hair peeking out steps out of the building and heads our way as Zach docks the boat. With his bucket hat, his blue button-up shirt, and well-loved khaki shorts, I can't help but think Finn would love to meet him and ask where his hat is from.

"Hey kid," the man waves, approaching us. "Happy you're finally taking me up on my offer."

Zach grabs his backpack and steps out of the boat to shake the man's hand. "Hi, Fred. You know I would have to eventually." He turns and gestures toward me and reaches his hand out. "Fred, this is Sidney."

I throw my backpack over my shoulder and let Zach help me out of the boat, reaching my hand out to shake Fred's once I'm standing on the dock.

"Nice to meet you, Sidney. I hope you know you're in good hands with this one," Fred says, winking and pointing toward Zach.

"It's lovely to meet you, too. I'm looking forward to whatever he has planned." I tilt my head toward him and give him a lift of my brow since I still have no idea what we are doing today.

"Well let's go find out," Zach says, grabbing my hand. "Fred, could you lead the way?"

Fred leads us down the dock and across the shore to the racks of kayaks. "Sidney, did you know he built these racks for me earlier this summer? My kayaks have never looked so good."

I turn toward Zach, who shrugs as he squeezes my hand. It's a quick squeeze, but my chest tightens at how quickly we've become comfortable with one another. How we can communicate without words, and that scares me. I'm only here for a short time, and I don't want any type of relationship, but this thing with him is starting to become all I can think about.

"Here we go, your chariots for this afternoon." Fred gestures toward two kayaks sitting near the water, one bright red and the other a lime green, before he pulls two life jackets from the kayaks. "Now, you kids take as much time as you need, but have these back about an hour before sunset. We wouldn't want you out there in these tiny things when it's dark."

Zach takes the life jackets and hands one to me, reaching and pulling my backpack off my shoulders and over his own. "Thanks, Fred. We'll definitely have these back by then."

"Perfect, do you need a run-through of the kayaks or am I good to leave you kids to it?" Fred asks, adjusting his hat.

"We're all set, I know where we're headed," he says, shaking Fred's hand again before he turns around and goes back toward the rental office.

Zach turns toward me, and I stare at him, thinking about all the ways kayaking on the River could go wrong. I can hear my heartbeat in my chest, and I'm starting to panic. "Zach, I—"

"Sidney, it's okay." He drops his life jacket and wraps his arms around me, pulling me as close to him as I can get with my life jacket stuck between us. He rests his chin on top of my head. "I can tell you're freaking out, and I'm not sure why, so I'm going to hold you here until you're ready, okay?"

I nod into his chest, and his familiar scent helps calm me down. He holds me there for a few minutes before I say, "I've never been kayaking before, and the River scares me." I feel safe admitting that to him, and if it was anybody else I know I wouldn't have. The way he cares for me makes me feel safe, and I know telling him about my fears won't lead to me being made fun of.

He squeezes me harder. "Lucky for you, I've become an expert in it over the last two years. I know it's scary, but since it's Tuesday there won't be many people on the water. The wind has also been pretty low today, so that won't bother us too much. I can teach you how to kayak before we head out, and we can go slow, okay?"

I take a deep breath and lift my head from his chest, gazing up at this boy who is slowly becoming my favorite person. "I would like that very much."

ZACH

I go over all the parts of Sidney's kayak with her and show her how to row on shore. She picks it up pretty fast, and before long she's comfortable enough to get on the water. After we put our bags in the hatches, I pick up our discarded life jackets from the ground and carry hers over, holding it open so she can put her arms through it.

"I can put my own life jacket on," she says, shaking her head, but she still holds out her arms one at a time for me to put it on.

"I know, but I wanted to do it." I get her arms through the holes and run my hands down her arms to her hands, giving them a quick squeeze. I can see the goosebumps left on her skin from the path of my fingers. "I like helping people," I say, turning her around to fasten the buckles. What I don't say is I mostly like helping *her*, but I don't want to scare her away.

"I can tell." She nods toward the racks of kayaks behind me before dropping her head, the rise and fall of her chest quickening and I step away quickly after doing the last buckle. The last thing I need is Fred gossiping about me making out on his beach.

As I put on my life jacket, I start to push her kayak into the water.

"Where are we going?" she asks, stepping into the water.

"It's going to be right out of this cove and to the right." I stand up and lean closer to her, pointing around the edge of the cove. "I'm going to have you lead."

"I don't know about that," she stops and grabs the top of her life jacket.

"Don't worry, princess. They're easy directions, and I want to be able to see you. What kind of lifeguard would I be if I let you go behind me?" I throw my arm around her and give her forehead a quick kiss, unable to contain my urge to touch her.

"Fine, but don't blame me if I go slow," she grumbles and heads toward her kayak. Once she's secure in her seat, I return to the shore to grab my kayak. Quickly getting back in the water and into my kayak, I paddle out to Sidney, who has already started heading out of the cove.

Like on the boat, it's not the easiest for us to hear, the kayaks putting more distance between us, and our communication is limited to me yelling directions her way every few minutes. This doesn't stop her from pointing to everything she sees on the shore or in the water. I can see the joy in her movements, and I can catch a few words if she turns her head. But mostly I watch her arms flailing and catching the paddle before she drops it. Her blonde hair shines under the sunlight, and it looks more blonde compared to the first time I saw her.

A crane flies into the water to our left, and she almost throws the paddle from pointing too fast. I hear her laugh echo among the waves.

"Sorry," she yells back at me, and she's grinning from ear to ear as she turns to look at me.

It takes everything in me not to yell back about how incredible she is, so instead I shout, "You're fine, princess. Take the turn after the red house."

Sidney turns back around and speeds up toward the turn, taking us into a small cove that has a cliff on one side. There aren't many houses in this cove and none on the cliff. The shore is less beachy and more rocky, with no docks. I paddle up next to her as she starts to slow down, not sure of where we are going.

"You up for a hike?" I nod to the cliff next to us.

She groans and throws her head back. "I didn't bring sneakers, Moretti. If you had told me what we were doing, I could've been prepared."

I reach over and rest my hand over hers. "That's okay, I'll carry you if I have to."

Her cheeks flush red, and suddenly I'm imagining the last time she was in my arms. Up against the shower wall as she moved up and down on me. I bet she's thinking the same thing because she licks her lips and pulls her bottom lip between her teeth before nodding at me.

I lead us over to the shore at the bottom of the cliff, and I let the front of my kayak hit the rocks before getting out. Grabbing the handle at the bow of Sidney's kayak, I pull hers onto the shore. She hops out and removes her life jacket, her red crop top bunches up so I can see a sliver of skin above her shorts. I feel like I'm in middle school again. Exposed skin shouldn't affect me this much.

Averting my gaze, I grab my backpack from under the deck and pull my kayak onto the shore next to hers.

"Are you sure we can leave these here?" she asks, playing with the ends of her braids.

"Yeah, this cove is all local residents." I point to the

small red house closest to us. "That one actually belongs to my boss, Mario, from the restaurant. He owns all of the land to the shore and told me I can hike here whenever, and no tourists will bother us."

"Well, aren't I a tourist?" Sidney lets out what sounds like a nervous laugh, and her grip around her braid tightens.

I step toward her and take her hand from her hair. "No, you are so much more than a tourist to me, princess." Then I lean down and kiss her forehead, inhaling the smell of her floral shampoo and sunscreen that coats her skin. I realize that confession might have been too much when I'm aware we have an expiration date, but seeing her so free on the water makes me question how okay I am with that.

Keeping her hand in mine I lead her toward a small path in the trees. Pulling her in front of me, we hike in silence, following the path further up the hill. Mario clears the path once a week, so there shouldn't be anything for her to have to step over, but I keep my eyes ahead of her watching out for anything she might not see. If she ends up getting hurt, I have my travel first aid kit in my backpack.

As we get closer to the top, the trees open to a rocky ledge at the edge of the cliff. Sidney stops suddenly at the tree line, and I'm too busy worrying about her feet to realize and I run right into her. My arms wrap around her chest as I pull her close to me, her backpack getting crushed between us.

"Oof—shit I'm sorry." She reaches up and runs her nails along my forearm, sending chills through my whole body. "You can let me go."

I'm breathing heavily now, and I can feel my heartbeat in my ears. "Give me one minute." I rest my chin on top of her head and close my eyes, willing my heart to slow down.

Logically, there's no way me bumping into her was going to send her over the edge, but I never think logically around her.

"Okay." I can hear the smile in her voice as she relaxes into me and brings her other hand up to my arm.

We stand there for a few minutes, her slowly scratching my arms, and when my heartbeat finally returns to a normal rate, I drop my arms. "Sorry about that."

"You're protective there, aren't you, Moretti?" She giggles and turns around to face me.

"Maybe a little. Be careful around the edge please." I drop my backpack and point over to the edge of the cliff.

"You got it." She turns and moves closer to the edge. "This view is beautiful. I've never seen the River from this height. We don't usually leave the campground."

"It's one of my favorite spots. Take a look around. I'm going to set up something for us." I start pulling things out of my backpack.

She moves around, taking in the view as I get distracted and take in the view of her. She's even more beautiful at this height, with the blue sky as her backdrop. My stomach knots and I feel myself starting to like her more with each interaction. I need to get my feelings under control before the end of the week and avoid being too clingy. Continuing to spend time with her is only going to make things harder, but as long as I'm the only one hurt, I don't mind the pain.

Focusing back on my task, I pull out a small lunch box. "I made us some peanut butter and jelly sandwiches, but I'm realizing I didn't ask you about dietary restrictions or allergies so I'm hoping you're not deathly allergic to peanuts."

"I'm not. I eat pretty much anything and everything. PB&J sounds perfect." She comes over and sits next to me on a log, dropping her backpack in front of her.

I hand her a sandwich and a bag of chips before sitting on the log across from her. I can't help but watch her as she slowly unwraps the sandwich and sets everything up on her lap. The sun's right above the trees that drape over this small area, sunlight peeking through enough to light up parts of her face that have me mesmerized. She pulls her water bottle from the pocket of her backpack, and the way she wraps her lips around it to take a sip before licking them makes me have to move my hands in front of me to cover my body's reaction.

She catches me staring at her and raises an eyebrow at me. "So, Moretti, I do believe we never finished our game of twenty questions."

"No, I guess we got distracted." I take a bite of my sandwich and wink at her. I see her cheeks flush red and she throws a handful of chips my way.

"Be serious, Moretti! I have questions," she playfully scolds me and points a finger my way.

"Okay, okay, what's your first one?" I ask, brushing the chips off of my shirt. I love it when she gets serious and stern with me.

"Tell me more about this whole hockey thing," she says, settling back into eating her sandwich.

I take a deep breath, thinking about what I should tell her, playing with my bracelets to soothe me. I want to tell her everything, but everything right now might be too much. Luke never wanted to hear anything about my past, always complaining whenever I brought it up and telling me to shut up and talk to my therapist about it.

"I mean, only if you want to," she says, interrupting my train of thought. "You don't have to tell me anything."

"No, I want to," I tell her. "It's kind of a lot, and you didn't sign up for that, so I'm trying to figure out how much to actually tell you." I don't know why I'm so honest with her, but maybe it's because I'm hoping she does actually want to know about me. Hoping that maybe I'm not the only one feeling so strongly.

"Well, I'd love to hear whatever you're comfortable sharing," she mumbles through a bite of her sandwich, covering her mouth with her hand.

"I told you a bit already. About how I was only doing it to appease my dad, right?" I say before my nerves stop me.

"Right," she confirms, taking a sip of water.

"You really want to hear all this?" I ask her one last time.

"Yeah, I do. Tell me the whole story." She nods her head and gestures to keep going.

"Hockey is my dad's favorite sport," I start. "He forced me into leagues the second I could skate, and after my mom died he started pushing me hard on it. I didn't mind playing, I always liked skating, but it felt like I was playing because he told me I had to. He had me playing so much, I got pretty good. I ended up getting into college with an athletic scholarship and majoring in business because it seemed easy." I think about all the ways I changed parts of myself to fit into this perfect hockey player picture my dad had outlined for me.

"And you went to school with Cyrus, right?" she asks. I pause to take a bite of my sandwich.

"Yeah, exactly." I nod through my bite. "Freshman year we were roommates. It was right when colleges were still figuring out what to do with COVID protocols. We basically spent all of our time in our room taking classes online, even though we were on campus. Hockey wasn't really a thing either, since the school suspended sports."

"Yeah, I remember it sucked having to sit in all those Zoom classes with people who didn't understand how Zoom worked."

"Cy and I actually had a whiteboard in our room." I draw a rectangle in the air with my finger. "We kept a tally of how many times someone did something embarrassing during a class."

"Final tally?" she asks.

"Over two-hundred." I shake my head.

"Damn, that's high." She laughs before turning the conversation back on track. "What happened with hockey?"

"The second semester, it slowly started to pick back up, and my dad acted like if I didn't get back on the ice as soon as possible I would fall behind. He kept talking about how he couldn't wait for me to make it to the NHL so he could get seats to games." I pause, thinking about all the times my dad changed the topic whenever we weren't talking about hockey. "He never once asked how I was doing."

"That's shitty," Sidney interjects, and I can tell it's not the way most people do when they're listening. She's not just nodding along at the right moments—she's seeing me and I can tell she really cares about what I'm telling her.

"Yeah, it was," I agree, nodding. "Not playing for a whole semester really got me wondering if I even liked playing. It took me a while, but by the end of sophomore year, I decided the answer was no. That's when I quit the team and dropped out. I lost my scholarship, and I didn't see the point in finishing a business major I had no interest in."

"That makes sense. I mean, college isn't for everyone and if you don't want to do it, you shouldn't," she says, shrugging her shoulders. When people find out I dropped out they always ask me why I didn't change my major or why I didn't transfer schools. Hearing Sidney validate my decision does something to my stomach that I can't describe.

"Exactly, but my dad didn't agree. He was livid when I told him I wouldn't be going back to school in the fall, and he kicked me out." I pause, collecting myself since this is the hardest part of the story. I can still hear him yelling at me when I close my eyes sometimes. I wipe my eyes before continuing, "He threw all my stuff into the front yard and told me I wasn't welcome back."

"Oh Zach, I'm so sorry." She sets her trash on the ground and gets up to sit next to me, rubbing her hand along my back. Her touch feels so good, so grounding.

"It's okay. Hockey was the only thing that kept us connected," I say, putting my arm around her. She comes closer, resting her head on my shoulder.

"After that, I realized how he was only using me to live out his hockey dream. I'm glad I dropped out. It's the best decision I've ever made, and it felt like the first decision I made for myself. The worst part is that some part of me still wants his approval, but I know I'm never going to get it. I can't imagine how he would have reacted if he found out I was bi."

"I can't imagine what that feels like. Where did you go after he kicked you out?" she asks, stealing a chip from the bag in my lap.

"I called Cy, actually," I tell her, moving the chips to her lap. "Every time we were at school he wouldn't shut up about this place, and he was the only real friend I had. I loaded up all my stuff in my truck and was up here half a day later. He let me stay with him until I found a place, and I've been there for the last two years. I guess that completes my tragic backstory."

"I don't think it's tragic." She sits up and turns toward me. "It makes you who you are. And it's really inspiring that you were able to stand up for yourself and do what you wanted. It's very brave," she says, popping a chip into her mouth with a nod.

I gaze at her in awe, at the girl I met a few days ago who let me spill my trauma on her and didn't say anything negative or make any jokes about it. She only listened and understood, and it feels like this weight has been lifted off my shoulders. I've talked with my therapist about this countless times, and while she's helped me understand the situation, telling Sidney's so different.

"You okay?" she asks me with a raise of her eyebrow.

I nod, afraid to open my mouth because I want to tell her more, but I'm nervous to keep going.

"Did you know you do that a lot?" She points to my face and swirls her finger in a circle, her nose wrinkling.

"Do what?" I laugh trying to grab her finger, but she moves away too fast.

"Stare at me," she laughs, glancing down at the empty bag of chips.

"I can't help it, princess." I reach up to tilt her chin up toward me. "It's too easy to get lost in my thoughts when I look at you."

She smiles at me, and my traitorous heart skips a beat. "What were you thinking about?"

I sigh, "About how much more I want to tell you."

She nods, and I think she's going to tell me she's had enough for the day. Instead, she says, "Okay, tell me. But let me grab something first."

NINETEEN

SIDNEY

I leave Zach with his mouth hanging open and skip over to my bag. I grab the candy and return to my seat next to him. He's watching me like he's not sure what to do with me. I'm sure he's lost in his thoughts again, and it makes me laugh that he has no idea how expressive his face really is.

"Okay," I say loudly to snap him out of it. "Now I'm ready."

"You're going to eat that now?" He laughs and points to the candy as I open it up.

"Obviously." I roll my eyes at him and swirl the paintbrush sucker in my hand. "What's a meal without dessert?" I lick the sucker and dip it into powder. I see his pupils dilate, bringing the sucker to my mouth and slowly sticking my tongue out to lick the powder off, his eyes on my mouth the whole time. "You may continue, if you can," I laugh, pointing the sucker at him.

"I regret buying you that," he sighs, removing his hat and running his hands through his hair before putting it back on.

"I don't, it's delicious," I gasp, holding the sucker up to my heart before dipping it back into the powder. "Tell me more about yourself, Zachary Moretti."

He shakes his head, "Well, you heard the tragic backstory—"

"Not tragic," I interrupt.

He rolls his eyes at me. "Sorry, the backstory. So a few months after moving up here and picking up the odd jobs here and there, I figured out what I really wanted to do."

"Wait, really? That's huge. What is it?" I ask, probably a little too loudly.

He covers his ears and throws his head back laughing, "Man, one hit of sugar and you get as loud as Gracie."

"What can I say? It runs in the family." I shrug. "Now, tell me about this breakthrough."

He takes a deep breath. "I want to open up an Italian restaurant," he says quickly, covering his face.

He must hear me gasp because he opens his fingers to peek through them.

"Is that a good gasp?" he asks.

"Definitely a good gasp, a great gasp. Tell me more, you can't leave it at that." I move closer to him, my knees brushing up against his leg. His hands drop from his face, and one lands on my knee, which he rubs with his thumb. His touch is warm and despite it being the middle of summer, a shiver runs through my body.

"It's because of my mom," he says, before pausing. The last time we discussed his mom we both cried. I breathe in deeply, preparing myself. "When she was alive, she always had me help her with the cooking. She taught me how to make all sorts of Italian foods from pasta to tiramisu."

"And you like cooking?" I ask, dipping my sucker again.

"I do," Zach nods. "I started cooking for myself again since I was living alone, and it was cheaper than ordering food every night. I realized how connected to my mom I felt when I cooked, and it brought me so much joy to cook for people. Cy has been the taste tester of my best and worst meals."

"I love that." I reach down to rest my hand over his. "Are you going to open one in town?"

He gives my knee a quick squeeze. "I don't think so. I recently hit my savings goal to go to culinary school, then after that I'll figure it out. I don't have a preference on where I end up. I just have to make it through school first."

"Is that why you are working at the restaurant?" I ask, putting these new pieces of information together with what Maeve said earlier about him.

"Yeah, I'm gaining some actual experience there, and I've been saving up my money since I have to pay for school myself," he tells me.

"When did you plan to go?" I ask, noticing the candy powder is almost gone.

"Actually, I already got accepted into the Culinary Institute of America. It's only two hours outside of New York City, and I'm moving down there at the end of the summer." He gives me a crooked smile with a small shrug.

"Zach, that's so exciting," I shout, lunging forward to wrap my arms around his neck. I want to ask if that means he's moving for good, if he'll continue to be a lifeguard during the summers, but I shouldn't care. I'm only here for a week, and I probably won't be here next summer. I try to be happy for him, but I can't hide that little bit of worry in the back of my mind.

His arms wrap around my waist, and pulls me sideways into his lap, burying his head in the crook of my neck. He holds me tight, his shoulders moving. I'm not sure if he's crying or not.

"Are you okay?" I whisper in his ear.

He leans back and separates us, the biggest grin spreading across his face. "Yeah, I don't know. Something about how happy you are makes me happy."

"Well, of course I'm happy for you. I can't believe you haven't been bragging about this since we met. I'm mad I didn't save any of this for you to celebrate." I pull my arms in front of us and show him the empty candy container.

"That's okay, I don't need the candy to figure out what it tastes like." He glances down at my mouth, then back up at me. I realize my lips and tongue are probably blue from the candy, and there's a slight tingle in my mouth from the sour flavor. Zach pulls me closer to him, causing me to drop the empty container, as my arms reach back up and around his neck.

"Be my guest, Moretti," I whisper and stick my tongue out between us, lightly grazing his lips. Then his mouth is on mine, sucking on my tongue. I wrap my fingers in his hair, knocking off his ball cap, leaning further into him. He pushes back, keeping us upright on the log, and kisses me harder. I hear him moan, and I can feel the effect I'm having on him beneath me.

Zach pulls away and grins at me. "Damn, princess. That's some *good* candy."

I laugh and pull him into one more quick kiss. "There's a reason it was my favorite."

"It just became my favorite, too," he smiles.

"Wait a minute." I jump off his lap and stand in front of him. "You mean to tell me you can cook and you brought peanut butter and jelly sandwiches for dinner?"

He shrugs at me. "I can't play all my cards on the first

day. You're going to have to wait until tomorrow to find out what I can cook."

I narrow my eyes at him. "That seems unfair, but I'll allow it."

He stands up and throws one arm around me in a half hug. "Thank you, now what do you say we hike back down and get these kayaks back to Fred before sunset?"

"What's after kayaking?" I ask him.

"You'll see," he says with a wink, picking up his backpack and our garbage before skipping back into the woods.

The hike back down and the kayak ride to Fred's feels much faster than the trip out to the cliff. I don't know if it's because I know the way, or because I'm starting to get anxious about what Zach has planned next. I asked him a million times on the hike and he kept saying *"You'll see"* with a twinkle of mischief in his eyes. He clearly doesn't understand that the planner in me is slowly dying from not knowing the details. Or he does, and he enjoys torturing me. Either way, it doesn't make me as mad as it usually does when my cousins do the same thing to me. I have a feeling I would let Zach get away with more than I ever let them.

Fred's already on the shore ready to greet us when we paddle back into the small cove. Coming out into the water, he helps pull the kayaks to the shore so we can get out.

"How did the ride go? River not too bad for you kids?" Fred asks as Zach steps out of his kayak and comes to help me.

"It went great. What did you think, Sid?" Zach asks, reaching his hand out toward me.

"It wasn't as scary as I thought it would be." I grab his hand and step out of the kayak and into the shallow water. "Thank you for the kayaks."

"Don't mention it, sweetheart," Fred says, pulling Zach's kayak fully onto the shore. "I'm glad to see all the young couples getting out and using them."

I'm about to correct Fred that we aren't a couple, but Zach squeezes my hand and answers instead, "Well, we've got to get to the next part of our night, but thank you again."

He reaches his hand out to shake Fred's, while still holding mine, and I get a strange feeling in my stomach. I thought I would be annoyed if he didn't correct Fred about our status, but something about him not saying anything and keeping my hand wrapped in his makes me giddy.

We collect our things from the kayaks and head back to the boat, where I take the seat across from the driver now, not wanting to be all the way in the back this time. I watch him untie the boat from the dock, the way he moves making my mouth water. I'm definitely a biceps girl because I can't take my eyes off his tattooed arm and how it flexes as he wraps the rope around it from his hand to elbow. My heartbeat quickens and I pull my bottom lip into my mouth.

"See something you like, princess?" Zach asks, making me jump at the sound of his voice. It's much deeper than it was a second ago.

I move my gaze from his arm to his eyes and simply nod in response. He hangs the rope on its hook and moves toward me, one hand on either side of my seat.

"How about I take us somewhere more private and we take a nice sunset swim?" he whispers, leaning down until I feel the heat of his breath on my lips.

"The swimsuit makes more sense now," I say in a breathy gasp.

He brings one hand to the string peeking out of my crop top and runs his finger under it, brushing along my skin and sending a thousand shockwaves through my body. "You have no idea how badly I want to see the rest of this suit." He leans in closer, and I close my eyes, but the feel of his finger and the heat of his breath is gone as fast as it was there.

I open my eyes and he's standing across from me with one hand on the wheel of the boat, smirking.

"You're evil, Moretti." I shake my head and try to glare at him, but it's useless because my face betrays me, smiling.

"You have no idea how evil I can be, princess." He winks at me and starts to reverse the boat away from the dock.

"Is that a threat?" I cross my arms because if my face can't act stern at least my body posture can.

He turns his head my way. "It's a promise."

TWENTY

ZACH

Teasing Sidney is way too easy and way too fun. I saw her watching me with the rope, the bright blues of her eyes reminding me of the hottest part of a flame, and I couldn't help but mess with her.

She probably thinks my line was just that—a line like one from her romance books. What she doesn't know is how true it is. I love the way she gets when I get close to her and talk so only she can hear. I can always see the rise and fall of her chest quicken and the red that creeps across her chest and up to her face.

I drive us between a few of the smaller islands and glance over at her, expecting to see her taking in all the different houses like when we were kayaking. Instead, she's got her head resting down on her arm against the back of the seat, staring at me. It looks like she could be asleep, but I know she's not because her blue eyes are piercing me.

"You don't want to check out the view?" I point behind her to a white-brick house on the shore.

"I am." I barely hear her as she smiles up at me, and I wish I wasn't driving this boat so I could kiss her. I tear my gaze away before I get any ideas, and I finally spot my destination up ahead.

It's a small cove in one of the smaller islands surrounded by a rocky shore and dense trees. There are no houses along the shore except for the one at the very center. It's an older house, with broken windows and peeling paint.

Sidney notices the house. "Does anyone live there?" she asks, pointing toward it.

"Nope, it's been abandoned for years now. This island is mostly wildlife since it's too small for people to live here," I tell her, turning the boat around to face the opening of the cove, giving us the perfect view of the sunset.

"You sure do know all the best spots." She peers over her shoulder and nods, impressed.

"When you live amongst more than a thousand islands, you tend to explore them." I shrug, bringing the boat to a stop and turning it off. I pull the anchor out from under the bow cushion and hook it up to the side of the boat, dropping it into the water.

Sidney has given up on asking me if I need help and watches me move around the boat. I appreciate that she's patient and lets me do my thing before jumping up and moving around. When Cy or Connor are out with me they always move too soon, and there has been more than one occasion where I've almost elbowed them in the face because of it. She sits there silently and waits for me to finish. I go slower than usual, too, making sure she always has a good view of my arms.

Pulling up the bottom of one of the seats, I grab a small cooler I packed earlier.

"Would you like a drink?" I open the lid and tip it toward her.

"Strawberry seltzer, please," she says, pointing to the

one I was hoping she would pick. I went to the store and specifically picked this flavor for her. It's the one I could taste on her tongue when we kissed. I hope she doesn't notice how glad I am that she picked that one.

I grab a mango seltzer for myself and close the cooler. "You ready to go for a swim, princess?" I grin at her and pull my shirt off over my head, throwing it straight at her face.

She catches it before it hits her and pulls it close. "You get in first, Moretti." She points behind me with her seltzer.

I climb onto the edge of the boat, and I see her start to open her mouth to yell at me as I do a backflip off the boat and into the water.

The water is cold but not as cold as the night when we went skinny dipping. I break the surface and turn back toward the boat, expecting her to be at the edge now. But she's not. She's standing where I last saw her, arms folded and shaking her head at me.

"You're such a showoff," she says, rolling her eyes at me while she takes a sip of her drink.

"You didn't rush to the edge to see if I was okay?" I throw my hand over my head and fall back into the water.

"No, because you wouldn't have done it if you could have gotten hurt." She moves to the edge of the boat, leaning over the side. She's right, though. I would never do anything that might harm myself, especially where she would have to take over and figure out how to help me in the middle of the River. It's unsettling how well she already knows me. It's almost like I never have to tell her anything.

I swim closer to the boat and peer up at her from the water. "Are you going to come in with me?" I ask, giving her puppy dog eyes and sticking my bottom lip out as far as it can go.

"You're ridiculous," she mumbles under her breath, rolling her eyes again. "Take these," she says, reaching down and handing me our drinks.

I grab them as she stands, backing up to where I can't see her lower half as she removes her shorts. I tread water and swim back from the edge of the boat to get a better view and see her reaching up and taking her crop top off over her head. My legs forget to keep me afloat and I start to sink into the water, taking in the sight of Sidney in a red bikini. I try to think of something clever to say but the sight of her leaves me speechless as I watch her come to the edge of the boat and jump into the water.

I can see the red of her bikini under the water, and I watch it grow closer until she's right in front of me. She surfaces seconds later, bringing her hands out of the water to wipe her face. She takes her drink from my hand.

"Cheers," she lifts it up and waits for me.

Opening mine quickly, I lift it up, too. "Cheers, princess."

She laughs and rolls her eyes, moving forward to hook her arm to mine before tilting her head back to drink. I mirror her move and it moves her a little too much in the water, so I pull my other arm around her back and pull her closer to keep her above water, not caring if I go under.

We make eye contact and she raises her eyebrow in a challenge, and I'm never one to back down. We start drinking at the same time and the carbonation from the seltzer starts to burn my throat, but there's no way I'm going to stop before her. From the determination on her face, she's about to finish this whole can right now.

Finally, she pulls the can away from her mouth and crushes it with a satisfied *"ahh"* and lets out the loudest burp I've ever heard come from someone her size. Her other hand instantly comes over her mouth and her eyes go wide.

I lower my drink and take a deep breath before matching her burp with one of my own, crushing my can, and tossing it back onto the boat. I reach down to pull her closer, her legs coming up to wrap around my waist under the water, we start to sink but I manage to keep our heads above the water. The sudden move causes her to drop her hand and she bursts into laughter.

"Oh my gosh I'm sorry, I didn't mean to burp that loud." She wraps one arm around my neck to steady herself.

"Don't be sorry, that was impressive." I grab the can from her hand and toss it on the boat, returning my hand to the small of her back. Her skin is soft under my touch. I never want to let go of her.

She smiles and I think for a second she's going to pull me closer, instead she throws her arms up over her head and falls back into the water. I watch her as she floats, her legs still wrapped around me. Her eyes are closed, arms spread out over the water with the sunset illuminating her in the prettiest shades of pink. I suddenly regret not becoming an artist because if I could paint anything, it would be this moment.

She opens her eyes, tilting her head back to take in the sunset, her breasts peek out of the water. The room in my swim trunks decreases rapidly. I tug on her lower back, and she brings herself out of the water to face me, arms still moving to help keep us up.

"I don't think you have any idea how free you look in the water," I tell her, running my hands up her back. She arches into the touch.

"I don't think you have any idea how free you make me feel," she whispers.

I want to tell her how the same is true for me. How I haven't felt this alive and worry-free since I was a kid, but I can't. Today has already been so much, I don't know what I would do if she decided she didn't want to continue our date tomorrow. I'm trying to find the right thing to say, and I'm realizing it's taking too long, and she's waiting for me. If I say something now it will be the wrong thing, but if I wait any longer she might think what she said scared me.

"Stop overthinking, Moretti," she says, interrupting my thoughts, "and kiss me."

I smile, in absolute awe that she's able to read me so well, and I do what she asks. Wrapping one arm around her waist and bringing the other up to her neck, I pull her closer until our lips meet.

The kiss is soft at first, before she parts her lips and licks along mine to open them. Our tongues collide and I tilt her head back to deepen the kiss. She still tastes like the blue raspberry lollipop, now mixed with strawberry. When I suck on her tongue, she moans.

She wraps her arms around my neck, leaning into me. She does it so fast I don't have time to register it. I fall back into the water, my whole head going under trying to keep her above water. We break the kiss, coughing at the intrusion of water into our lungs.

"Sorry, I forgot we were floating," she laughs.

"How about we get back on the boat and grab another drink?"

"Good idea," she says, unhooking her legs from my lower back. She disappears under the water, reappearing at the back of the boat and climbing on.

I rush to catch up with her and quickly pull myself out of the water, noticing her staring at my arms as I climb on board. I don't draw attention to it. But when I stand up on the back to stretch, her eyes go wider.

I grab a towel and toss one her way, "Another seltzer for you, princess?"

She jumps and shakes her head, bringing the towel to her wet braids before wrapping it around her waist. "Yes, please."

TWENTY-ONE

SIDNEY

I grab the seltzer from Zach and make my way to the bow, crawling onto the small space there. The cushion is comfortable, and I bet if I laid down I would fall asleep here as the boat rocks in the water. I would always fall asleep in my Uncle Owen's boat when we would go out, the rocking of the waves lulling me to sleep.

I lean against the edge, tipping my head back and letting the ends of my wet braids hang over the edge. The sunset lights up the sky in the prettiest shades of pink and yellow, making it feel like I'm in a dream. Zach stands between the boat windshields, leaning against one, staring at me. The sunset behind him creates a maddeningly delicious glow around him.

"Come here," he whispers. "You're too far away." He taps the top of my feet, which are stretched out in front of me.

I take another long sip of my seltzer and set it down in a cup holder beside me, tucking my legs underneath me. I drop my hands to the cushion and crawl toward him.

"*Fuck*," he says, turning to set his drink down. I can see the bulge in his swim trunks has gotten noticeably bigger since getting out of the water, and the pulse between my legs quickens.

Once I'm to the edge, I sit back on my heels and peer up at him with a grin reaching my hands toward the ties of his swim trunks.

He reaches out and grabs my wrists before I can pull them any further. "Hold on, princess."

"You don't want this?" I ask him, guilty thinking I must have read his signs wrong.

"Believe me, I do. I'm not the first though." He bends over and grabs my jaw to lift my head so his mouth is hovering above mine. "Do you know how badly I need to taste you?" The heat of his breath against mine only makes me squirm.

"No," I let out a breathy sigh.

"So fucking bad, it's all I've been able to think about since the shower. I wish I had been the one to clean you up instead of letting you taste yourself." He closes his eyes and takes a deep breath. I reach down between my legs and into my swimsuit. Quickly sticking a finger inside myself, I hold back a groan so he won't know. Right as he releases his breath and opens his eyes, I remove my finger and bring it to his mouth.

There's a flash of surprise before he opens up and sucks my finger into his mouth, tongue dancing around the tip of it before swirling around, and releasing it. He tightens his grip on my jaw and pulls me closer. "God, you're already so wet for me, and you taste like heaven."

He licks his lips, and we're close enough that I feel the brush of his tongue against my lips. "That's not nearly enough. I need *more*." He's almost growling at this point, and I'm surprised his hands haven't found their way under my suit yet. But I know Zach won't do anything I don't want.

"Then *do it*," I whisper back at him, nipping his bottom lip. That's the move that breaks him. He cups the back of my head and pulls me into a kiss. I move up to my knees to follow him and he pulls me up, devouring my mouth with his. I can taste myself on his tongue, and I moan into his mouth.

His other hand moves to my ass, squeezing the skin that's uncovered, before moving further down my leg. Not breaking the kiss, he pushes me back down on my heels and moves his hand from the back of my head to my other knee, and then pulls. I let out an *'oof'* as our kiss breaks and I'm suddenly on my ass. The move is fast and exciting, and it makes me think this is what all my past relationships were missing. This thrilling desire to devour each other.

Zach kneels on the floor of the boat and kisses my legs as he makes his way down. His hands run up my thighs to my hips and I'm wondering why my bathing suit is still on. His fingers graze the edges of my bottoms, and I drop my legs open to get a better view of him. I'm almost 100 percent sure I hear him growl, before his mouth is on my inner thigh. He kisses and sucks his way up to my center. But he moves to my other thigh instead. I lift my hips up to try to get him closer to where my suit still covers me.

He chuckles and pins my hips down. "Is she impatient?"

"I'm—please Zach," I beg and move my hips more.

"I wasn't talking about you, princess." He runs one finger along me, and I almost come from that alone. "This pretty pussy is just begging to be eaten."

I can't take it anymore. I drop my head to the cushion

behind me and throw my arm over my eyes. "Oh my god, if you don't do something, I'm going to die."

"We wouldn't want that, now, would we?" I can hear the smile in his voice, and he hooks his fingers into the sides of my swimsuit. "Lift," he demands.

I lift my hips and he wastes no time pulling my bottoms down and off, tossing them somewhere behind him.

"Fucking magnificent," he whispers. "I need you closer," he mumbles, grabbing my hips and pulling me toward the edge of the cushion, lifting my legs up to rest on the windshields. "Don't break my windshield, princess."

"I'll try no—" I can't get the rest of the sentence out before his mouth is on my pussy. It's warm as he moves his tongue around my lips before licking up to my clit. He sucks it into his mouth, and my hips jerk off the cushion.

His arm falls across my stomach and presses down to keep me still as he continues to lick and suck. He slowly moves one finger from my clit to my entrance before pushing inside.

I moan and arch and push against his arm keeping me in place as he pumps his finger in and out of me before adding a second one.

"That's it, princess. You can scream as loud as you want out here." Then he's back on my pussy sucking my clit as he expertly fingers me.

"Holyfuckingshit," I scream and moan as the orgasm builds. I can't catch my breath and my heart is going to burst out of my chest, and it's all becoming too much. I'm about to have one of the best orgasms of my life, and I'm in an open boat on the River. This was not on my bingo card this year. The whole thing should scare me. I'm doing all these things I never would have dreamed of a month ago. But really it only makes me crave it more.

He pulls his fingers out of me, replacing them with his

tongue to fuck me while he pinches my clit. This is the most alive I've ever felt while hooking up with someone before. The overwhelming feeling crashes over me as I release and come all over his face. He laps it up, but I can still feel it dripping down to my ass.

I hear him hum against my pussy, licking it clean, and I jerk when he slowly licks around my clit. He chuckles and lifts his head from between my legs. "How are you doing, princess?"

I can't form words at the moment so I simply lift my arm from my face with a thumbs up.

He kisses each of my thighs before standing up and leaning over me. "Sidney, open your eyes."

I listen to him and open my eyes. I can see the shine of my release on his scruff, realizing what happened. "Oh my god, did I squirt on your face?"

He grins ear to ear. "Yeah, and I'm going to need you to do that again for me some time because I just found my newest addiction." He reaches down and cups my head, pulling me up to meet him for a kiss.

I push back against him as we kiss, moving us backward until I'm stepping back onto the floor of the boat. His hands are in my hair, running down my back, cupping my breasts. I reach up and push back so he moves more, breaking our kiss.

"What are you doing?" he asks, pushing back against my hands.

I push him backward until his legs hit the edge of the seat and he falls backward into it. I tilt my head. "You had your taste, now I want mine." I drop to my knees in front of him, reaching for the ties of his swim trunks.

He watches me untie them and move to pull them off. "You really don't have to, I'm good knowing you got off." He runs his hands through his hair, still damp from the water. I can see his chest moving rapidly, and his face is flushed.

I pause, his trunks just low enough that I can tell where that delicious V shape of his hips leads. "Do you want me to stop?"

I can tell he goes over his options before he settles on, "No."

"Then, shut up and come in my mouth, Moretti," I say, yanking his swim trunks down over his thighs to the floor, freeing his cock. I wrap my hand around the base of it and peer up at him one last time. He gives me a small nod, and then I wrap my lips around the head.

"*Fuuuuuuck*," he groans as I take him deeper and start to work him in time with my hand and mouth. I take him almost completely out of my mouth before swirling my tongue around the tip. There's a small bit of precum already there, and it's the perfect mix of salty and sweet. I work my tongue around the head and down his soft underside. He moans and leans back into the seat, causing his hips to move forward more. Every time he moans, a sense of pride washes over me, and wetness pools between my legs.

I reach up and cup his balls in my hand and massage them before slipping one finger to stroke behind them. He pushes into my mouth, and I see his hand gripping onto the edge of the boat, knuckles white.

I sit back on my heels, separating myself from him completely, reaching up to remove the hair ties from my hair. I run my fingers through my braids, letting them fall apart, and Zach lifts his head toward me, his eyes questioning.

"I don't want you to hold back," I tell him, grabbing his hand from the edge of the boat and tangling his fingers in my hair.

"Are you sure?" he asks me with a breathy gasp.

"I'm sure. I can handle it." I smirk and take him back into my mouth. I need him to feel as free as I do in this moment.

His grip on my hair tightens, as I bring my hands back to his balls and shaft, licking my way around the head. I glance up at him through my lashes and realize he hasn't taken his eyes off of me. The sight of him watching me turns me on so much that I adjust my position trying to seek any type of friction between my legs.

"Fuck, princess, you're squirming so much," he says, reaching down, he removes my hand from his shaft. "Touch yourself."

I don't need any more encouragement. The second my fingers slide over my clit and down to my center, Zach thrusts his cock back into my mouth. The combination almost causes me to come, and I moan around his cock. I pinch my clit, and he guides himself further into my mouth, tilting my head back to open up more for him.

"Look at you," he runs a thumb over my hollowed out cheek. "Such a good girl sucking my cock while fucking yourself."

I moan and take him to the hilt, another orgasm already building. He guides my head up and down his cock, while pulling my hair enough for it to sting, but not hurt. I slide two fingers inside of myself, stroking my clit with my thumb.

"Shit, Sidney, I'm close," he gasps. He starts moving his hips faster and suddenly the orgasm crashes into me, coating my fingers. I moan around his cock, and then he's coming down my throat. I hum as I swallow and swirl my tongue under his shaft. His hips jerk as the last of his come coats my tongue.

Slowly releasing him from my mouth, I push up onto

my knees and rest my arms on top of his thighs. He's staring down at me like I'm the buried treasure he's been searching for and takes my face into his hands and pulls me up further for a kiss.

He hums as he sucks my tongue before breaking the kiss. "Holy. Shit."

TWENTY-TWO

ZACH

S he laughs and her cheeks are so scarlet, they're almost maroon. "Yeah. Holy shit."

I throw my head back and let out a loud whoop and catch her rolling her eyes at me. She yelps as I reach down under her arms to pull her up onto my lap. Instantly I realize how bad of an idea that was because her wet pussy rubs all over my dick.

"Oh my god, don't you dare move." She puts her hands on my shoulder and digs her fingers into my skin. "You didn't think that through, did you Moretti?"

"No, I didn't," I admit. We both sit there for a moment, catching our breath and staring at each other. The sun has almost completely set, and the last bit of sunlight lighting up her face is doing things to me that I can't explain. Today has gone better than I could have ever imagined, and I have no idea how this beautiful creature slowly killing me is still single.

She pushes off of me and stands, her bikini top is the only thing still on her and I instantly miss the warmth of her on my lap. I always miss the warmth of her skin on mine, and I don't think I'll ever be fully happy unless I'm touching her.

"Where did you throw my bottoms?" she laughs, looking around the boat.

"I think they're over by the driver's seat." I point and reach down to pull my trunks back up, tucking my dick away. She pulls out clothes from her backpack. "Are you cold? Do you want a hoodie?" I get up and pull up the seat I'm sitting on, pulling out one of my sweatshirts from the storage area.

"I really just want to change out of my suit, if you don't mind?" She holds up a pair of black underwear and a black bra, and I realize this is the first time I've seen her underwear since she's always in swimsuits. The idea of her wearing that matching black set makes me want to lay her back on the bow of the boat and make her scream so loud they hear her back at camp.

"No, no that's totally fine." I turn to fix the seat. "Just don't—" right as I turn back around she already has her top off and her boobs are out. I groan and throw my hands over my eyes and fall back into the seat. "Sidney, please warn a man before you try to kill him."

"Sorry," she giggles.

"It's fine, princess, really. My dick just wasn't ready to see your boobs." I keep my eyes closed and adjust myself in my trunks, already half-hard from the sight of her.

"Wait, really? That fast?" I can hear the shock in her voice and it makes me want to show her how long I could last with her. She makes me feel invincible, and I want to show her that.

"Really. I lose my mind when I'm around you." I'm talking to the darkened night sky now, not ready to see if she's fully clothed yet. "Are you dressed?"

"Almost." I hear her moving toward me, and her legs

brush up against my knees. "I am a bit cold. Is this for me?" She starts to pull the sweatshirt off my lap, and I reach out to grab her wrist.

"Let me," I say and stand up in front of her, taking the hoodie. I see she's wearing sweatpants and she didn't put a shirt on. Pulling the hoodie over her head, I graze her sides with my fingers and she shivers. The hoodie swallows her and falls almost to her knees, her head pops out of the top and her hair has only grown more wild. I run my fingers through it, "Fuck, I don't know if this is better or worse than you completely topless."

She laughs and reaches her arms around my neck and pulls me down for a quick kiss. "Well, get used to it because I'm not giving this back."

"That's fine by me, princess, you can have my entire wardrobe."

"You're funny, Moretti." She smiles up at me. "Hey, how bad is my hair right now?"

"Well, it doesn't not say I-just-had-my-world-rocked," I respond, pulling on the ends of one of her curls.

"Shit, I'm going to be interrogated when I get back," she groans, dropping her forehead to my chest and the softness of her curls on my bare chest makes my heart skip a beat.

I wrap my arms around her. "I could braid it if you want?"

She pops her head up, wide-eyed. "You can braid? I can't even braid my hair."

"Yeah, my mom liked it when I would help her." I drop my arms from around her and pull her toward one of the seats. "Here, sit down." The moonlight lights up everything perfectly, but I turn on the boat lights to see her better.

She sits and turns so her back is toward me, and I run

my fingers through her hair, parting it down the middle. Her head falls back and her eyes shut as I work to recreate her French braids from earlier. They won't be nearly as perfect as those were, but it will be dark when she gets back and hopefully they won't notice. The last thing I want to do is put her in an uncomfortable situation.

"Hair tie?" I ask and reach out a hand and hold the end of the braid in the other.

She pulls both off of her wrist and hands them to me. I tie the one braid and move to the other side of her head, putting the other tie between my teeth. She relaxes into my hands as I braid and she lets out a small hum.

"You okay there, princess?"

"Mhm, this is really relaxing, I thin—" A yawn interrupts her sentence. "Sorry, I could fall asleep like this."

"Maybe it's time to take you back?" I finish her second braid and tilt her head up toward me so I can see her eyes. They're half closed, and her pulse quickens underneath my fingertips. I should take her home, but my desire to hold onto her for a little bit longer is outweighing the logical part of my brain.

"Yeah maybe," she says through another yawn. "But could you rub my shoulders? My body isn't accustomed to all the movement we did today."

"Sure thing," I kiss her forehead and move to rub her shoulders. Her head falls to the side, and I sneak my hands under the hoodie. I rub her shoulders until she's on the brink of sleep. Her head has started to drop.

"You relax, and I'll take us back to camp now, okay?" I move to grab my hat and run my fingers through my hair before placing it backward on my head.

"Okay," she mumbles, turning in the seat and bringing her legs up to her chest, tucking them in under my sweatshirt. She reminds me of a turtle—an adorable Zach-covered turtle.

I grab another sweatshirt and toss it on, bringing in the anchor of the boat before heading out of the cove. The boat ride back is calm. Since it's Tuesday night, there isn't much activity on the water, and I don't have to worry about any major waves. The air is chilly, but it's not cold, and there's almost no wind. The moonlight reflects off the water, and the sight is beautiful. I turn to check on Sidney, and she's staring right at me with her head resting against the back of the seat. I could get used to the sight of her eyes on me every day, but we don't have that time. Instead I take a mental picture, telling myself it will be enough once this week is over.

Soon, I'm pulling into the Sutter State Park marina to dock the boat. I go to turn the engine off and she stands up and puts her hand over mine.

"Don't, I can make it up there by myself," she says, picking up her backpack.

"I really would rather make sure you get back there safe," I say.

"It's okay, I don't want you getting ambushed by my family. You'd never get to go home."

"Sidney, I—"

"No, really, I mean we have the other half of our two-day-date tomorrow, right?" She tilts her head, holding my hand now.

"We do," I nod reluctantly.

"How about tomorrow night you can take me up to camp when you drop me off?"

I don't want to argue with her, so I nod. "Sure, we can do that, princess." I lean in to kiss the top of her head. "I had a really nice time. Thank you for spending it with me."

"I did, too. Thank you, Zach." She squeezes my hand and adjusts her backpack on her shoulder.

My other hand comes up to cup her face, and I pull her closer, but not all the way. She closes the distance and reaches up behind my neck to pull me the rest of the way into a slow, passionate kiss.

She pulls away first and moves to the edge of the boat. I grab her hand before she can get too far and place the bag of candy from this morning into it. "Don't forget these."

"Oh my god, thank you. They really are going to love these." She leans back and presses a quick kiss to my cheek before turning back and stepping out of the boat. She takes a few steps before turning over her shoulder. "What time did you want to meet tomorrow?"

"9:30 will work. Bring a book, too. Does that sound good?"

She smiles from ear to ear, "That's perfect. Goodnight, Moretti." She gives me a small wave and skips off, the candy bag swinging in her hand.

"Night, princess. See you soon," I call after her, before I pull my boat out of the marina and head home. The whole time I let my mind wander thinking of what a future Sidney would wear, and if she would let her hair grow out or keep it short. The view of her at my favorite table in my restaurant, eating as I cooked her the entire menu. These images don't scare me as much as I predicted they would, and that's what really frightens me.

TWENTY-THREE

SIDNEY

When I returned to camp last night, I was instantly bombarded by the girls. They came at me so aggressively I turned around and ran the other way, not getting far since Maeve's much faster than me with her longer legs.

They were ecstatic about the candy, and we walked down to the Point while I filled them in on almost all the details of my date with Zach while they each ate a lollipop.

I was starting to warm up to the idea of being the center of attention for once. There was something about Zach where I wanted to tell anyone who would listen. I wasn't sure if all my new confidence was coming from him or if the Cali Sidney experiment was working, but I didn't want it to end any time soon.

Maeve insisted I wear my sundress today, the irony that it's a dusty rose dress with deep red roses all over it is not lost on me, but I also don't care if I match Zach. Per his wishes, I made sure to put my Kindle in my bag. I lift my butt up off the bench I'm waiting on and smooth the dress down, willing it to cover the backs of my legs.

"Stop fidgeting so much," Abby says next to me. "You look great."

"I don't remember this dress being so short," I sigh and pull on the ends of it.

"That's kind of the point," Maeve chimes in with a pop of her bubble gum.

I snap my head and glare at her. "You're both making me nervous. Please go back up to camp."

Maeve stands up and reaches her arm out to Abby. "Come, my dear, we must let Sidney get railed in her sundress in peace," she says in a British accent while looping her arm in Abby's.

"I will not be getting railed in my sundress," I groan.

Abby glances at Maeve, then back down at me. "Sid, if you don't get railed in that sundress then we are going to have to take Zach to the hospital because that means there's something seriously wrong with him."

I drop my head to my hands and try to hide the blush now covering my face. I seriously can't believe we're discussing this when last week I would have never dreamed about talking to my family about potential hookups. My heartbeat is just starting to slow when I hear the sound of a boat making its way into the marina, and it immediately picks back up.

"Looks like lover boy is here." Abby points over to where Zach makes his way into his spot in the docks.

"Here goes nothing. I'll see you tonight," I say, standing up and making my way down the dock.

"Have fun," Abby calls behind me.

Followed by "Use protection!" from Maeve.

I give them the finger over my shoulder, keeping my eyes on Zach who I can see laughing and waving at them. He's dressed similarly to yesterday with his backward cap and T-shirt, but he's wearing navy shorts instead of swim trunks. He's grinning from ear to ear and I'm instantly calmer when I see him, all my nervousness washing away. I was expecting the opposite would happen, but he's different from anyone I've ever dated before.

"Morning, princess," he says, reaching his hand out to help me into the boat. "The forecast looks perfect for today, and might I add that you do, too." He twirls me when my feet hit the deck of the boat, dipping me in his arms leaning down close to me. "Did you wear roses for me?"

I throw my arms around his neck to keep from falling over and whisper back, "Sorry, but no. Roses are a very common dress pattern." I smirk at him and shrug.

His brows furrow and he frowns at me. "I reject that narrative, if you don't mind."

I roll my eyes at him, pulling him closer to me. "I don't mind," I reply, bringing my lips to his to taste the minty flavor mixed with the smell of sunscreen and lavender. It's become so familiar over the past few days, I've started to crave it. His arms are warm and strong around me as he holds and kisses me.

Remembering where we are, and the audience we probably have, I break the kiss and move to the passenger's seat.

"Where are we headed today?" I ask, crossing my legs and dropping my backpack to the floor.

Zach moves to grab the wheel and starts to reverse the boat out of the marina. "I thought I would show you around town."

"Perfect. I haven't been to town during the day in a few years, actually. We get too caught up at camp most of the time." The only times I've been to town in the last two years were to go to Cyrus's house for a party, but we didn't wander around town since it was at night and all the shops were closed. Although two summers ago, I didn't end up going to the party. Instead I picked everyone up and drove them home, having to pull over three times on the way home for three different people to throw up.

He picks up speed once we're out of the marina, and I realize my hair is not going to like the wind. I reach down to my wrist and I'm met with only my skin. I must have forgotten to put my hair tie back on after I showered this morning. I sigh and throw my arm up over my head, willing my hair to stay in place.

Zach sees me struggling and laughs while shaking his head. Reaching up he takes his hat off his head and leans over to place it backwards on my head before returning to driving. The hat is warm and too big on my head, so I reach up and adjust the strap to make sure it stays put.

"Thank you," I shout over the wind and he turns to wink at me as his hair blows in the wind. The sight sends all kinds of feelings straight to my core, making me readjust in my seat.

Soon we are pulling up to a dock situated right in front of the small Black Willow Bay Memorial Lighthouse. Zach docks, and I wait for him to finish before standing up. If he wanted to stay here all day and tie and retie ropes, I wouldn't say no.

"Ready to go?" he asks, turning around and reaching his hand out.

I pop up and throw my backpack on, grabbing his hand. "Let's do it."

He interlocks our fingers and helps me out of the boat, leading me down the dock and past the lighthouse to the town's main street. My hand feels so right in his, and I love the way he rubs his thumb over my skin. There isn't too much activity in town, but I can see people coming in and out of shops. The restaurant across the street on the corner is setting up tables on their patio. He pulls me closer as we stroll, and flexes as I wrap my other arm around his firm bicep. It's a good thing I'm holding on because my knees are starting to feel weak. We cross the street and continue past the shops and toward the residential houses. It feels like we've been doing this for ages with the way our bodies know how to move around each other without it being awkward.

"Wait." I turn behind me. "Are we not going down that way?"

"Nope, we are going straight down here." He points ahead.

I try to peer down the street, like our destination is going to be marked with a neon sign.

"It's a farmers' market." He leans down and kisses the side of my head.

"There's a farmers' market here? I love those," I yell, jumping up and down, using my grip on him as leverage. I see his eyes darken, and I realize I'm not in my average outfit and that this sundress is probably not the best for jumping.

He snaps his gaze forward. "I actually have to go. It's a part of my deal with Mario, my boss. I go to the market every Wednesday and pick up fresh produce for the restaurant. I hope you don't mind that I'm taking you along to run errands."

"No, I love that. I want to know about all the errands Zach Moretti runs." I squeeze his hand and lean my head toward him. I'm not lying either. I really am excited he's showing me something personal to him. I could see myself going to the market with him every week, if that was possible, but it's not. I have to remember not to get wrapped up in fantasies when this isn't going to last past this week. No matter how good things are with him, we have an expiration date. That's how summer romances work. At least on the River it feels like time moves slower. For now, I'm going to enjoy this time I have with him and learn as much as I can.

We walk for a few minutes, Zach pointing out fun facts about the different houses and their residents. One is home to a couple that still has their Christmas lights up and refuses to take them down. Then there's Cyrus's childhood home, where his parents still live, next to a house that Zach says is haunted, but he can't prove anything yet.

We cross the street to a small park where there are pop-up tents lined along the brick walkway that goes deeper into the park. There's an ice cream truck parked on the street before the pathway, and he takes a quick turn to the window.

"Zachary, happy farmers' market day," the older man calls from the window.

"Morning Joe. One pup cup please." Zach orders from who I assume is the owner since the side of the truck says 'Joe's Ice Cream.'

"A pup cup?" I lean in and whisper to him, "Do you have a secret dog I don't know about?"

"All will be revealed, Sidney. All will be revealed," he says like he's some kind of video game NPC who is supposed to give me hints about my mission.

"That's seriously so unhelpful." I roll my eyes, shaking my head at him.

"Here you are." Joe leans out of the window and hands Zach the pup cup, taking a dollar from him. "Enjoy the market!"

"Thanks, Joe," he calls and pulls me toward the park. "Come on, you'll see soon."

TWENTY-FOUR

ZACH

I head into the market, pup cup secure in one hand and Sidney's hand in the other. Since I'm here every Wednesday, I've gotten into a routine of which booths to visit first, and my first stop is always Joe's for a pup cup. Having Sidney here is different. It feels like this is the way every Wednesday should go.

"Why can't you tell me what you have planned?" she asks as we move past a booth with fresh produce.

I've learned she gets mad at me when she doesn't know the plan, but I can't help it. I love the annoyed glances she throws me, the way her nose wrinkles when she does it. It's the same wrinkle that happens when she laughs. Like she isn't really mad at me.

"I said you'll see it will all make sense soon," I reassure her. I stop at the front of the booth, and a German Shepard pops out from under the table.

"Oh my gosh," she shouts and drops my hand to bend down to pet the dog.

"Sidney, this is Loki." I squat down next to them as Loki licks her face, and she laughs, trying to keep herself balanced. "And this is Loki's pup cup," I say, handing the treat to her, placing one of my hands on the small of her back.

Her eyes go wide, taking the cup from my hand. I don't know if it's from my touch or the fact I'm giving her the honor to be the dog's favorite, but I don't care as long as it makes her smile.

She puts it in front of Loki, who instantly sticks his nose in it. She laughs and her nose wrinkle makes an appearance as she tries to hold the pup cup still for Loki. I watch her, laughing and petting him behind his ears. I'm so caught up in her that I miss Jill coming around the corner of the booth and almost run into her as I stand up.

"Zach, you spoil him too much," Jill says with a shake of her head, her gray bob bouncing back and forth. The pockets of her overalls are filled with various flowers and shears and there's dirt smeared all over her.

I lean in to give her a side hug. "You know I wouldn't miss an opportunity to give my favorite market dog a treat."

"Who is this you've brought today?" Jill fixes a few of the flowers on the table and nods down at Sidney. I've never brought someone to the market with me before, not even Luke. It's a special place for me, and I don't want to share it with just anyone. Jill's eyes are on me, and my face heats, knowing she probably realizes the significance in me bringing someone here.

Sidney's head pops up at the question, and the sight of her down on her knees with my hat on almost knocks me over. Every time I look at her, my heart stops. I quickly recover and reach down to help her stand. "Jill, this is Sidney Murphy, my market date."

"Lovely to meet you, Sidney," Jill says, reaching out to shake Sidney's hand.

"It's nice to meet you, too. These flowers are beautiful, and your dog is adorable," Sidney says. Loki cozies up beside her, nudging his head into her hand.

"Thank you, I wish I could say I grew both but I can't. Speaking of, since you were so kind to Loki, I have something special for you. Let me go grab it." Jill bounces with excitement before running off toward the street where her truck is parked. I can see the bed is full of flowers from here, and Loki is quick to follow her.

"What does she mean by something special?" Sidney asks, moving around to the back of the booth to browse the flowers.

There's a line of trees behind her, and I take this opportunity to get closer and step behind her for as much privacy as this market will give us. Standing directly behind her, I can see the tattoo peeking out from her puffy sleeve.

Leaning down, I drop my voice so only she can hear, "I can see the tattoo on your back in this dress, and I want to bend down and bite it."

"*Zach*," she whispers, a hint of warning in her voice, and I can see the goosebumps rise on the back of her neck.

I ignore it and continue, "It's perfectly you. A butterfly with one book wing shouldn't turn me on as much as it does. Add the fact that you're still wearing my hat and this little floral dress?" I take a deep breath, running my fingers along the bottom of her dress where people won't see, and lean closer. "You have no idea how badly I want to lay you down next to these flowers and devour you. But I can't do that with all of these people here, can I?"

"No, you can't," she says on a breathy exhale, and blood rushes to my cock.

"I bet if I reached up underneath this dress right now I'd be able to feel how much you want that too, wouldn't

I?" I tease the bottom of her dress more, brushing the side of her leg.

Sidney glances back at me over her shoulder. "I don't know. I guess you're going to have to find out before Jill gets back, aren't you?" she says with a raise of her eyebrow, and I love how she thinks she's calling my bluff.

I step closer, crowding her between the basket of flowers and my body. She has no idea how badly I've wanted to touch her since I saw her. It's almost criminal. We've already spent so much time together this morning, and I haven't felt her come around my fingers yet. She keeps her eyes locked on mine as my fingers move from the edge of her dress, in between her legs, and along the edge of her underwear. "Look forward, princess. We don't want this whole farmers market to know how wet you are for me."

She turns forward and reaches for a flower right as I dip one finger underneath her underwear and slide it along her pussy. She gasps and crushes the stem of the flower as my cock presses against the fly of my shorts.

"Careful, princess, we don't want you drawing attention over here." I stroke up to right below her clit and back down, curving the tip of my finger inside of her before pulling it back out. "Fuck, Sidney. I suspected you'd be wet, but you're fucking soaked." I close the last bit of distance between us and press my hard cock against her. "Do you feel what you're doing to me?"

Sidney throws her head back against my chest, and mumbles, "Jesus Christ, fuck me."

I let out a small laugh. "Believe me, if I could get away with lifting this dress up and slipping my cock in right here I would. But I see Jill and Loki coming back, so we don't have enough time to do that right now." Removing my finger from her underwear, I step next to Sidney and reach for the sunflowers. "Did you know the world's tallest sunflower was over 30 feet tall?" I ask, turning toward her. She glares at me, her cheeks and chest matching the red of the roses on her dress.

"I hate you right now," she says, trying to hide her smirk, right as Jill reaches the booth with a basket of red roses.

"Here they are," Jill exclaims, setting the basket on the table.

"They are beautiful. You really didn't have to go get those," Sidney says, standing on her tiptoes to see all of them.

"Nonsense, it's the least I can do since you two brought Loki a treat," Jill adjusts the roses in the basket. "These are the best ones I've grown this summer, and I was going to wait to grab them"—she plucks one out and hands it over to Sidney—"but they match your dress so well, my dear."

"Thank you." Sidney blushes and brings the rose to her nose, closing her eyes and inhaling.

"We'll take half a dozen, and three of these sunflowers please," I tell Jill and pull my wallet out of my pocket. Sidney snaps her head my way, and I wink at her.

"Nope," Jill says, pushing my money back toward me. "These ones are on me, enjoy the market."

"Thank you," I say, taking the flowers from Jill.

We spend the next forty-five minutes wandering around the market and gathering produce for Mario. I can't keep my hands off Sidney now that I've felt her, and my hands keep finding their way under her dress whenever she steps further into a booth or behind something. I suspect she started doing it on purpose when she would move in front of me around the tables while glancing back at me and biting her lip. I wanted to pull that lip out from between her teeth and bite it, but I'd save that for later. My fingers haven't crept back into her underwear since that first time, but I've learned she's wearing a cheeky pair with a lace edge, and she likes it when I run a finger down her arm.

She ended up carrying the sunflowers and roses as my arms became full with bags of produce, including a small carton of strawberries for her.

Every time I asked her for a sunflower, she would only raise one eyebrow, handing it over. Her eyebrow almost goes all the way to the edge of my hat on her head, and it kills me every time.

I give one sunflower to Mrs. Q, who gives me tomatoes from her secret stash. Another goes to Mary, who stocks me up on the freshest parsley and a reminder to tell Mario to call her. The last one goes to Joe as we leave the market.

Sidney walks next to me now with only the roses clutched to her chest, smiling up at me.

"You have something you'd like to say, princess?" I ask, nudging her leg with one of the bags.

"Nope," she says, popping the "p" in a way that makes me want to kiss her.

We walk in silence for a few minutes before she finally breaks.

"Fine," she says with a sigh. "That was pretty impressive."

"Which part? The one where I got the best ingredients using my charm or the one where I was able to get my hand under your dress?" I smirk over at her as she gasps and hits me in the shoulder.

"Shut up Moretti! You know I meant the *charm*. I was trying not to inflate your ego," she says, shaking her head and rolling her eyes at me. If I had a dollar for every time I got an eye roll from her, I could probably pay for school without any loans. She doesn't realize how charming she is.

"Princess, you do that every time you look at me," I tell her with a laugh.

She takes a deep breath before changing the subject. "Where are we headed now?"

I lift one of the bags and point forward. "To the restaurant—gotta drop these bad boys off. Then I'd like to have lunch with you, if you want." I glance at her, and I love that she's already staring at me, her blue eyes hitting me straight in the heart.

"I would love that," she replies, burying her face in the roses. But I can still see the blush she's trying to hide from me.

TWENTY-FIVE

Zach leads me through to the back of the restaurant. It's the perfect little Italian place right on the water. I think back to the last time I was here a few years ago when Maeve tried to order wine, and Aunt Shan immediately yelled at her.

He's saying hi to everyone as we pass through and out to the back patio, and I'm in awe at how perfectly he fits into the community here. There are tables outside with the best view of the water. The iron fence is covered in vines with flower baskets hanging on the other side, and the awning above shades the area.

"Here's our table," Zach points his bags at a small table in the corner right up against the fence with three seats. "Have a seat and read. I need to bring these back to the kitchen and grab us some food. I'll send Tyler over to get you something to drink."

Sitting down in the corner seat, I drop my backpack and pull out my Kindle. I see Zach stop in the doorway of the restaurant, setting down the bags and pulling out the strawberries, before heading back my way. Placing the container on the table, he leans down and grabs my cheeks. He finally pulls me into the kind of kiss that my body has been craving all morning. I lose myself to the feel of his calloused fingers against my cheeks and the softness of his lips, letting out a small moan. I feel his smile against my lips as he breaks the kiss.

"You're good with anything to eat, right?" he whispers, barely moving away from me.

I open my eyes to see his beautiful green ones lit up in front of me. I can only nod before he's gone again into the restaurant.

My entire body is on fire, but I try to ignore it and focus on reading and snacking on strawberries. After reading the same paragraph six times, I finally give up. I can't focus on anything when I'm a live wire. From Zach teasing me all morning and that kiss that left me craving more, I can't sit still. I always assumed romance books were exaggerating when it came to sundresses, but I'm so grateful they weren't. This dress was a great decision, but I will never tell Maeve or Abby. Cali Sidney is having way too much fun finding out how far her sexual preferences will take her.

Needing something to do with my hands, I pull out my phone and open up the group chat with my cousins to see I've already got unread messages from them.

Maeve named the conversation "Get Sidney Laid".

RYAN

can we not?

MAEVE

fine

Maeve named the conversation "Waiting on Lifeguard Updates".

> RYAN
>
> thank you
>
> FINN
>
> what time did they leave?
>
> ABBY
>
> around ten
>
> JORDAN
>
> proof of life is required pls

I roll my eyes and hit the camera button. Flipping the camera to myself I stick out my tongue and hold up a peace sign before sending it. It takes a minute, but it delivers to the group and I can't help but stare at it. I forgot I was still wearing Zach's hat, and I love the way I have a piece of him with me. He doesn't know it, but I'll be keeping this as a souvenir.

> MAEVE
>
> EXCUSE ME IS THAT HIS HAT?!
>
> LIAM
>
> are you at Mario's? Bring breadsticks back!
>
> ABBY
>
> IT'S TOTALLY HIS HAT
>
> FINN
>
> omg omg omg
>
> QUINN
>
> SIDNEY HELLO???
>
> LUCY
>
> where's Zach??

They all react to the photo with hearts and exclamation marks, and I decide to leave them hanging, putting my phone away as a waiter approaches.

"Good afternoon, I'm Tyler. I'll be your waiter today. Can I start you off with some water?" Tyler smiles at me and holds up a pitcher of water.

"That's perfect, but could I also get an unsweetened iced tea?" I move my empty water glass closer to him.

"Sure thing," he says, filling my water.

"So, you work with Zach?" I ask him, desperate to find out any information I can.

"Yeah, but not this week."

"Why not this week?"

"Well on Monday he asked for the rest of the week off, and Mario was more than happy to let him since he's literally never taken a sick day." Tyler turns to check behind him, then leans down closer, lowering his voice, "I'm starting to see why he might have done that." He motions the pitcher my way with a raise of his eyebrow and heads back into the restaurant.

I'm sure he wasn't implying Zach asked for a full week off so he could spend time with me, right? I really don't want to get my hopes up about him when this is only supposed to be a fun vacation fling. The more time we spend together, the more it's going to hurt both of us, but I can't help how badly I crave him.

Tyler quickly brings me my iced tea, plates, and breadsticks, and I relax, enjoying the view of the River and people-watching on the patio.

I'm not sure how much time passes, but Zach finally comes back carrying a metal pizza stand in one hand and a pizza in the other.

He's grinning from ear to ear, and he looks messier. He has flour in his hair, on his shorts, and sauce on his cheek.

"Lunch is served, milady." He bows slightly, setting the pizza in the middle of the table. I think he's going to sit across from me, but instead, he sits in the chair right next to me and pulls it to the corner of the table, his leg brushing up against mine. The slight brush isn't enough, so I turn toward him to move my leg closer.

Every time he gets near me I want *more*. He smiles and grabs the edge of my seat, pulling me toward him. Close enough that he reaches down and lifts both of my legs over his left leg, and I feel the warmth of him through his shorts. He doesn't remove his hand from my leg, stroking my skin with his thumb.

"You've got a little something…" I point to my cheek and then to Zach, who reaches up to the wrong side of his face. "Here, let me do it." I go to wipe the sauce from his face, but then I get a better idea and grab the side of his face, looking around before pulling him closer to me. Leaning forward, I lick the sauce off his face. His hand tightens around my leg. He lets out a low growl that makes me laugh as I sit back in my seat.

"Careful, princess," he warns as his hand slides higher up my leg, his fingers finding their way to my inner thigh, his pinky lightly brushing the edge of my underwear. I gasp and tilt my hips toward him as he moves his hand back to my knee. One touch from him, and I'm instantly on edge. "We should really feed you before we get too adventurous."

He doesn't take his hand off my knee, reaching for the pizza that I completely forgot about. Drawing my gaze away from him, I notice the pizza is loaded with different vegetables and meats, almost like he couldn't decide what he wanted to put on it. Biting into the pizza I can't hold back the moan that escapes.

"You like it?" he asks, and I realize he hasn't gotten a slice yet.

"It's fucking delicious," I say, taking another bite. "This is the best pizza I've ever tasted."

He exhales loudly and drops his head before peering back up at me with those bright green eyes. "I really hope you mean that."

I grab his hand under the table and squeeze it. "I do. You picked the right profession to pursue."

His shoulders relax and he grabs a slice of the pizza for himself.

"So, tell me more about yourself," he says, rubbing his thumb over my skin.

"Okay, well. I'm in the middle of the Murphy cousins, Abby is my only sister, and my mom can never go more than two weeks without thinking of getting another dog," I tell him.

He smiles and does a small shake of his head. "No, Sidney. I mean tell me about *you*, not your family."

"About me?" I stare at him, unsure of what to say next. "I'm not very interesting," I mumble through a bite of pizza.

"I don't think that's true," he says, giving my knee a slight squeeze. "Tell me the first thing that comes to your head."

"Um." I hesitate, all the facts I know about myself are suddenly missing from my brain. I try to think of something fast, but there's nothing. I don't like talking about myself. When I get excited about the small stuff I like it feels like people are always judging and laughing at me. I feel like if I don't say something soon he is going to get up and leave. But he sits back and waits for me. "I like puzzles?"

"Are you asking me or telling me?" he laughs.

"Telling you. I like puzzles," I say more confidently.

"What kind of puzzles?"

"Why?" I say automatically, ready to defend myself like I always have to. "Sorry, sorry. I'm not used to talking about myself like this, it's going to sound stupid."

He sighs, "I'm not asking about you to fill the silence. I'm comfortable sitting here and saying nothing with you. But I also want to know what kind of games you play on your phone and what your go-to movie theater snacks are."

"That's easy. Popcorn with M&M's mixed in," I spit out.

"See that's what I'm talking about," he shouts, clapping before returning his hand to my knee.

His excitement makes the very mundane thing I said seem not so mundane. His joy doesn't feel forced or faked, and I think he genuinely cares about these small details.

We finish the pizza as I tell him about things I like—books, movies, puzzles, and TV shows. His hand never leaves my knee, and I've never been so content.

Finishing the last bit of pizza, I lean back in my seat and drop my head back, closing my eyes. The breeze from the River on my face, the feeling of fullness in my belly, and the warmth of Zach's touch on my skin is everything I never knew I needed. I'm beginning to think I might be in some serious trouble.

TWENTY-SIX

ZACH

L unch was a bad idea.

Watching Sidney eat something I cooked and moan at each bite had me as hard as a rock. I don't think she noticed, thankfully. I kept her legs closer to my knee so she wouldn't brush my dick. She ended up eating most of the pizza since I could barely focus on eating because I was losing my goddamn mind.

Everyone in the kitchen gave me shit when I barged in and started cooking since I was technically not supposed to be back there. All of them already knew I brought Sidney in, telling me to get back out there and out of their way. I didn't care, though, because the satisfaction I got from cooking for her was worth it.

Heading down the street now, she's glued to my side. My arm drapes over her, and the roses are clutched to her chest like she's scared to drop them. Her head rests against my shoulder, and everything is right in the world, if only for this moment. If we were lying down I'm sure she'd be asleep, and I could listen to her breathe and watch the rise and fall of her chest, knowing she was safe with me.

"You're not going to fall asleep standing up, are you princess?" I squeeze her shoulder and move her to make sure she's awake.

"I'm fine, I'm fine," she says, her elbow connecting with my side. "Just a small food coma." She closes her eyes and wrinkles her nose. I have to stop myself from stopping in the middle of the sidewalk to kiss her.

I press a quick kiss to her forehead instead, slowing our pace as we approach our next destination. The blue house turned gift shop is one of the most eccentric places in Black Willow Bay. The porch and front yard are scattered with birdhouses, garden decorations, and other items.

Sidney perks up and bounces. "I love this shop."

"I actually live here." I lean down and point at the second floor with the arm that's draped around her.

"You're lying." She stops, her mouth wide open.

"Zachary, there you are," Marcy shouts from the porch before I can answer Sidney. She's dressed in one of her most colorful dresses, with rainbow strings hanging down from her waist. Her long gray hair sparkles in the sunlight, the way it has ever since she put tinsel in it.

"Marcy, you know I can't stay away," I call to her, leading Sidney up the path to the porch. "This is Sidney. Sid, this is Marcy, my favorite landlord."

Marcy was one of the first people Cy introduced me to when I moved up here. Since then, she's become one of my favorite people, like a pseudo-grandma. She taught me how to play dominoes, and we have a standing lunch date on Tuesdays. Yesterday, she made homemade mac and cheese, and I told her about my plans with Sidney before I left. She told me if I didn't bring her by today, she was going to evict me.

Marcy stands up from her porch chair and rolls her eyes at me. "I'm your only landlord, and it's a pleasure to formally meet you." She shakes Sidney's hand. "I do recognize you from all the times you've visited."

"This is one of my favorite shops. I can't believe you remember me," Sidney says, flustered. I can see a hint of pink on her cheeks, and I don't know why she's so surprised someone would remember who she is. I don't think I'll ever be able to forget her.

"Don't underestimate yourself, sweetheart," she winks at Sidney, who lets out a small laugh.

"We really should get these in some water." I pull one of the roses from Sidney's bouquet and inhale the smell of it.

"Of course," Marcy nods with a smirk. "Come down to visit if he bores you," she says to Sidney before sitting back down.

"Will do," Sidney says with a laugh, letting me lead her around the side of the house where there's a separate entrance for my apartment.

Right as I turn the corner, I see Marcy giving me a thumbs up. The introductions between them went well, and if she didn't end up liking Sidney I'm not sure what I would do. She never liked Luke, and I always brushed it off, but it turns out she was right. Now I trust Marcy's opinions of people with my life.

Unlocking the door, I hold it open for her and let her lead us up the stairs. She's a bouncy step-skipper. Her sundress moves up and down, and I get small flashes of those cheeky underwear I've been feeling all day.

Fuck me.

They're a dusty pink. I grip the railing and tell myself I'm going to stick to the plan and not push her against the door and fuck her the second we step into my apartment.

She beats me to the door and goes inside. Luckily, I cleaned the entire apartment last night after getting home from our date. I step through the door and stop dead in my tracks.

She stands in the middle of my living room, and suddenly, I realize what I've been missing from this apartment. Marcy keeps saying I need to find the right decorations, giving me various items from her store to try. But none of them ever do the trick, and now I understand why. I didn't need a decoration to make this apartment complete. I needed her.

A small part of me wonders if I could convince her to extend whatever we are doing past this week. To come visit me or have me visit her. Once she leaves this apartment it is going to feel even emptier than it does now, and there won't be a decoration Marcy will be able to find to fill that void.

She spins around, flowers still tight to her chest. The sun coming in from the windows hits her in all the perfect spots. I want to take her picture and frame it, but I'm too distracted by her to grab my phone.

"Vase?" She tilts her head at me.

I snap out of my Sidney trance and head to the kitchen to grab the only vase I own. After filling it with water, I place it on the small island Marcy installed for me, she puts the flowers in and sits on the stool.

"What's next?" She pops her elbows on the table and her chin in her hands.

"We are going to make dessert for after dinner."

"Now?" She raises her eyebrows and glances down at her wrist, checking her imaginary watch.

"It has to cool for four hours," I clarify, shrugging. "So better to do it early, and I wanted to make it with you."

She cracks her neck, then her knuckles. "Okay, put me in coach, I'm ready."

TWENTY-SEVEN

SIDNEY

Z ach pulls out all of the ingredients we will need to make tiramisu as he walks me through the steps. We have to start with the ladyfingers, then the mascarpone cheese, and put it all together. He keeps telling me little tidbits about the ingredients and how to tell when different steps are ready, but it's all going in one ear and out the other. I'm too mesmerized by the way he's moving around his kitchen. It's like baking porn.

He's done most of the work so far and keeps asking me to hand him stuff as he goes. I've now been quietly banned from being the baking assistant since I wasted almost a full carton of eggs to separate three yolks. To Zach's credit, he's really patient with me, and when I start to get frustrated, he soothes me by rubbing his hands along my arms.

Now I'm standing next to him watching as he pipes the ladyfinger mixture onto a baking sheet, wondering why it's so erotic. I can see his forearms flex every time he squeezes the bag, and his fingers wrapped around it gives me flashbacks to when they were wrapped around my neck.

"Princess, you good?" He taps the tip of my nose with his pinky, and I realize I've been zoning out watching him.

"Never better," I say, releasing my lip from my teeth and standing up straight. "Why?"

"I asked if you could grab the powdered sugar for me a few times. Seems like you might've been distracted," he teases, giving my shoulder a nudge and winks at me.

"Oops, my bad," I reply, my face heating as I grab the bag of powdered sugar and bring it closer.

"Think you can handle dusting these with some sugar?" He puts down the piping bag and steps to the side.

I nod and reach into the bag, grabbing a small amount and sprinkling it over the ladyfingers.

"That's perfect." His praise causes my body to heat further. He moves behind me, placing his arms on the counter on each side of me, sending a full-body shiver down my spine. I almost throw the sugar in my hand all over the counter.

I try to concentrate on what I'm doing, but his scent surrounds me as he steps closer. "Are you trying to make me mess up?"

"Not particularly." He leans down, and I can feel his breath against my ear. "Do you know how perfect you look in my kitchen?"

My head falls back against his shoulder. "Zach, please," is all I manage to say. I'm about ten seconds away from throwing these ladyfingers on the floor and hopping on this counter and telling him to do dirty things to me.

"Please, what?"

"Touch me." It's so quiet I barely hear myself.

He lowers his lips to my exposed neck and runs his tongue along it. "Here?"

"No." I press my ass back into him, and I can feel the

hard length of him. I've been craving more of him since he started teasing me at the market.

Zach hums and moves his hands from the counter to my hips, and I swear he burns a hole right through my dress with the heat of his hands. "Do you mean"—his hands move lower, fingers finding the edge of my dress—"here?" He cups my ass and squeezes.

"Moretti, are you trying to kill me?" I groan in frustration.

I can feel him smile against my neck. "That's the plan, princess." His hand reaches around and grabs the pan, leaving me missing the heat of him against me.

"What the actual *fuck*?" I snap and turn around, crossing my arms and glaring at him. He's acting like he hasn't been leaving me on the edge all day as he sets the oven timer.

He stands up and leans back against the oven, mirroring my crossed arms. "Is there something you'd like to say?" He grins as he asks it, and I think I could get away with killing him. I'd only have to make one call to Abby and tell her to bring backup. I have no doubt the Murphys could hide his body successfully.

"Is there a reason why you won't fuck me?" I ask, and I'm not sure if that's Cali Sidney or horny Sidney, but I don't care. We've already hooked up multiple times, and I'm dying to feel him inside of me. Just like Maeve said, I need to get railed in this sundress.

He laughs and runs his hand through his hair before returning to crossing his arms. "If I started this day by fucking you, I don't think I'd be able to stop. I'd want to spend all day with you in my bed. I'd need to learn every curve of your body and which touches make you moan like the night in the shower." I'm holding my breath as he pushes off the oven and steps in front of me. "But I also want you to learn about my life, and I want to learn about yours. I can't do that if I keep you in my bed all day."

I release the breath. "Fine. I can't argue with that." I refuse to let him know how much that statement melted me to my core. The idea of spending all day in bed with him is so tempting, but the fact he wants me to know more about him? It's one of the sexiest things I've ever heard. "What's next?" I turn and close the bag of powdered sugar.

"You." He points to me. "Over *there*." He points to the island stool.

"Am I being demoted to spectator?" I huff and stomp my foot, overplaying it a little to make him laugh.

"Princess, if I have you over here, my whole plan is going to be shot, and I need to finish this tiramisu," he laughs, shaking his head.

Reluctantly returning to the stool, I prop my head in one of my hands and reach up to take off Zach's hat. I've been wearing it all day, and I don't need it anymore since we're inside. I'm sure I have horrible hat hair by now.

He reaches over the island so fast I jump when his hand rests on top of my head. "Don't. You. Dare. Take. That. Off." His eyes darken, and he slowly removes his hand from my head.

I drop my head to the counter and groan. If he keeps doing sexy things, the rest of this day is going to move so slowly.

TWENTY-EIGHT

ZACH

Sidney sits and watches me as I make the mascarpone cheese, her eyes hungry, and not for dessert. I wasn't lying when I told her I wanted her to learn about my life.

I'm stirring the egg yolk and sugar together, waiting for the sugar to dissolve, and searching for the strength to open up. Telling her about hockey and culinary school yesterday felt so right, and I desperately want to tell her everything. About my favorite toys growing up. How I had my sexual awakening when I saw Pirates of the Caribbean for the first time. I don't want to overstep though, and the sugar should be dissolved in about five minutes. I give myself that much time to work up the courage and let my libido calm down from teasing her.

I move to the next step and figure out how I want to start. I don't usually tell people about my mom, but she makes me want to. I'm going to test the waters first, if she wants to know more she'll follow up. If not, I won't bring it up again.

Finally, I say, "My mom taught me how to make this."

"How often did you cook with her?" Sidney asks, and a

wave of relief washes over me. Her genuine interest shows by the way she leans forward.

"All the time," I reply as memories of her bouncing around our kitchen flash through my head. "She liked to cook big Sunday dinners, always with dessert, of course. This recipe has been in my family for generations."

"Was this the favorite dessert you made?" she asks.

"It was," I pause. "That's why I wanted to make it for you." I move to the final step of the cream and wait for her to respond. When she doesn't say anything I lift my head and I'm met with her glossy eyes. I lift the spatula and point it at her, "Are you trying not to cry right now?"

She huffs and wipes both of her eyes. "Obviously, you just said one of the sweetest things I've ever heard. How could I not?"

I set down the bowl, moving around the island to give her a side hug. "I'm sorry, I was trying to keep the tears away this time."

"I cry at cute commercials." She laughs in my arms. "I'm kind of a lost cause."

"You're my favorite lost cause," I say into her hair. She leans into my arms, and it's like she was always meant to be there.

"I promise I won't cry anymore. If you want to tell me more about your mom." She takes a deep breath and wipes her eyes one last time before I let go of her and pick up the discarded bowl.

When I finish the cream, I place it in the fridge to set, telling Sidney about my mom. I haven't talked this freely about her in over ten years. My dad never liked bringing her up, and mentioning her around my friends was always met with sad eyes. There's a collection of home movies and photo albums I keep in my closet so I don't lose the memory of her, but talking about her with Sidney is so much better.

I get to share the funny things she did and when she would pull the mom card to make me clean up my messes. How she got me an apron that said "chef's assistant" on it, which Sidney now wants, and how I had a designated step stool to reach the counter, which made her say "aw" for a few seconds.

Once I put together the rest of the tiramisu, I put it in the fridge, where it will have to chill for four hours. Closing the door, I realize how light I feel. It's like this weight I didn't even know was there has been lifted off my shoulders.

"Okay," I turn and face Sidney, who hops up off the stool. "Now we wait, and I have a few other things planned in the meantime."

"And what, pray tell, might these things be?" she asks me with a wave of her hand.

"You really want to ruin the surprise?" I ask her, cleaning up the last few messes around the kitchen.

"I want to say no and act all cool, but you're killing me and I might break out in hives if you don't give me a quick overview," she says fast and firm. I love that she's not trying to hide who she is. It makes me feel less guilty for not hiding who I am. We're comfortable around each other, and I don't feel the need to change myself so she'll like me.

"First, I wanted to take you to a few shops. There's the cheese place and Cy's parents' bookstore." She gasps and I hold up my finger, not done yet. "Then I was thinking we could pick up dinner from this barbeque place I love. We would bring that back here and have the tiramisu for dessert. How does that sound?"

"Cheese, books, barbeque, and dessert?" She steps into my space and throws her arms around my neck, tilting her head back. "Zachary Moretti, you just described my perfect afternoon." Then, she pulls me down into a quick kiss before scooping up her backpack and skipping away toward my front door and down the stairs.

I rush to put my shoes back on, but I'm starting to realize she's a fast little thing, since I don't catch up to her before Marcy can intercept her. I hear Marcy from around the corner already sucking Sidney in.

"Do you want some lemonade, dear?"

Yup. I'm screwed. I should've moved faster.

"Sure, that would be great," Sidney replies.

I'm starting to think I should have warned her about Marcy. I once saw her keep a family at her shop all day because she kept giving them lemonade and snacks.

I finally catch sight of her sitting on the porch in one of the chairs as Marcy disappears into the store.

"Got caught up?" I point to her all cozy in the chair, taking a seat on the steps of the porch.

"I didn't know she was going to invite me to sit down," she leans closer and whispers to me. "I can't say no to old people. It's a major flaw."

All I can do is roll my eyes and laugh at her before Marcy returns with cups and a pitcher of lemonade, pouring one for each of us. Marcy's lemonade has quickly become one of my favorite drinks. Sometimes, she makes pitchers for me to keep upstairs.

Marcy sits back down and turns to Sidney. "He didn't bore you too much, did he?"

Sidney laughs and my heart swells at the sound. "No, no. He was plenty entertaining, I got to learn a lot about him."

"Allow me to add to that." Marcy nods and sits up straighter.

"Marcy, you really don't—" I try to get out before she waves her hand at me.

"Oh, hush boy, this girl should know who has been carting her around town all day."

I told her about yesterday, but I never told her I was showing Sidney around town today. "How do you—" I start, but Marcy interrupts again.

"Do you really think that Joe wouldn't call me the second you showed up with her?" Marcy nods back toward Sidney, who is turning beet red and trying to hide her laughter behind her glass. "Now as I was saying," she turns back to Sidney. "Zachary here showed up at the best time for me."

"Oh really?" Sidney smirks, and I have to surrender and let Marcy do her thing.

"Yes." She pats Sidney's knee. "My dear sweet Irvin had just passed away, old age, you see, and I was not fit to go up and down those damn stairs to that apartment. One day, Cyrus comes in asking around for a friend who was searching for an apartment and seeing if I knew of anyone with space to rent."

Sidney nods along as Marcy tells the story, her arms flying all over the place. She spills some lemonade on Sidney, who casually wipes it off.

"Conveniently enough I was about to put mine up for rent and convert the garage into an apartment of my own. Zachary was here a few weeks later, with nothing but a few duffle bags to his name. He helped me fix up the garage and before he took over living upstairs. I don't think I've ever told him how much it helped having someone around after Irvin passed away." She turns to me and puts her hand over her heart. She hasn't ever told me directly, but I had an idea since we've gotten so close.

"You know I was happy to help, and I still am." I tip my lemonade at her with a nod of my head.

"I know, you helped me get that damn boat out of the driveway." Marcy laughs and turns back to Sidney. "Irvin loved being out on the water. When Zachary got the lifeguard job, I begged him to take it. You've seen the boat?"

"*My Ladybug*? I have, it's a beautiful boat," Sidney replies and her cheeks get redder, probably like mine, thinking about what we've done on that boat.

"Yes," she says whimsically. "That was what Irv called me. I didn't have it in me to get rid of it, but I couldn't have it sitting in my driveway anymore. I told Zachary I would cover the costs of everything as long as he got her back out on the water. She was out that very next day."

Sidney wipes her eyes and tries to hide it.

"Dear, don't cry." Marcy rubs her arms and pulls her as close as she can over the arms of the chairs. "These are all good things."

"I know," Sidney says through a sniffle. "It's so sweet. Your husband, the boat, the nickname. I cry a lot, I'm sorry."

"Don't apologize for your feelings, feel as much or as little as you want," Marcy says firmly and turns toward me. "Don't you dare make her cry for any negative reasons, boy."

"Wouldn't dream of it," I say, throwing my hands up in the air.

TWENTY-NINE

SIDNEY

Marcy keeps me and Zach on the porch for what feels like the next two hours, telling me mostly about her life and some stories about Zach. When she gets to what sounds like a pretty juicy story about one of his exes, he pops up off the stairs like someone lit a fire under him.

"That's enough, Marcy. I have some other spots I want to show to Sidney before dinner," he almost yells over her. She rolls her eyes at me.

"Okay, fine. You two go enjoy," she waves her hands toward us.

"It was really great hearing all those stories. Hopefully, I can hear that last one later." I wink at her.

"Nope, nope," Zach says quickly, putting a hand on my lower back to push me toward the street. "That's not a Marcy story, definitely not."

"Come on," I whine and let him lead me to the sidewalk. "That was the one I wanted to hear the most."

"All in due time, princess. And I want to tell you that,

not have you hear it secondhand from Marcy." He leans down to whisper, "And she's really such a gossip."

I laugh and lean into him, locking my hand with his as we head down the street toward the cheese shop. It's one of my family's favorite shops to visit each year. I'm not sure if Cy told him that, or if Zach just likes it, but I haven't been yet this year so I'm not complaining.

We enter the shop, the familiar bell dinging as I make a beeline for the candy section, on a mission for my favorite.

"Already know where you're headed? Have you been here before?" he asks, following behind me.

I locate the chocolate-covered gummy bears and grab three bags from the shelf. "You might be underestimating how long my family has been coming up here. This is basically *our* shop."

"Three bags?" He nods toward my now full arms of candy.

"Yes, three bags. One for me, one for Abby, and a second one for me when I get sad the first one is gone." I point to each of the bags in my arms. "Now we need cheese."

I wander around the shop and grab my favorite bricks of cheese and a few cheese spreads, all while Zach follows behind me, taking anything I pick up. He insists on buying everything, and I let him after going back and forth with him about it.

We head to Wilson's Books next, the small bookstore that Cy's parents own. I'm not sure why he doesn't work there. I would be there all the time if I were him. When we cross through the front door, I tug on Zach's hand to stop him, and take a deep breath to inhale the smell of the bookstore.

"I'm guessing I've hit another favorite?" He steps beside me and pulls me close to him, and the mix of the book smell and Zach's smell makes me never want to leave.

"Definitely. I'm going to need at least an hour," I tell him, trying not to think about how limited our time is.

"Take all the time you need, princess, I'll be right behind you." He gives me a quick squeeze before I head off into the stacks.

Zach sticks to his word and follows me around the shop without complaint. I spend most of my time in the new releases section pointing out the ones I own, the ones I plan on reading, and the ones I have actually read. He asks me questions about each of them and picks up one for himself. I already own the new ones I would want, so I make my way upstairs to the used books.

Going up the stairs, I hear him groan behind me, and when I turn around he's staring down at the stairs. It's much quieter up here, and the stacks are filled to the ceiling with books. I wander through the shelves, when it occurs to me he hasn't done any of his teasing in a few hours. It might be time to change that. I've always had a fantasy about bookstores and libraries, and Cali Sidney says we should make that a reality right now.

I stop and crack my neck, rubbing it and sighing. "Hey, could you carry this for a little bit?" I ask him, taking the backpack off my shoulders.

"Sure thing." He reaches out and takes it, throwing it over one of his shoulders.

I take this opportunity to run around the corner into the next aisle. Zach's at the end of the aisle a few seconds later, right as I bend down to grab one of the books stacked on the floor. It's one of the slowest bends I've ever pulled off, and I manage to keep my legs straight. When I hear him groan behind me, I know he sees what I want him to.

"Sidney," he almost growls and it sends a shock straight between my legs. "Where are your panties?"

I pop up, elbow resting on my hip, and said panties dangling from my fingertips. I managed to slip them off when I got into this aisle. "You mean these?" I smirk, tossing them his way.

He drops the bag of candy and cheese to the ground and snatches them out of the air. But he's frozen, so I take the lead and slowly glide toward him. His eyes move from my underwear to me, and he drops the rest of the belongings on the floor.

"Do you want to play, princess?" He tilts his head and smirks at me, a devilish glint to his eyes.

"I do." I nod, reaching down to pull the bottom of my dress up my leg.

He's on me in a second, hand at my hip and pushing me up against the bookshelf, making a book tumble to the floor. "You *really* have to be quiet here. I can't have Cy's parents catching us." His voice is husky, and his chest heaves so much it rubs against the tips of my breasts, causing them to harden to little points.

"I can do that," I say with a shaky breath.

"Good, because I don't think I'm going to be able to go another minute without kissing you," he confesses, and his lips are on mine, devouring. I instantly open up to him, our tongues clashing fast and hard. I moan into his mouth and his hand comes up to the base of my neck, weaving into my hair while still managing to keep the hat on. He tugs the slightest bit, and I tilt my head back, letting him go deeper. I didn't think I would be this sexually adventurous, but he brings out that side of me.

He kisses along my jaw and down my neck, sucking and licking along my collarbone. All the energy from this morning is still inside me as I arch into his touch. His other hand, still holding my underwear, reaches around and cups my ass, pushing me into him. I can feel him hard against me, and his arms around me feel like the warmest and safest place I could be.

I grind into him, seeking the friction I desperately need between my legs, and my dress inches higher with each grind. He lowers his gaze until he's resting his head against my shoulder.

"Can I taste you?" He barely gets out the sentence between his jagged breaths.

"Yes," is all I say before he drops to his knees in front of me, and I might die in this bookstore. It's honestly not the worst way to go, surrounded by one of my favorite things.

He throws my leg over his shoulder, running his hands up my thighs, taking my dress with them. I lean back into the bookshelves and drop my head back, feeling the heat of his breath over my pussy. Just when I think he's going to change his mind, he brings his mouth to me.

My hand flies to my mouth to muffle my moan, as he hums against me. He doesn't waste any time parting me with his tongue and licking his way to my clit before sucking it into his mouth. I involuntarily grind against his face, his hands moving me to keep going. Between his licking and sucking, my orgasm quickly builds, and I need release more than I need anything else right now.

I reach down to rake my hands through his hair, pulling him closer as I grind against his face. He sucks harder and keeps me against him, devouring me like I'm the best thing he's ever tasted.

With another flick of his tongue against my clit, I press

my hand harder into my face and moan as I come apart around him. He slows and licks around my lips before standing back up in front of me. I'm panting, and his hair is a mess, and I can see the shiny wetness from me on his scruff.

"*Fuck*," he says through gritted teeth.

"*Fuck*," I agree and lean up to kiss him.

"Let's go get dinner." He steps back, wipes his face with my underwear, and pockets them before picking up our discarded bags and books and shuffling off.

"Wait," I whisper-yelling after him, "give me my underwear back!"

"Sorry, princess. You lost those the second you threw them at me." He spins to wink at me before he's off down the stairs.

THIRTY

ZACH

We get back to my place after picking up dinner, and I set it up at my small table as Sidney uses the bathroom. I check the tiramisu, it's setting pretty well, but it has about another half an hour to go before it's ready.

I put Sidney's vase of roses in the center of the table and readjust them to be perfectly spread out, then I mess with them some more. I still have all this pent-up energy from eating her out at the bookstore.

I haven't been this adventurous in my past relationships, but there's something about her where I can't wait to get my hands on her, no matter where we are. Almost like my body knows something is missing when I'm not touching her, and everything she does makes me crave her more. From the way she's constantly rolling her eyes at me to the sound of her laugh, I can't get enough.

I'm grateful Cy's parents didn't come upstairs because he would kill me for doing that—well for getting caught doing that.

I adjust myself in my shorts, half-hard from remembering the way she squirmed against my face and how she moaned into her hand when she came. I wanted her to be loud the first time she came today, but I guess we'll have to go again later if she's up for it.

I hear the sink running and do a quick scan of the table to ensure everything is set up the way I like before she comes out.

I take one glance at her, and I'm not sure how I'm going to survive dinner. Why did I want to show her around? Why didn't I want to spend all day in bed with her? I need to talk to whoever made that decision because they need to be fired.

"Moretti, you're staring again." She struts over to me and pokes me on the forehead.

"Sorry, can't help it." I wink at her.

"Don't apologize," she says, shrugging and sitting at the table. "I like it."

I sit down across from her, determined to at least maintain some kind of control by keeping her far enough away while we eat. We picked up way more food than we needed, including a variety of meats and sides.

"Are we going to be able to eat all of this?" She gestures to all of the food with her fork, getting some of the mashed potatoes first.

"Probably not," I admit. "I wanted you to taste a little bit of everything. I'll be set for lunch this week with whatever you don't want." I reach for the ribs and mac and cheese. "Plus, don't forget about dessert."

"Don't worry, my dessert stomach will stay empty even if I eat all of this," Sidney mumbles through a mouthful of potatoes. "Oh my gosh, these are so good," she moans through her next bite. The room in my shorts officially reduces to zero as I watch her lick her spoon clean. This is going to be a very long dinner.

Half an hour later, my suffering is almost over as I plate the tiramisu. I never would have guessed watching someone eat could turn me on so much. First during lunch and then now, I swear she eats slower and more sensually than anyone ever has in the history of the universe.

Sitting down, I take a bite as I watch her take hers. She somehow eats it slower than she did our dinner. I can't take the anticipation anymore and drop my head to the table.

"If you hate it, please don't tell me," I say to the floor.

"Zach, it's delicious," she mumbles.

"Princess, swallow first before you speak." I lift my head to see the fork still in her mouth. Her cheeks flush red, and I decide maintaining control is overrated.

I stand up and move my chair to the side of the table and get as close to her as I can. Mirroring our positions from lunch, I reach down and pull her legs over mine. Running my hand over her thigh I realize how much I missed her soft warm skin.

"Sorry." I still my hand to check in with her. "Is this okay?"

She laughs and goes for another bite. "Yeah, Zach, it's okay. If it wasn't, I would have pushed you away." She squeezes her legs closer to her, pulling me closer and almost out of my seat. "Are you going to have any more? This really is one of the best desserts I've ever had, and I'm not just saying that."

"I had a bite, but it'll be good for a few days. I'd rather have a different dessert right now," I inch my hand higher up her thigh, right under her dress, and she parts her legs for me.

"What kind of *other* dessert?" I can hear the playfulness in her voice as she takes another bite and smirks at me.

Leaning closer, I nip the bottom of her ear and whisper, "One that will make you scream with pleasure."

She drops her fork and her hands are around my face in a second, turning me to face her. "Are we finally doing this?"

"If by *this* you mean, am I finally going to feel you come around my cock? Then yes, I'd like to do this." My gaze slips to her lips, her bottom one caught between her teeth, and it takes everything in me not to move to remove it.

"Fucking finally," she exhales, pulling her lips to mine.

Her hands slip into my hair, and she brings me closer. I'll never get over how passionately she kisses me, like I'm her oasis in a desert. The heat of her under my hands makes me crave more, and I stand up out of my chair without breaking the kiss.

She doesn't let go of my hair and moans when the position lets me explore her mouth deeper. I reach down and pull her legs, and the chair, in front of me. Leaning down, I guide her legs around my waist and scoop her into my arms. Her arms fall around my neck, and I can feel the heat of her center through my shirt.

I walk us to my bedroom, where the sunset lights up the room through the windows. It makes it feel like some magical world, removed from reality. One where I could get lost forever, where I would have no other worries besides making Sidney come.

I bend down and lay her on the bed, pulling her off me before standing above her. She's a masterpiece on my bed, lit by the sunset. Her skin is flushed red, her lips are swollen from our kisses, her dress pushed high enough I can see how wet her pussy is, and my hat still rests on her head. She should be in a museum. Artists should study her, but instead she's in this room with me.

Her lust-filled eyes land on mine as she drags her hand down her dress, right between her legs. I realize this is what the sight of *my girl* is like. It always was supposed to be Sidney, I just didn't know it until now.

THIRTY-ONE

SIDNEY

My eyes are locked with Zach's as I reach down between my legs. He's standing at the foot of the bed, like something from a dream, the way the sunset lights up the room. The soft yellows and pinks are highlighting his face, making me imagine the sight of him standing there naked. His comforter surrounds me with his scent, and I can't wait to be immersed in them. I'm so turned on that the second my fingers reach my clit, I moan loudly, and I hope his windows are shut. He steps forward, but my foot comes up and connects with his chest, stopping him.

"Not so fast, Moretti." I reach my other arm up and point at him. "Strip."

"Yes, ma'am." His hand flies to the back of his shirt, pulling it off in one clean sweep. His belt, shorts, and boxer briefs follow, all in one go. His cock springs free, and the sight of it suddenly makes me feel empty. I slide my hand down and slip a finger into myself to relieve the hollow feeling. I throw my head back further into the mattress, causing his hat to fall off of my head.

I look back up at him, and he's fisting his cock in his hand, his eyes on mine. I bring my other hand up to cup my breast, and I realize I'm still fully dressed. Sliding my finger free, I quickly move to my knees, reaching to pull the zipper of my dress down.

Zach steps forward, and his hands lock around my hips. "Let me."

I drop my hands from the zipper and let him take over. He pulls me flush against him, and my hands fly to his chest to steady myself. I rake my fingers through his chest hair. It's so soft compared to the hardness of his chest. His nipples harden as I swirl my fingers around them. His cock twitches against my stomach, and I feel a sense of satisfaction that my touch can do this to him.

He reaches down and pulls my dress up and over my head before tossing it on the floor. My bra falls from my breasts as he unhooks it and steps back, running his hand over his face as I kneel on his bed naked.

"Fuck, Sidney. You're so much better in this light. Fuck the moonlight. We should only have sex during sunsets," he says with a small laugh. Then his hands are back on me, his mouth meeting mine.

"Condoms?" I ask him between kisses as he crawls onto the bed with me, pulling us further up the bed.

"In the nightstand." He points to the small nightstand next to the bed and falls to the other side of me.

Reaching over, I pull it open and gasp. "Moretti." I turn back to him. "How many toys do you have?"

He relaxes into the pillows and shrugs. "What? I like to be prepared."

"You have like, every toy I can name plus some." I pass by the box of condoms and pull out an unopened rose vibrator. "You don't have a vagina. Why do you have this?"

"I *don't*," he points at himself, "but you *do*," then he points at me. "Care to try it out?"

I glance at him and then at the toy in my hand debating my options before finally dropping it back into the drawer. "Not this time."

"Maybe next time?" Zach asks with a tilt of his head.

"Definitely next time," I nod, pulling out a condom and a small bottle of lube. "Just so you know, I'm negative for everything and on birth control," I say, turning to face him again. "Since we kind of skipped that earlier."

"Right, sorry about that. Guess we were too excited. I'm all negative too," he nods. "Minus the birth control."

I laugh. "It's okay." I hold up the condom between my fingers. "But can we still use this to be safe?"

"Yeah, that sounds good," he agrees.

I place the condom and lube on the nightstand and turn back around and throw my leg over his, pulling him closer to me. I bring my mouth back to his, missing the taste of him already. Right now it's mostly his minty taste, but with a hint of sweetness from dessert, and it's every-thing I need.

His hands move over my leg, bringing it higher on his hip and lining up our centers perfectly. The head of his cock brushes my pussy, and I arch into the touch, seeking more.

"I need to taste you again," he growls into my mouth as we grind together.

"Please," I say through a shaky breath, my soul leaving my body every time he tells me that.

Releasing my leg, he moves me to my back and lowers himself down to my pussy. He doesn't waste any time licking me from my opening to my clit. My back arches off of the bed as I cry out.

"That's it, princess," he says as he kisses my inner thigh. "Scream for me."

His mouth is back on me, sucking my clit. My moans fill the room, and I don't hold back. I'm not far from an orgasm, already so turned on all I need is a little bit of contact. The second he inserts one, then two, of his fingers, I'm done for. He strokes inside me and licks outside, and I come around his fingers so hard I see stars behind my eyelids.

Catching my breath, he kneels above me and reaches for the condom and lube. I watch as he opens the package and rolls the condom down his thick length, pouring out a drop of lube and rubbing it over himself.

"Flip over." He motions with his hand. "On your knees."

I do as he says and quickly move to my knees as anticipation courses through my veins. I can't help but notice how in sync we are at this moment, like he knows everything I want and need before I do. I arch my ass back toward him. He comes up behind me and places a hand on my hip. He rubs his cock through my pussy, soaking it with my wetness, before lining it up with my entrance.

"You sure about this?" he asks before pushing forward.

"Zach, if I don't feel your cock inside me in the next ten seconds, I'm going to murder you," I snap. "Respectfully."

I hear him laugh, slowly pushing into me before filling me all the way to the hilt. His hands grip my hips, moving me in time with his thrusts. Our moans sound like the sweetest symphony I've ever heard.

Leaning down over me, he cups my breast in one hand as he whispers, "I need you closer."

Pulling me back with him, he adjusts us to an upright position with my legs spread around him.

"Fuck, you feel so good around me," he says into my neck as his hand moves down to circle my clit, while he fucks up into me.

I moan, my head falling back on his shoulder, my hands digging into his thighs. The feeling of him inside me and surrounding me is almost too overwhelming. I don't know why. I've had sex before, but it never threatened to ruin my whole existence like it seems to now with Zach. It's like our bodies already know each other, and have for years. Like they were created to do this one thing for the rest of our lives.

He brings his mouth to my neck and sucks, and I don't care that it will probably give me a hickey because it feels too damn good. I reach down to where we are connected, feeling him move in and out of me. He moans and pinches my clit hard.

"Fuck, don't stop," I gasp between breaths. "I'm so close."

"Wouldn't dream of stopping," he moans, tilting my head to the side so he can kiss me, picking up his pace. The orgasm builds, and soon it's crashing into me. A tingle shooting through my entire body like I've been lit on fire from the inside. After a few more thrusts, his orgasm follows, and I feel him pulse inside of me.

He holds me against him as we both catch our breath, slowly lowering us back to the bed before he slips out of me.

"Sidney?" Zach's voice cuts through the silence.

"Yeah?" I ask, staring at the ceiling.

He turns his head toward me. "Would you judge me if I brought the leftovers to bed?"

I sit up on my elbows and glance down at him, and I'm met with the biggest and greenest puppy dog eyes I've ever seen. My only response is to burst into laughter and fall back onto the bed.

"What?" He moves up on one of his elbows. "I don't want you to think I'm a slob," he exclaims.

I roll off the bed and head for the bathroom, still laughing. "I can't," I say, shaking my head, sitting down on the toilet to pee.

Zach comes into the bathroom behind me through the open door, rolling the condom off and tossing it in the trash can. "You can't what?" He turns on the faucet and runs his hands through the water, and then over his softening cock.

"Well, first, I can't believe you came in here while I'm peeing." I point to the door, him, and me. "Second, I can't believe you're already thinking about food after we just had sex."

He cocks his hip and places one hand on it, and I can't help but laugh. "First," he starts. "My mouth was just on your pussy. I literally don't care that you are peeing. You're supposed to pee after sex."

Okay, true.

He continues, "Second, me being hungry is how you know it was good sex. I've worked up an appetite." He stands proudly and crosses his arms.

I shake my head at him. I really can't argue with that logic. "Oh my god, I love " I catch myself and quickly change course. "Love the way you think. I'll have some leftovers, too. Now, get out." I point to the door and wave my hand at him so I can finish cleaning up.

I don't know what possessed the L word to slip out of my mouth, and I'm hoping he bought my cover-up. I'm sure I didn't mean it like love-love, but more like a love you have for your friends who make you laugh, and who you enjoy spending time with. I've only ever told one person I loved them. It was my first boyfriend because fifteen year old Sidney thought she understood what love was. It turns out she didn't. Since then, I've been careful not to say it unless I really feel it, which I haven't yet. I'm not falling for this lifeguard on vacation. At least, I think I'm not.

THIRTY-TWO

ZACH

I wake up to my alarm and a warm body pressed into mine. I had every intention of taking Sidney home last night, but the night got away from us and we both ended up falling asleep.

Over her head, I can see the empty plate on the night-stand next to the condoms and lube. We managed to eat most of the leftovers last night. It turns out Sidney gets as hungry as I do after sex, and considering we ended up having sex two more times, it makes sense that we ate most of it. I couldn't stop touching her, and we never managed to get our clothes back on.

I lift up the covers and confirm we're still naked, her ass nuzzled right against my thickening cock. Thinking about last night really isn't helping the situation.

Right as I'm about to get up and go make coffee, she stirs and scoots further back into me. My hand flies to her hips to stop her, groaning as she rubs against my cock.

"Sidney, you can't do that," I say, clenching my jaw and fighting the urge to grind against her while she's still asleep.

She turns her head back to me, eyes full of lust, biting her lip. "What if I want to?"

Seeing as how she's more awake than I thought, who am I to argue about morning sex? "Is that how you like to be woken up?" I pull her closer to me and grind my cock between her ass cheeks. "With a nice orgasm and my cock inside of you?"

She moans, and her arm flies back into my hair. "Yes, please. I need you."

I move at lighting speed after that, grabbing a condom and some lube. I slip into her from behind, making sure to be gentle with her. She moans as I reach around and rub her clit. She feels so right around me, like we're two pieces of a puzzle, like we're meant to do this. It's soft and sensual as I fuck her and kiss her neck. She comes apart at my fingertips and the feel of her coming around my cock sends me over the edge.

Our breathing slows, and I slip out of her body right as she turns around to face me.

"Morning," she laughs, raking her nails through my scruff. I lean into her touch, relishing in the feel of her skin on mine.

"Morning." I run my hand up her back and pull her closer for a kiss. Right before our mouths connect, my phone alarm goes off again causing both of us to jump back. I reach behind me to turn it off, but it falls to the floor. Groaning, I roll over and pick it up, and Sidney slaps my ass.

"Damn, Moretti, that ass looks great in the morning," she laughs, and I hear the sheets move as she sits up on the bed.

"I'd tell you what I'd do with your—fuck Sidney, we gotta go!" I practically fall off the bed when I see the time on my phone.

"Wait, why? What's wrong?" Her eyes are wide from the center of the bed, perfectly wrapped in my sheets, and I'm pissed I only took off working from the restaurant.

"That was my *oh-shit-you-better-leave-or-you-are-going-to-be-late* alarm. I'm lifeguarding today, and it's a thirty minute commute." I pick her dress up off the floor and toss it at her.

"Fuck," she yells and hops off the bed. "I need my underwear back. I can't go back to camp without them."

"Not a chance," I smirk and grab a pair of my smaller boxer briefs from my drawer. "You'll fit in these. I'm keeping them." I see my hat on the ground and pick it up. "You should also wear this, it's yours now."

She glares at me and wrinkles her nose, but she takes the boxer briefs and hat, getting dressed while I run to the bathroom to discard the condom I've still got on.

Soon we're running down Main Street hand in hand to the *My Ladybug.* Sidney holds on to the hat, running in the same outfit from yesterday, and laughs every time I dodge us past a shop sign or someone walking their dog. I've never had this much fun running late for work, and it's only because I'm doing it with her.

We get to the marina with a few minutes to spare. I pull the boat into the dock and tie it up before shaking Sidney to wake her up. She ended up curling up on the passenger's seat and fell asleep about five minutes into the trip, and I can't help but take pride in being the reason she's so tired.

"Hey princess, we're here." I squat in front of her and shake her leg.

She yawns, stretching wide before freezing and curling back up in the seat. "Shit!"

I scan her for injuries, thinking maybe she pulled a muscle when she stretched. "What's wrong? What hurts?"

"My fucking family is here," she mumbles into her arms.

I slowly peer behind me, and sure enough, she's not wrong. Over on the grass, I see the majority of her cousins at a picnic table. Finn and Jordan are tossing a football, but the rest of them are staring straight at us.

"They've seen me? I can't hide in here all day?" she asks, head still buried in her arms.

"I'm afraid so. You're going to have to strut down this dock like a catwalk," I stand up in front of her and reach my hand out. "Let's go."

She sighs, uncurls herself, and grabs my hand. I don't drop her hand as we get out of the boat, not wanting her to face this alone.

"You first." I gesture in front of me. She glares at me before standing straight up and heading down the dock toward her family.

Maeve's the first one to stand up, starting a slow clap that everyone quickly joins. Soon they're all clapping, and there are a few whistles, too. Other campers start to turn our way to see what all the commotion is about.

Sidney stops and turns back around to me. Her face is beet red. I can see a million emotions run through her brain, and it's like we are having a silent conversation. One where she's embarrassed to have been caught, but I know she feels more pride than she's willing to admit. I encourage her to embrace the attention because she's always got mine.

She nods, turning to face her cousins again, dropping into a curtsy. They get louder and cheer for her, and she turns around and gestures toward me. I smirk and bow, and the clapping is so loud that Sally has come out of the office to see what's happening.

I scurry toward Sidney and stop next to her. "One last kiss?"

She smirks at me. "Well this can't get any worse, so why not? One kiss."

One of my hands comes up to the back of her head and the other to the small of her back as I dip her and lean down to kiss her.

Her arms come together around my neck, and I kiss my girl in front of the whole marina.

THIRTY-THREE

SIDNEY

Heading back up to camp, I'm barely able to get a word in as everyone bombards me with questions about yesterday, and how I showed up doing the walk of shame. I really do love my family, but right now they are getting on my last nerve. They're all adults, and if I need to explain to them why I didn't come back last night, then I can't help them.

I don't want to tell them all the details, and I don't owe them anything. Yesterday, I got to learn more about Zach than I could've imagined. I was sure this was going to be some fun vacation fling, and I'd be able to move on next week and start fresh in LA. Waking up in his arms this morning surrounded by his scent and warmth felt like a missing piece of me had been found. I'm starting to think the L-word slip last night might have not been a friendship one, and I'm treading into some dangerous territory.

I pick up my pace and try to out-run everyone, but it's no use since my shorter legs don't take me very far. When I hear Liam whisper, "Is it a walk of shame if she came back on a boat? Like would that be a boat ride of shame?" I finally snap.

Spinning around to face them causes them all to collide, tripping over each other like the puppies in *101 Dalmatians*.

"First," I hold one finger into the air. "It's not a walk of shame because I love this dress," I say in a sing-song voice, channeling my inner Kesha.

I see Abby and Maeve high-five, no doubt proud their prediction came true.

"Second," I hold up another finger, and my face heats thinking about what I'm going to say next. I'm hoping if I'm blunt enough, it will shock them, and they'll stop asking me about it. "We had sex and that's all I'm going to tell you, so stop asking me questions."

Everyone stares at me for a few seconds before Finn whoops, "That's our girl!" He runs toward me so fast I only have a second to prepare before he throws me over his shoulder and runs toward camp.

I do my best to keep Zach's hat on my head and cover my ass, which I realize doesn't work when I hear Lucy yell, "Wait, are you wearing his underwear?!"

After a quick shower, I realize Zach and I didn't have time for breakfast so I grab a bowl of strawberries at my parents' site. They're down at the Point letting Sammy swim, so our site is quiet right now. My small moment of peace and quiet is quickly ruined when the girls come around the camper and sit down with me. They place their towels and beach bags down, and the smell of sunscreen surrounds me.

None of them say anything and stare at me. "Can I help you?" I gesture at them with a half eaten strawberry.

They all turn to Abby, who straightens. "We know you said you weren't going to tell us more, but the others aren't here so you are going to tell *us* more, right?"

I sigh. "Fine, but it doesn't leave this table."

"Scouts honor." Lucy throws three fingers in the air, and we all break out into laughter.

I tell them about the whole day, from the farmers market to his cooking. I leave out some of the details that I want to stay between me and Zach, but they get the spark notes version of those parts. When I finally finish, my strawberries are long gone, and my cheeks are starting to hurt from smiling so much.

"Wait," Hannah chimes in. "Do you like *like* him?"

"Hannah, we aren't in middle school," Quinn chastises, then directs her gaze at me. "But please answer the question."

I throw my hands over my face and close my eyes, mumbling, "I think so."

They all let out shrieks, and everyone over at Aunt Shan's site turns our way.

"Everything okay over there?" Uncle Owen calls over.

"All good, Dad," Maeve holds up a thumbs up. "Just a bee."

"What's next, then?" Abby asks.

"I don't know. He's working the rest of the time we are here, and we didn't exactly get a chance to discuss our next date due to the audience this morning." I pointedly glare at each of them.

"I have no regrets." Maeve slams the table and points at me.

"Do you think you could continue talking after we leave? It's only a three-hour drive," Lucy points out.

"Yeah, but he's going to a school near Poughkeepsie this fall," I remind them, feeling guilty they still don't know I'm moving.

"That's only like another hour, you can do that." Quinn nudges my shoulder, and I glance up at Abby. She widens her eyes and gives a subtle nod to the group.

This would be the perfect time to tell them it would actually be a lot harder to continue a relationship with Zach after we leave here since I'm moving, but I can't. I don't want to ruin this happy moment and spoil it with tears and promises to FaceTime and text. I'd like to live in my denial bubble a little bit longer, thank you very much. The idea of telling them has my stomach twisting in knots. I want to barf.

"I don't want to do any type of distance," I say, settling on this version of the truth. I see Abby roll her eyes at me, which is fair.

"Well, don't write it off yet," Lucy says and stands up from the table. "Want to go down to the beach and see him?"

I do. I really do, but I can't. I need to distance myself from Zach today, or Sunday is only going to be harder. "I'm actually going to stay here. I could really go for a nap," I point to the tent behind me, which isn't a lie. I'm exhausted after last night. "And please don't bother him when you go down there." I bring my palms together in front of me, begging them.

"We won't. We'll be down there if you want to join us," Abby stands next and the others follow her.

I get up and head to my tent, unzipping all the windows before collapsing on the air mattress.

Hours later, I realize how badly I needed a day at camp. My nap didn't last too long, but I was able to read and get a few pictures for my Bookstagram account to post later. I played with Gracie and her bubbles and sat around with the aunts and uncle as they told stories I've heard a million times before. I also got to play a quick game of dominoes with my grandparents, which Grandpa won.

It was nice to sit, relax, and recharge. With all the attention being on me the last few days, my social battery was almost empty.

I find myself looking down toward the beach anytime I hear voices in the distance. I know Zach's working and can't leave the beach, but some small part of me is hoping he'll appear at the end of the road.

On my hundredth look, I see everyone coming back, towels wrapped around them and hair wet. The second Maeve spots me sitting and reading, she runs my way, with Abby not far behind her.

She stops abruptly in front of me and Abby runs into her. "Maeve, what the fuck?"

"Oops, my bad, sorry Abs," Maeve throws her arm over Abby's shoulders and gives her a side hug.

"It's fine, just warn a girl next time." Abby rubs her nose. "Give it to her," she says pointing my way.

"Give me what?" I set my book down and glare up at them.

Maeve smirks and her hand comes shooting out, almost hitting me in the face. I see a small folded piece of notebook paper laying in the center of her palm.

"What's this?" I ask, taking it from her.

"Read it and find out," Maeve says in a sing-song voice and skips away with Abby, leaving me to open the note alone. Holding my breath, I unfold the paper:

Be ready at 8:30. Wear comfy clothes
-Z

Be ready at 8:30. Wear comfy clothes
-Z

THIRTY-FOUR

ZACH

Not seeing Sidney all day was torture. Knowing she was so close to me but I couldn't go see her. Then, all of her cousins came down without her, and I couldn't help but wonder why. I almost went over to them to ask, but I didn't want to come off as clingy. After we broke up, Luke told me I was too clingy, which never seemed to bother him when we were together.

Luckily none of them came out to the raft when I was out there. I was half expecting them to come to question me, but they all left it alone. The most I got were some winks and thumbs up.

Right when they were about to leave, I stopped Maeve and Abby and asked if either of them had a pen and paper, to which Maeve pulled both out of her bag immediately. I wrote a quick note and told them to give it to Sidney, and then they were gone. I couldn't text her since we never traded numbers, and I wasn't going to ask her cousins to give it out without her permission.

Now I'm driving back to the campground in my truck, after having gone home to shower and have dinner, and I have no way of knowing if they gave the note to her. She might not want to go out with me again, but I really hope she's waiting for me when I get there.

Pulling into the campground, I pass the registration booth and drive around to the Murphy's camp. I spot Sidney and her cousins at one of the sites, outdoor hanging lights illuminating the area as the sun sets.

I can see she's laughing, so I roll my windows down and let the sound of it fill my truck. I slow down to a stop in front of the site. They all stop and turn my way as I open the door and stand on the foot rail of my truck.

I rest my elbows on the roof and cup my hands over my mouth. "You ready to rock'n'roll, princess?"

All heads whip back toward Sidney who stares at me with the widest grin. She dressed comfy like I said, in the hoodie I gave her and sweatpants. Memories of that night come flooding back. If I'm not careful, the whole camp-ground is going to be able to see my dick through my sweatpants.

Sidney hops off of the picnic table and heads my way. Jumping backward, I round the front of the truck and see she's running toward me now. I open my arms right in time for her to jump into them and her lips to collide with mine.

I hear cheering from behind us, but it doesn't matter since my worries that she might not want to go out tonight dissipate with each flick of her tongue against mine.

She pulls away first. "Sorry, I guess I missed you more than I thought."

"I missed you, too." I kiss her again, letting her legs drop to the ground. "You ready to leave, or do you need anything else?"

"I'm all set. Let's go before they get even more annoy-ing." She nods behind her and pulls me to my truck.

I open the door for her, helping her climb in before moving around the front and getting into the driver's seat. She leans out the window and waves at everyone before I pull away from the site.

"Wait, where are we going?" She turns toward me, pulling her feet up onto the seat with her.

"I was thinking about the drive-in?" I reach over and place my hand on her knee, and she moves closer.

Her hand comes over mine, squeezing. "Shut up, I love the drive-in," she shouts. She notices "Delicate" by Taylor Swift playing on the truck's dashboard and reaches to turn up the volume. "Oh my gosh, I love this song." Her head drops back against the seat as she sings along. "Seeing her play this live was a magical experience."

"Right? Getting to scream the chant was the best." I squeeze her knee and glance at her. She's stopped singing and her mouth is completely open.

"Wait, you saw her live?" she says in one of the most serious tones I've heard from her.

"Hell yeah." I throw my hand up in the air. "Cy and I are total Swifties. We dressed up and everything. The glitter stayed in my hair for weeks." People always seem to have a hard time processing that we're Swifties, but we lost our voices as badly as anyone else at the concert.

Sidney still looks like she's trying to process it when she asks, "Where did you see her?"

"Philadelphia."

"Shut. The. Fuck. Up." She enunciates each word, getting louder until she's yelling with her hands in the air. "I was at Philly, night one."

"Seriously? I was at night two," I yell.

"WHAT?" She screams so loud, I'm thankful the windows are still down. "You were there for the "Bad Blood" Security Guard night? That's so unfair, I had to watch so many grainy videos of Taylor yelling at that guard during the middle of the song.”

She drops back into the seat and crosses her arms. I can’t help but laugh as she pouts because she’s so damn cute right now.

“Yeah, our whole section was so confused,” I tell her. “Cy got it on video, too. You should ask him to show you.”

“I don’t know what I want to focus on, the fact that we missed each other by one night or that you got the “Bad Blood” night.”

“It’s almost like...” I start.

“Don’t say it,” Sidney warns.

“There was an invisible string,” I say through a laugh, unable to help myself after making the corniest joke I’ve ever told.

“You said it, and I didn’t actually hate it.” She laughs and shakes her head, pulling my hand back over to rest on her knee.

At the drive-in, Sidney picks the horror movie double showing, and we drive around to the screen to find a parking space.

She hops out of the truck and gasps when I pull down the tailgate. When I got home, I set up the truck bed with multiple sleeping bags and various blankets and pillows.

“Stop. Zach, this is perfect,” she says, hugging me. I wrap my arms around her hips, picking her up and placing her on the tailgate.

Stepping between her legs and pulling her close to me, I cup her cheek, “You’re perfect.”

Her cheeks heat below my fingertips, and she pulls me

into a kiss, I'm really starting to regret not taking her back to my apartment.

I'm the first one to pull away this time. "I'm going to go grab popcorn and drinks, you stay here and get cozy." I kiss her nose and head toward the concession stand.

I end up with a large popcorn, a large soda, and three candies. M&M's for the popcorn, then a sweet and sour choice in case she wants something else. Right as I head for the doors, I see the backs of two familiar heads quickly disappearing into the bathroom. My eyes must be playing tricks on me, but I would know that red hair anywhere.

I adjust my course and head straight into the bathroom, snacks in hand. My suspicions are confirmed when I see Cy and Connor staring at me like deer in headlights.

"Hey, man, great night for a movie, right?" Connor says. "That's a great selection of snacks, I gotta get some popcorn."

"Cut the bullshit," I snap. "I told you I was bringing Sidney here, so why the fuck are you here?"

"What? Can't we also want to see a movie tonight?" Cy throws his hands up in the air.

"Correct," I clip, glaring at them and Connor's face gives everything away when it turns the color of his hair.

"It wasn't our idea," Connor exclaims a little too loudly, his voice cracking.

"What do you mean your—oh fuck." I rush out of the bathroom and out the doors to where I left Sidney. If it wasn't their idea to come here, that only leaves one group of meddling Murphys.

I do my best to jog to the truck without dropping any of our snacks and round the bed of the truck right as the trailers are starting.

"Sidney, I think your—" I freeze when I see Sidney

crouched on the sleeping bags, a blue and orange Nerf gun pointed right at me.

THIRTY-FIVE

SIDNEY

I drop the Nerf gun and crawl forward to grab the snacks from Zach. "Hurry get in and get low," I whisper, pulling on his sleeve.

"Why are you whispering, and where did that come from?" He matches my whisper and points at the discarded Nerf gun.

I crawl to the back of the truck bed and pull a bag out from behind the pillows, "I found it when I was searching for something to defend myself with." I pull a second Nerf gun from the bag and toss it to him.

"Shit, I forgot I had these. Cy and I used them to prank another park." He catches it and examines it before pointing it away from me. "I take it that defending yourself means your family is here?"

"Did you see them? I wasn't sure if I actually saw them," I say as he moves to the edge of the truck to peer over the edge. He resembles a video game character, and when he turns back around he's grinning from ear to ear.

"I saw Cy and Connor, who claimed it wasn't their idea

to come here." He grabs a handful of popcorn and returns to peering out over the truck.

"No, this has Abby and Maeve written all over it." I move to the opposite side of the truck and mirror his position. I should have known I was never going to survive this week without them crashing at least one date.

I remember being thrilled when I turned seventeen and could go see rated-R movies with dates, not having to worry about the two of them coming in during the trailers and sitting behind us. Then they would question why I never told them anything about my dating life in college and I would stare at them until they shut up. It seems like they decided to pull out some of their old moves and follow us here.

"What do you want to do? We have like ten minutes before the movie starts." He crawls over to crouch beside me, and it's making me feel things I wish it wasn't. All of my past dates told me to ignore my family and that they would go away if we left them alone. Meanwhile, Zach didn't question me when I tossed him the Nerf gun, and now he's letting me lead? I swear he's trying to make me fall in love with him.

"I can't see them, so we figure out where they are and shoot them." I hold up my Nerf gun and shrug.

"Brilliant." He leans forward and kisses me quickly. "Let's go get them." Then he's out of the truck and holding his hand toward me to join him. The position makes me feel like Jasmine in *Aladdin* when he shows up with the magic carpet, and I am not swooning right now.

I hop out, and he lets me lead us around the truck. We're creeping forward, bent over on a mission, Zach's hand holding onto my hip burning a hole right through my sweats. We pass a few of the other trucks in the row before he pulls me down, getting low behind the hood of a larger truck.

"That's Cy's truck over there." He points around the truck to a green one a few down.

I peek around and spot the truck he's talking about and see Uncle Owen's right next to it. Ryan must have convinced him to let him borrow it since we all drove up with our parents. I can see the whole lifeguard crew is here in addition to my family. They're in the two trucks, some are in camping chairs in front, all facing Maeve, who appears to be laying out some sort of plan with the way her hands are flying around.

I turn back around to Zach. "You go around Cyrus's truck. And I'll go to the other side. We attack and run."

"Do we need an attack signal? Like a Hunger Games call?" he asks, turning toward me. He purses his lips to produce the most perfect rendition of the whistle from *The Hunger Games* that I've ever heard. I'm honestly still in shock that he's on board and hasn't made fun of me at all for wanting to do this, no matter how childish it may seem.

"Perfect. There's no way I can whistle like that so that's all on you." I point to him, and he smirks with a thumbs up before we are on the move and getting into position.

I can hear all of them talking, and they're so loud I hope I can hear Zach's whistle. My hands are practically shaking around the Nerf gun. I've never had the chance to mess with my family my way. If this goes poorly, I'm never going to hear the end of it. I don't want to become an embarrassing story they tell each year.

After what feels like forever, I hear the whistle followed by a caveman cry. I run out from my hiding spot.

Everyone's facing where Zach appeared and is now shooting them with foam Nerf bullets. I take this opportunity to make sure I hit Maeve and Abby first, aiming randomly after that. They all scream and duck for cover. Liam drags Lucy in front of him as a shield and I see Connor cut off Maeve to dive into one of the trucks.

Zach runs out of ammo first and beats his chest like Tarzan before running at me and throwing me over his shoulder.

I shoot my last few bullets as Zach runs away screaming, "Long Live Team Sidchary!"

Movement near my head jostles me awake. I try to open my eyes, heavy from sleep, but they close fast, ready to return to the dream I was having.

"Sorry, didn't mean to wake you," I hear Zach say, his fingers combing through my hair. It's so soothing that I hold tighter to whatever my hand is hovering over. I grasp the fabric under me, and my knuckles brush something warm and hard. "Careful there, princess," he hisses, tensing below my touch.

I open my eyes fully to see I've koala-hugged him and he's sitting against the back of the truck. My leg is wrapped around his, and I realize my hand was brushing his stomach.

"I fell asleep?" I peer up at him and move my hand fully along his stomach now, running my fingers over his happy trail.

He sucks in a breath before answering. "Yeah, about halfway through that second one. The credits have been over for a bit now, but I didn't want to wake you." He brushes a strand of hair that's fallen over my eyes. "I'm not really sure how you fell asleep during a horror movie. It was actually pretty impressive."

"I guess I was just really cozy. I had a great cuddle

buddy." I move my leg higher up and can feel the outline of his length beneath my leg.

His hand comes down and stops my movement. "You really shouldn't start something you can't finish," he warns.

"Who says I can't finish this?" I move my hand higher up his shirt. The feel of his skin under my fingertips is so familiar. I swirl my thumb in a circle once I reach his nipple. His cock hardens under me, and I silently thank the inventor of sweatpants for this moment.

Zach groans, and his head falls back against the windows as I continue to circle his nipple. "*Fuck*, that feels so good."

"Everyone's gone?" I ask right as I pinch it. His head snaps down to me, eyes almost black.

"Everyone's gone," he glances around and behind us to the concession stand. "The employees, too. Allison's girlfriend works here, and I told her not to wait around."

"Want to hear a secret?" I whisper and move my hand to his other nipple, slowing down to rake my nails through his chest hair.

"Only if you trust me," he hisses through his teeth.

I stop my movements and grin up at him. "I've always wanted to hook up at the drive-in."

THIRTY-SIX

ZACH

Sidney's confession brings my dick from half-hard to fully hard as I grab her hips and move her to my lap. She lets out a small yelp, settling over me. I can feel the heat of her through our clothes.

"Good," I rasp as I guide her hips to start moving over me. "Because I've missed the feel of you around my cock."

"It hasn't even been a day," she gasps, her hands coming to my shoulders to steady herself.

"Princess, it could only be a minute, and that's still too long. You're not too sore?" I check with her, moving my hands up and under her hoodie.

"No, I'm good," she says through a gasp as her head falls back when I move further up her sides and brush the underside of her bra. I reach back to unclasp it and lift up the rest of her hoodie over her head, along with her bra.

The moon isn't full anymore, but it's full enough that I can see every part of her perfectly. Our days are limited, so I take my time running my fingers along the shape of her breasts, memorizing them. Her nipples are the palest shade of pink they could possibly be, and they harden at my touch. I see Sidney watching me now, her eyes dark and heavy with lust.

"Do you have a condom?" she asks.

I stretch to grab my backpack in the corner of the truck bed and quickly pull out a condom and a small travel bottle of lube, and her eyebrow shoots up. "I told you I'm always prepared," I explain as she goes to grab the condom out of my hand. I pull it away. "Not yet, I need to taste you first."

She wraps her hands around my face to pull me into a kiss, and I can taste the hints of chocolate and popcorn from earlier. She moans and grinds harder against me, and I have to pull her up on her knees before I come in my sweatpants. My dick is already leaking and begging to be inside of her.

I tug on the side of her sweatpants, and she quickly lifts each leg, pulling them off fast and leaving her naked over me.

"Your turn," she whispers and tugs on my shirt, which quickly comes off and joins her discarded clothes. She reaches for my sweatpants but loses focus when I grab her ass in one hand and use the other to guide her breast to my mouth.

I swirl my tongue around her nipple and sprinkle kisses around and in between her breasts, slowly trailing my way down her stomach. I start to lower myself and keep her steady above me until I'm finally laying flat in the truck bed with her pussy right above my face. I can see her already dripping, and I run a finger through her lips. She moans, and I glance up at her, reaching my hand up to dip my finger into her mouth. She swirls her tongue around it and sucks the taste of herself off of me, and it's now one of my favorite sights. I add it to the Seven Sexual Wonders of Sidney, along with the sight of her mouth wrapped around me and the expression on her face when I first enter her.

I move my hands to her hips and start to pull her down to my face.

"Zach, you really don't—" she starts to protest, and I can feel her resisting my pull.

I stop. "Do you not want me to?" I glance from her pussy to her face.

"No, no, I do. I don't want to crush you." She covers her face as she says it, and I don't like that she feels embarrassed about this.

I reach up and pull her hands away from her face. "Princess, I'd be honored if you would make me the happiest man alive and sit on my face. Now hold on to the truck." Then I pull her the rest of the way, and she cries out when her pussy comes over my mouth.

It's the sweetest thing I've ever tasted, and I don't know if you can get addicted to someone's taste, but it's starting to seem like you can. I work my way around her lips and start sucking on her clit. She's still resisting, so I start to move her over me, and she moans louder, rocking against my mouth.

I have to keep my hands on her hips so I don't reach down into my sweatpants and fist my own cock. I'm not sure I would need it though. I could come from this alone. The sounds she makes when I suck harder, the moans I hear from her as I release her clit, and her cries as I lick down to her entrance have me on edge.

She picks up her pace, finally confident. I was planning on stopping before she came, but I don't think I'll be able to pull myself away. I slip one finger inside of her, coating it in her wetness. Reaching behind her, I tease my fingertip around the tight hole of her ass. I move my mouth back up to her clit and suck hard as I push into her. She comes so fast I don't have time to lap up her release, leaving my facial hair wet and shiny.

I kiss my way back up her stomach and over her breasts until I'm sitting back against the truck, painfully aroused as she catches her breath.

"I apologize for doubting that," she laughs, wiping my chin.

"I'd never lead you in the wrong direction," I reply and bring my mouth to hers for a kiss.

The kiss turns frantic quickly, and she guides my sweatpants down my legs. It seems like we both had the same idea of not wearing any underwear tonight, and I can't help but smile at how we're so in sync.

As soon as my legs are free, she grabs the condom and lube. Her pussy brushes along my dick, and it takes all of my willpower not to grab her and thrust inside.

"Sidney, please hurry," I beg.

She slows down and leans back to take my dick into one hand and rips the condom open with her mouth. "Or what?" She holds the condom up in one hand and strokes my dick slowly, swirling her thumb around the slit and spreading the bead of precum that's there.

My head drops back against the window, and I thrust into her touch right as she lets go. My head whips back up, and I reach behind her head, my fingers threading through her hair as I pull her close to me. "Or I'm going to make sure you won't be able to walk for the rest of your trip." I crash my mouth to hers and take the opportunity to grab the condom from her hand and work it down my length as our tongues tangle.

"That's not the threat you think it is," she gasps between breaths.

I find the lube, rubbing it over myself before lining up with her entrance, pushing in slowly at first. I break the kiss to witness one of the Seven Sexual Wonders of Sidney as I thrust all the way into her.

"*Holyfuckingshitohmygod*," she moans, starting to move over me.

I cup her ass to help guide her, continuing to thrust up into her. She's so perfect around me, and I never want this moment to end.

Rubbing her ass, I lift my hand to give her a small spank. Her pussy clenches around my cock the second my hand connects with her ass.

"Fuck yes, do that again," she gasps, pushing her ass into my hands.

I spank her twice more, and each time brings me closer to coming as she clenches around me.

"I'm so close, Zach. I need more," she pleads. I rub my hand over her ass.

"More what?" I ask, not sure if she wants to be spanked more or if she wants to switch positions.

"More anything, just more." She leans down and kisses me, and I know what she means.

Us together feels so good that I want more, too, but don't know what I want more of. I want to touch her everywhere at once, for her to be there at night if I have a bad dream, for her to wake up beside me every morning, to have her in my kitchen and live amongst my things. I want *more*. I know I can't have more, though. She's leaving in a few days, and there's nothing I can do about it.

Instead of saying all that and risk ruining one of the few nights we have left, I reach between us and find her clit. We both look down at where we're connected, and it's one of the most overwhelming feelings I've ever had.

I press harder and bring her forehead to mine. "Come around my cock, princess. Let me feel it," I say, thrusting up into her.

Sidney screams through her release, her pussy clenching around me so perfectly that it only takes a few more thrusts until I'm unloading into the condom.

We stay wrapped up in each other for a moment, catching our breaths. The chirping of crickets is the only other sound around us. She leans against me, resting her head on my shoulder as I rub my hand along her back, slipping out of her.

"Come home with me?" I ask in the night air, unsure if she'll want to, after our welcome back this morning.

"Okay." She nods against me, and at this moment I know I'm never going to be able to let her go.

THIRTY-SEVEN

SIDNEY

The heat from the sun warms my face, as I listen to the sounds around me. I can hear the waves crashing into the rocks, seagulls fighting over food, kids playing in the sand, and Zach laughing as he talks with Allison and Taylor.

Last night we went back to Zach's apartment, falling asleep the second we crawled under the covers. I slept curled in his arms, and it was one of the best nights of sleep I've ever had. I woke up to breakfast in bed with eggs, toast, and coffee.

There wasn't anyone waiting for us when we pulled into the marina, and no one asked me any questions when I got back to camp. My mom was surprised to even be seeing me and simply asked if I was being safe, which I assured her I was.

People are finally seeing me as an adult, which makes my impending move to LA seem not so bad after all. My confidence is the highest it's been in years, and I refuse to analyze it any further than that.

Suddenly the warmth from the sun disappears, and I

open my eyes to see Zach standing above me, the widest smile on his face and his green eyes shining brighter than ever. My face can't help but break into a matching grin.

"I'm headed out to the raft in a few. Come out and keep me company?" he asks, pointing out to the water.

"Sure thing, Moretti. I'll see you out there," I reply and sit up on my beach towel.

He grins and does his best to skip away in the sand, almost falling into a moat one of the kids created. I laugh and stand up to stretch, adjusting my red bikini. I told myself this morning when I put it on it was for me, but the second I got to the beach and saw Zach's eyes light up, I realized I picked it for him.

I head to the water, Maeve and Abby quickly trailing behind me.

Maeve does a small jog and dives, disappearing under the water. The only reason I know where she is underwater is because I can see her bright pink bikini.

"You headed out to the raft?" Abby asks, and we take our time going deeper into the water, pointing over to where Zach's now getting into the water.

He removed his lifeguard tank top, and the sight of him diving into the water and reemerging headed straight for us makes my heart skip a beat.

I hear Abby laugh behind me and swim away toward Maeve, who I'm sure is already halfway to the raft. I could confirm that, but I can't take my eye off Zach as he slowly swims my way.

"Hey princess, fancy meeting you here." He smirks and splashes water at me.

"Shut up, let's go." I roll my eyes at him and start swimming.

We swim in silence, and I can tell he's going slower to keep pace with me. Which is maddeningly sweet, like everything he does is. This fling has an expiration date, and he's only making it harder for me to stick to that.

We reach the raft, and it's only Cyrus, Maeve, and Abby. Zach lets me climb up first, following closely behind.

"Hey Sid," Cyrus calls out, hopping down from the guard chair. "Ready for tonight?"

"Hell yeah! I'm excited to have my drinks made for me all night." I turn around and cock my eyebrow at Zach.

"Shit, I forgot about that," he groans, running his hands over his face.

"Speaking of that," Cyrus chimes in. "Us lifeguards had a vote, and Zach here is going to be your only DD and waiter this evening." He pats Zach's shoulders, and I can tell he's trying not to laugh.

"What the fuck? When was this decided?" Zach throws his arms in the air.

"Think of it as hazing the newest lifeguard. There's no way we are helping you cater to them all night." Cyrus shrugs.

"How am I supposed to fit all ten of them in my truck?" he grumbles.

"Put them in the bed and hope you don't get pulled over," Cyrus laughs and runs off the raft, executing a perfect corkscrew jump, soaking all four of us.

Zach climbs up into the chair and drops his head into his hands. "Please tell me all of you drink beer and only beer."

I glance over at Abby and Maeve, who I have never seen drink a beer, and we all burst out into laughter. He's in for a really rough night.

Right around nine, Zach's pickup truck pulls into the campground and into our site. He hops out, and I'm immediately annoyed at how well dark jeans and a black Henley compliment him.

"Okay, climb in Murphys. I guess five in the truck and five in the back. If you're in the back, try to stay low so no one sees you." He moves to open the back doors, and everyone climbs in. I head for the back seat.

Zach raises his eyebrow at me and shakes his head, grabbing my hand and leading me around the truck to the passenger's side. He checks over my shoulder before pressing me up against the car and bringing his mouth to mine.

My hands fly into his hair, and I pull him closer to me, kissing him deeper as our tongues dance around each other.

"You look amazing," Zach pants, breaking the kiss.

I glance down at my high-waisted black jeans and red cropped tank. "Really? I don't—"

"If we were alone right now, I'd be on my knees for you," he whispers into my ear, and suddenly my whole body is on fire as he leans past me and opens the door.

Hannah, Jordan, Finn, and Abby managed to fit into the back seat of the truck. While the rest piled into the bed, some of them laying down to stay out of sight. Around here, there are hardly ever any cops, so I'm sure Zach isn't too worried about getting pulled over. I get comfortable in the front seat, and Zach's hand immediately finds its way to my knee.

We spend the whole drive to Cyrus's telling Zach stories about past parties. One year Liam and Lucy got so drunk they switched clothes and tried to convince people they were each other. Another year, Maeve tried to dance like Kat in *10 Things I Hate About You* and ended up breaking Cyrus's dining room table. Last year, Quinn almost got into a fight when someone said something mean about Abby. Zach laughs and inquires about each story, asking to hear more. His hand doesn't leave my knee the whole way there.

ZACH

I park outside of Cy's house, and the Murphys pile out of my truck like it's a clown car. I don't usually get to attend these parties since I work at Mario's at night and I'm always too tired to go back out. I hear my fair share of stories the next day, but I'm pretty bummed I missed experiencing Quinn almost fighting someone last year.

I get around the front of the truck in time to catch Sidney hopping out. I throw my arm around her, pulling her close to me. There's no way I'm entering this party without her next to me. I need everyone here to know she's with me, even if it's only for a short time.

"Hey, Murphys," I call out, and they all stop on the walkway to turn around. "I'll be with Sid all night. If you need a drink or want to go back to camp, find her. Otherwise, have fun and try not to fight anyone." I wink at Quinn, who rolls her eyes and heads inside.

The music grows louder the closer we get, and the smell of beer hits me like a wave when we cross the threshold. The Murphys scatter in different directions, leaving me with Sidney and Abby.

"How am I supposed to know what everyone wants if they all disappear?" I look down at Sidney and then at Abby, who both roll their eyes at the same time. It honestly gives me the chills how much they look alike. I've never really noticed how close they are to twins, but I don't have a desire to kiss Abby the way I do Sidney.

"Come on, we'll help you with the first round." Sidney grabs my hand and pulls me through the crowd to the kitchen.

We get five drinks from the keg in the center of the room and five more from the plastic storage bucket filled with a jungle juice mix. The smell is so strong it almost makes me gag as college flashbacks enter my mind.

Abby grabs a handful of the drinks and sashays away to pass them out, while Sidney and I head toward the living room with the rest where the furniture has been pushed back to create a makeshift dance floor.

Finn and Liam are already sweating from dancing, and they chug their drinks, handing the cups back to me for a refill. Sidney is tugged into the center by Lucy and Jordan, dancing lazily as I officially start my evening as the Murphys' waiter.

Two hours later, I've lost count of how many drinks I've refilled. It has to be over thirty by now, and I'm fully anticipating having to clean my truck tomorrow when one of them throws up.

I enter the dance floor, handing Maeve her refill. She screams to thank me and I can barely hear her over the music. Sidney spins around and throws her arms in the air, spilling some of her drink on the people dancing next to her.

Watching her dance has been amazing but also torture. The way she moves to the music is so carefree, her curls bouncing as she jumps around. She's sweating from moving so much, and I can see the shiny sheen of sweat that glistens on her skin dipping down toward her chest. The sight of her makes my dick twitch, and I have to adjust myself.

She stumbles toward me and throws her arms around my neck, craning to meet my eyes. I smile down at her as she closes her eyes and spins around. She dances in front of me, and my hands fall to her hips to move with her. I feel like I'm at a middle school dance, trying not to come in my jeans from the hot girl grinding her ass all over me.

I throw my head back and close my eyes and let myself get lost in the music and Sidney as we dance in time with each other, never missing a beat when the other changes positions. If someone had told me a week ago I would be here completely infatuated with a girl I just met, I never would have believed them.

She spins toward me, and she says something. I can't tell what she said, so I guide her back into the front foyer where the music is quieter.

"What did you say, princess? I can't hear you in there." I brush back a piece of her hair stuck to her sweaty forehead.

"I said," Sidney sways in my arms and slurs her words. Maybe the next drink should be some water. "That you are an excellent dancer. And—" she stops mid-sentence and her eyes widen as she sees something behind me.

I turn around to see what scared her and see my ex-boyfriend sauntering through the front door. Luke spots me immediately, and I can tell he's already drunk by the way he can't hold himself upright.

"Well, well, well if it isn't Zach Moretti," Luke slurs, heading toward me and Sidney.

"Evening, Luke," I nod and try to remain civil, moving Sidney behind me. I know Luke when he's drunk, and it's like he aims to be hurtful. I don't need him being an ass to her right now.

"You trying to hide her?" Luke peers around me at Sidney. "Afraid to say I was right? There really is too much competition when it comes to you, everyone's fair game." My blood boils, and if I say something right away, it isn't going to be pretty. I try to collect myself before speaking, but Sidney beats me to it.

"You can fuck right off, Luke, I never liked you." She steps around me and lunges for Luke.

She's fast, but I manage to grab the back of her jeans before she can get to him, pulling her back behind me. "Princess, don't engage with him, he's not worth our time."

"I was worth your time a few months ago." Luke gets louder and closer, drawing a crowd from the living room, and someone turns down the music. I see Maeve and Connor emerge from the dance floor out of the corner of my eye. I really don't need this right now.

Suddenly, Cy comes pushing through the crowd from the kitchen. "Luke, get the fuck out. You know you're not welcome here anymore."

Luke throws his hands up in the air. "You even got my friends turning on me."

He steps closer, getting right up in my face. He reeks of alcohol. "You had to go and take my job, too? Couldn't handle only breaking up with me? Plus, you didn't even get the best Murphy. She's so *meh*."

"Oh, fuck that," I hear Maeve before I can respond, and damn these Murphy girls are fast. She's pulling out her hoop earrings and shoving her cup at Connor, who drops it and wraps his arms around her waist, pulling her flush against him. He's taller than her and the difference causes her legs to kick in the air. "Let go of me, you tall ginger," Maeve shouts, trying to squirm out of Connor's grasp.

"Not a chance. We don't need a Quinn repeat." Connor shakes his head and backs up with Maeve in tow.

More people have gathered now, and I see all the Murphys have found their way to the commotion. I want nothing more than to give Luke a black eye, but I also want to get him out of here with as little violence as possible.

"Go home, Luke, before you do something you're going to regret." I nudge Sidney back toward the living room. Hopefully he takes my advice and leaves. Nothing good will come of him staying here.

"Yeah, run away and fuck your camp slut. She's going to end up leaving you anyways. She's only around for a quick fuck. I bet you'll have someone new next week," Luke shouts behind me, and I lose control as I feel my fist connect with his face.

THIRTY-NINE

SIDNEY

I'd be lying if I said seeing Zach punch his ex to protect my honor wasn't the sexiest thing I've ever seen. I've known Luke since he started working as a lifeguard, and for him to reduce me to a camp slut felt like a punch to the gut. He's lucky Zach was the one who hit him because I don't fight fair, and his pretty boy face probably would have walked away with more than a split lip. Not to mention I'm pretty sure Maeve would have loved to get her hands on him, too.

"He's gone. Zach okay?" Finn asks, coming into the kitchen with Liam. Both of them were on Luke the second he hit the ground and escorted him out.

"I'm fine, but I'm going to have a few bruises, I'm sure." Zach lifts his hand in the air to show them, removing the bag of peas from it.

"Keep those on there." I pull his hand back down to the bag of peas.

"Sorry, princess." He leans down and kisses my forehead, and my face heats.

"What's his problem anyways?" Liam asks.

"Long story short, he's got a lot of shit to work through and blames it all on me." Zach shrugs.

Liam nods like he gets it, which he doesn't since he's barely been in a relationship, and leaves the room with Finn to head back to the living room.

"He really blames everything on you?" I ask, adjusting the peas on his hand to make sure they're covering his knuckles.

"Yeah, I was too compliant during our relationship, adjusting my likes to fit his. He wasn't too happy when I stopped doing that. On top of his insecurities about me being bi, he says everything's my fault," Zach says.

I nod, and the next question is out of me before I can tell myself to not be selfish. "You're not doing that with me, right?"

"No, I'm not." He moves his free hand over mine, which is resting on the bag of peas. "He's right, though, you are leaving. I guess we both are, though. Have you told your family about it?"

"No, I haven't." I shake my head, avoiding his eyes.

"Why not?" he asks, rubbing my hand. I feel guilty that he's comforting me, when I should be making sure he's okay.

I mumble, "Still scared." I shrug, beginning to sway in front of him.

"That's fair. I'm sorry for what he called you. I don't think of you like that," he says.

I finally lift my head, and I can see tears on the edges of his eyes through my own. I'm not nearly as drunk as the rest of my cousins, but the drinks I have had make me more emotional. We have a silent conversation like the one on the dock, and I stare into his green eyes trying to tell him how much he means to me. How I'm sorry we only have a week. He stares back at me with understanding, and

I know he's sorry, too, but I'm not sure if it's for the short time or the feelings.

Abby pokes her head around the corner, breaking us from our trance. "You two up for beer pong? Or does that need more time?" She points to Zach's hand.

I turn toward him, not sure if he wants to talk more, or if doing something will help get his mind off of Luke and us.

"Me and Sid versus you and Cy?" he asks Abby, who raises her eyebrow at me.

I laugh and pat his shoulder. "Sorry, Moretti, I only play with Abby. We're kind of a package deal in beer pong." I skip over to Abby and hook my arm around hers, turning back to him. "But I understand if you can't handle losing right now." I try to say it in the most cheery way I can, hoping it stops the tears from escaping from my eyes.

He shakes his head and heads our way, stopping right in front of me. "Oh, it's game on, princess."

I'm starting to worry Abby and I might end our winning streak when it's down to one cup each. I can't explain why Abby and I are so good together. I'm never this good when I play with other people. There must be some type of special sister power that has helped us keep a three-year streak.

Everyone's gathered behind us, waiting to see if Zach and Cyrus will finally be the ones to defeat us. Cyrus just landed his ball into our cup, and if Zach doesn't make this shot we have a chance to take it home. With Cyrus's house rules of no rebuttals, we are only three shots away from winning.

Abby holds my hand, and I hold my breath as Zach

lines up his shot. We lock eyes and I can see the smallest bit of mischief twinkle in his bright greens, then he's tossing the ball my way. I watch it slice through the air and hit the rim of the cup, then bounce off onto the floor.

Their side of the room groans, and Abby and I high-five and prepare ourselves for our turn.

"Any last words before we end this thing?" I ask Zach as Abby steps up to shoot.

"You're awfully cocky for someone who needs to make two shots." Zach crosses his arms, and my mouth waters from the sight of his tattooed forearm, his sleeves now pushed up to the elbows.

I shrug. "Call it a gut feeling." Leaning forward, I put my hand on Abby's shoulder and whisper, "You've got this, take your time."

"I don't need time," Abby smirks and the ball is out of her hand a second later, landing right in the center of Zach and Cyrus's cup.

The cousins cheer behind us, growing silent as I step up for my turn. I hold up the ping pong ball in front of Abby. "Blow?"

Abby rolls her eyes and blows slowly on the ball. It may be dramatic, but I can't help myself. I stare straight at Zach and take my shot without looking at the cup, and only know I made it when the crowd behind us bursts into applause.

Abby tries to pick me up and spin me, only getting me a foot off the ground. "Yes, Sid! That's how it's done," she shouts, setting me down and shaking me. "Who am I supposed to play with next year when you're not here?"

The words hit me like a truck, and Abby freezes when she realizes what she said. The room starts to close in on me, and I can't breathe. The tears from the kitchen start to flood my eyes. I need to get out of here. I turn to run and see all my cousins staring straight at me, the same confusion written on all their faces, before I'm pushing through the crowd and out the front door.

The summer night air doesn't help, and I run down the steps and lean over the bushes, hands on my knees. I can't tell if I need to barf or if my stomach is merely having fun trying to kill me.

I can hear everyone yelling my name before they come filing out the front door.

"I'm so sorry. I didn't mean to let it slip." Abby's first to me, and her hand rubbing my back doesn't help make me feel better.

Everyone's talking at the same time, and I can't focus. My tears are blurring my vision, and the moment I've been putting off this whole vacation is finally presenting itself. It's the universe's way of saying, *"Well if you don't do it, I'll do it for you."*

"Okay, everyone, shut up," Maeve yells, silencing the group. "Sidney, what's going on?"

I finally pick my head up, and my legs give out as I drop down to my knees in the grass and cry.

Everyone sits down around me as I cry into Abby's shoulder and Maeve rubs my back.

"Sidney, why are you crying?" I hear Lucy ask, followed by what I assume is Liam hitting her based on her yelp. "Fuck, sorry, didn't know I couldn't ask."

I can't help but laugh, and I wipe my eyes, careful not to rub too hard and lose my contacts. "I think I'm crying because I'm drunk." I glance up at all of them. "And because I have something to tell you."

I take a deep breath, and Abby grabs my hand. "I got a job in LA, and I'm moving there next week. I don't know if I'll be able to come here next year," I say as fast as possible, afraid if I don't get the words out quickly I'll never say them.

"Oh thank god," Quinn throws her hand over her heart. "I thought you were dying or something."

"Me too," Maeve shouts, and then turns to me. "Wait, if you are only moving, why didn't you tell us?"

I sigh. "I don't know, I didn't want you to be mad at me." I throw my hands up and bury my face in them.

"Why would we be mad at you?" Hannah asks.

"Well, I guess because no one really leaves. I don't want you to forget about me," I confess, and saying it out loud sounds dumber than it did in my head.

"That's some bullshit," Ryan says. "You know we aren't going to pull your Murphy card, right? You're still our family if you move."

This somehow makes me cry again, and Finn reaches out to pat my knee. "You moving also means we get to plan trips to come visit. I hope you have enough room for all of us."

I laugh and lean my head on Abby's shoulder. "I guess I'm also scared to go out there."

"Well that's why you have us," Jordan says from the back of the group. "That way you never have to do anything scary alone."

"I love you." I meet all of their eyes, filled with love and understanding. I'm not so sure why I was so scared of telling them about this. This went over pretty well, and no one yelled at me for leaving.

Different variations of "love you too" all overlap as everyone speaks at once before we all fall silent. The party's in full swing, and I see Zach leaning against the front door frame with Cyrus next to him.

He lifts one hand from his crossed arms to wave at me, and my world is slowly coming back to me with my family and him around to keep me grounded. It won't always be that way, but I can enjoy it for the night.

I can hear the song change, and the opening of "Mr. Brightside" comes pouring out the front door. It may be cheesy, but this is our song. One year Liam got really into 2000's music and only let us play songs from that era the whole trip. This one got played the most, and it kind of became our theme song.

We all glance around at each other and grin. Liam is the first to jump. "Let's go! We're going to fucking miss it," he shouts, sprinting for the house, all of us getting up and running after him to the dance floor.

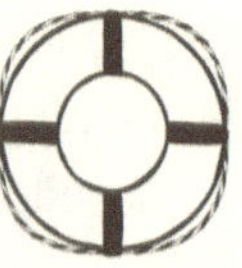

FORTY

ZACH

Rounding up all the Murphys to take them back to camp took twenty-seven minutes. I timed it. I ended up carrying Hannah and Jordan to the truck bed, where I left them to star gaze. The rest of them took more convincing it was time to leave. If I tried to pull Sidney and Maeve off the dance floor a minute sooner, they were going to murder me. She started drinking more after telling her family about her move, and yelled at me when I tried to give her water, so I gave up. I've heard her tell each of her cousins how much she loves them and how she's going to miss them, and I can't help but wish she was saying the same thing to me.

Sidney has been blasting Taylor Swift from the front seat since she got in, hanging her head out the window. My finger is secure in her belt loop to make sure she doesn't hang out too far. The first few songs got her emotional, and she started to cry again before Abby started yelling lyrics in her face to distract her. Surprisingly, it worked. Pulling into the campground, I turn the music down and tug Sidney back into the car.

She grumbles, as I roll up the window, "Noooo, I want to stay outtt."

"Sid, we gotta get ready for bed." Abby leans forward from the back.

"Boooooooo," she whines, and I can't help but grin at how cute she is when she's pouting.

I park at her site and go around the hood to open her door. Everyone climbs out and thanks me for tonight. I reach my hand out toward Sidney, but she hops out too quickly and stumbles into me.

"Come on, princess, let's get you to bed." I turn to Abby. "Which one is your tent?"

"It's over here, follow me." She gestures for me to follow, and I wrap my arm around Sidney's waist to keep her upright.

Abby unzips the tent and turns on the lantern inside, lighting up the small space. She helps me get Sidney inside, sliding down my arm to the air mattress.

I go to stand, but she grabs the sleeve of my shirt. "No, don't goooo."

"Sid, he has to go home," Abby sighs from the other side.

Sidney sits up, still hanging on to me. "Abigail. Have you seen this man?" She points at me, a sudden serious drunken tone to her voice, her eyes half closed.

Abby rolls her eyes. "Yes, I have. Multiple times."

Sidney cups one hand over her mouth and leans toward Abby to whisper, "What you don't see is how good of a cuddler he is." She glances up at me, not realizing her whisper isn't a whisper at all. "And he's a good kisser."

My cheeks heat, and I love that I'm getting a front seat to drunk Sidney. "I really need to go home, princess."

"And he calls me princess," Sidney shouts, throwing her

arms up in the air and falling back onto the air mattress. "He stays."

"Okay, I'm going to sleep in the camper." Abby grabs her pillow and stands up. "You two have fun, just leave my side alone."

"You really don't have to, I can leave," I whisper to Abby so Sidney won't hear me.

Abby sighs at the sight of Sidney, who's trying to remove her pants in the least efficient way I've ever seen. "No, you can't. Stay, but be out before breakfast or else the adults are going to never leave you alone."

"Thanks for the tip," I say.

"No problem, have a good night, Sid." Abby leans around me and waves at her sister before leaving and zipping the tent back up.

"Zach stays," Sidney shouts, tipping backward as her leg comes flying out of her jeans.

"Yes, Zach stays. Let me help you," I laugh, shaking my head at her. I help her get her jeans the rest of the way off and leggings on. It takes us ten minutes to get her contacts out since she won't let me touch her eye.

I crawl behind her and do my best to fit both of us on the single air mattress. She moves back and fits into my arms so perfectly. I can't help but bury my nose in her curls inhaling her floral scent.

"So cozy," she mumbles, pulling my arm closer to her. "I'm going to miss this."

My chest tightens. I don't think she would be saying something like this if she was sober, so I'm not going to say anything. But we both know she's not going to be staying here. Neither of us are.

We lie like that for a few minutes, and I hear her breaths deepen as she falls asleep. I look around the dark tent and can easily differentiate her belongings from

Abby's. Abby's side is messy with clothes everywhere, while Sidney's is organized and put together. I notice my hat on top of her duffle bag, and my heart skips a beat thinking about how she looked in it.

I close my eyes and settle into her pillow. "Hey Sidney?" I whisper, not sure if she's fully asleep yet. When my question is returned with a light snore, I know she can't hear me. "I might be falling in love with you," I say into her hair and kiss her head before falling asleep, knowing it won't change by the end of this week.

The weather is cloudy and chilly today, which is great for us because that means fewer people at the beach. Usually when it rains, we end up playing Uno in the shack, but there's no playing today with Cy, Connor, and Taylor moving around like zombies. It's probably best we have the least amount of people to watch as possible. They've all got their sunglasses on and Taylor's currently in the shack "making sure we have enough first aid supplies." We've basically given up on going out to the raft today.

I managed to leave this morning before any of the adults spotted me, leaving a note next to Sidney with my hat that said I would see her today and suggesting she wear the hat. Right around noon, I see she read it when she comes down the hill with the hat on. She's wearing shorts and a long sleeve shirt, and I can't help but wish she was wearing more of my clothes.

She's with Maeve, and they're swinging Gracie between them. Gracie sings something I can't place, and I can hear Sidney laughing and attempting to sing along. I can't help but smile as they head toward the guard chair.

"Morning, ladies," I call down from the chair, waving

at them. Cy and Connor flinch from the picnic table like I screamed it.

"We thought we would come to check in on you guys to see how you were holding up this morning." Sidney peers up at me and pats Cy on the back.

He groans and drops his head to the table. "I've been better."

"How are you two so cheery?" Connor grumbles, pointing between the girls.

"Like we'd ever give you the secret to our hangover cure," Maeve tries to cross her arms, but Gracie reaches up to tug one back to her.

"What are you up to today?" I ask before Connor can bite back at Maeve. The last thing I need right now is to have to listen to their bickering.

"Bracelets," Gracie yells and jumps, practically pulling Sidney and Maeve down as she jumps as high as she can.

"We are going to head up to the rec center since today isn't the best day for swimming. Gracie has been itching to make a bracelet," Sidney clarifies, and my hand goes to the bracelets around my wrist from past campers. I want to ask them to make me one, but I don't want to seem needy.

"Nice, they have the best strings up there," I say instead.

Gracie starts to pull Sidney and Maeve, toward the rec hall. I watch them all the way, and right before they step inside I see Sidney glance back at me.

"Dude, what's up with that?" Connor barely lifts his head to ask.

"What do you mean?" I ask.

"I mean," he says, glaring up at me over his sunglasses. "You've been totally MIA, Tyler said you took the whole week off, and you didn't leave her side at all last night. So I'll ask again, what's up?"

I run my hand over my face, not sure how to explain to them how completely fucked I am. "I don't know. I guess I'm trying to spend as much time with her as I can before she leaves."

Cy perks up at this confession. "How bad is it?"

I scoff and try to play it off, but he knows me too well. "Bad."

SIDNEY

Heading back down the hill after making bracelets, I tell Maeve I'm going to make a quick stop to see Zach and I'll catch up with her and Gracie in a minute. This is our last full day, and I want to make sure I have plenty of family time today, since I've been ditching them a lot this week. I'll be seeing them again in no time for the holidays, so I only feel a little guilty about spending so much time with Zach.

He's out of the chair now, so hopefully I can get a moment of alone time with him without the other lifeguards eavesdropping. I woke up this morning alone in my tent with a note next to me. His hat was on my head before I sat up, wanting to feel some part of him close to me.

Everyone's back up at camp playing lawn games and relaxing. I have to be back up there soon to help prepare things for dinner. Tonight is the cousins' assigned night to cook, which means the ten of us not married or in committed relationships are in charge. Last year it went spectacularly wrong when Finn and Liam spilled the salt potatoes after trying to figure out a more efficient way to drain them. Needless to say, we aren't doing salt potatoes this year.

Zach sees me approaching and jogs over, wrapping me in his arms the second he gets to me. Any nerves I had about inviting him for dinner tonight are instantly gone with this one hug.

I squeeze him tighter, and I can hear his heartbeat through his hoodie. "Thank you for last night," I say, peering up at him. I'm going to miss the feel of his arms around me, and I don't want to let him go.

"Of course." He smiles down at me and I could never get sick of the way those green eyes pierce my soul. "I'm sorry I wasn't there when you woke up. Abby told me not to stick around too long."

"That was probably for the best," I say with a laugh breaking the hug. I pull the new green and blue bracelet from my pocket, holding it between us. "I made this for you."

Zach's smile somehow gets bigger and he holds his arm out. "Care to do the honors?"

I wrap the bracelet around his wrist and I'm thankful when there's enough room to tie it. I tried to use my wrist for scale, but his is bigger than mine, so I had to guess. This one fit around mine and Gracie's wrist by the end, so I was pretty sure it was going to fit.

He holds up his wrist and twists it around, inspecting it. "This is my new favorite bracelet, thank you, princess."

"Of course," I nod. "I also wanted to know if tonight—"

"Yes," Zach cuts me off.

"You don't even know what I was going to ask."

"Are you going to be there?"

"Yes, I am," I laugh, shaking my head.

"Then count me in. Tell me when and where."

My knee bounces, shaking the whole picnic table. I'm only growing more anxious waiting for Zach to show up. I've never brought someone around my whole family before, and I don't know how they're going to react.

"Sidney, if you don't stop, these cucumbers are going to go everywhere," Maeve scolds, catching a cucumber as it rolls off the table.

"Sorry, sorry," I apologize, placing my hand over my knee.

"Looks like lover boy is pulling up now." She points behind me to where Zach's truck pulls into my site, and my stomach feels like it's falling out my ass.

I drop my knife and quickly hustle over to him, trying not to think about how I leave tomorrow. I'm not sure why I invited him to dinner when this thing between us can't last. I wanted one last memory with him, and I would like to live in denial for a few more hours. Denial and I have become such great friends over this last week, I might ask it to move in.

He steps out of his truck, and I hate how delicious he looks in shorts and a plain blue T-shirt. His hair looks like he's been running his hands through it nonstop as he heads straight to me.

"I assume I'm here for dinner?" He stops in front of me but doesn't touch me at all like he usually does. His hands are playing with his bracelets, and I realize he must be as anxious as I am.

I hook my arm around his and link our hands together, squeezing tight. "Correct. It's our turn to cook, but you can hang out while we get everything ready. I didn't really think this through." I lead him toward Aunt Shan's site where everyone is preparing dinner.

"What, I don't get to help?" He relaxes and the playfulness returns to his voice.

"Please help us," Finn shouts from the grill, acting like he's never flipped a burger in his life.

"Finn, stop. You're fine. You did great last year," I yell at him and turn to Zach. "You really don't have to help, I just wanted you here."

"Oh, I want to help. What are we cooking?" Zach cracks his knuckles and neck, surveying the organized chaos of our dinner night.

"We are doing pulled pork and burger sliders, mac and cheese, roasted veggies, and salad." I point behind me to Maeve and the salad station I abandoned. "Finn could use the most help with the burgers."

Zach sees Finn, who's trying to scrape a destroyed burger from the grill. "Yeah that's a good call."

Over the next thirty minutes, I try to keep my cool as the parents realize Zach is here. They all know who he is from the beach, and Cyrus has been up here a few times to visit, so seeing a lifeguard here isn't uncommon. But this time they all know about *us*. My dad and Uncle Owen try to act casual by grabbing a beer and checking in on Finn, but they are trying to figure Zach out. If I run over there and try to stop it, I'm only going to draw more attention to the situation.

After Maeve yells at me five more times for shaking the table, I give up on the salad and go help Abby with the buffet setup.

I hear my dad laugh, and I realize Zach is doing fine on his own. He could be telling a story with the way his arms are moving, and more people have crowded around him to listen. He effortlessly takes the burgers from Finn and flips them as he talks.

My heart aches in my chest watching him fit in so well.

Usually, new people only get stern and serious faces, followed by questions about their intentions like it's the 1950s. Zach somehow gets none of it, like he's known my family for ages instead of only nine days.

Eating dinner goes just as smoothly. I barely get a word in sitting across from Zach as people ask him questions and listen to his stories. He could have a really promising career as a stand-up comedian if he wanted to.

We didn't talk much during dinner, but he kept his feet touching mine under the table, keeping me grounded and less anxious about the whole situation. Inviting him to camp was the worst idea I've ever had. Seeing him banter with my family is making me second-guess the ending of this vacation romance.

Luckily, I'm not on dish duty since I did the breakfast dishes this morning so I'll finally get some alone time with Zach. He's talking with Ryan and Liam now, so I try to casually sway over and stand next to him.

"You want to go on a walk?" I ask, giving him a small hip bump.

"Sidney," he cheers and throws one arm in the air, placing the other around me. He pulls me close and floods my senses with his warm lavender scent. "I would love to go on a walk."

"Awesome. Sorry to steal him away from you guys," I apologize to Ryan and Liam.

"He's your guy, Sid. You can steal him anytime," Ryan laughs, rolling his eyes at me.

I grab Zach's hand and lead him down the road. We don't say anything, and Ryan calling him "my guy" shouldn't have made my stomach feel like it's been twisted inside of me. I really wish I didn't have to leave this place, or him.

FORTY-TWO

ZACH

Sidney leads us to the farthest bench at the Point. I don't think she knows I know what she's doing, but I do. I could tell her energy was off the second I got out of my truck. It's no secret she leaves tomorrow and is off to California soon. Plus, I'm leaving in the fall, so it's not like it would be easy if we wanted to keep whatever this was going. We haven't discussed anything past tomorrow, and I have a feeling she isn't going to want to do a long-distance thing, but I have to let her tell me that. If she wants to try it out, I'll do it. I'm not ready to let her go yet.

We sit down, and it's the perfect view of the sunset, still a few minutes away from fully setting. She doesn't lift her head, though, and starts to play with my bracelets instead.

"You know I've never actually watched the sunset from here before," I tell her, watching her flinch at the comment. I lift my finger under her chin and tilt her head to meet my gaze. I can tell from the sadness in her eyes my first instinct was right. "Princess, you have to talk to me."

She takes a deep breath, and her hand wraps around mine. "I'm so sorry," is all she says.

"What are you sorry for?" My hands cup hers, and I need to hear her say it to believe it.

"About everything?" I can see the tears gathering in the corner of her eyes, and I tug her to my chest. I can't watch her cry or I'll cry too.

"This, whatever we are, it's done, right?" I ask, and she nods into my chest. "Can we talk about it?"

She nods again, and it takes a few sniffles before she can talk. "I never expected to like you this much," she says into my shirt.

I rub her back. "Me either."

"Don't say that. It's only going to make this worse," she whines, and I don't know why she expected any of this to be easy.

"I'm not going to lie about my feelings for you, Sidney. You've been the best part about me moving up here. You just happened to have arrived right at the end."

She lifts her head, and I see her eyes filled with sadness, tears running down her face. I want to lift my thumb to her cheek and wipe them off, but I don't have that kind of strength in me.

"Would you be interested in trying long-distance?" I ask her, because if I don't ask I'll always wonder if this could have worked.

"No. I don't want that," she sighs. "I need to explain this better, I'm sorry."

"Take your time, I have nowhere else to be." I lean back and give her room. I can see the emotions on her face, pain, and sadness, and that's the last thing I want her to feel.

"For years, I've only ever been a Murphy cousin. There were brief moments when I would date someone, so it was Sidney and that person, but never just Sidney." She moves back to playing with my bracelets. "I've never been on my own, and I don't think I've ever really explored who I am, as Sidney. My whole goal of this trip was to step outside of my comfort zone and see who I could be."

"What was I? Just another goal?" I ask. She told me about wanting to be on her own, but it doesn't make this hurt any less.

"Zach, no. No, that's not what you were," she pleads and cups my face, turning me toward her and no doubt seeing the tears forming in my eyes. "I only told myself I would do things this trip that I usually said no to. Saying yes to you was one of the best things that could have happened to me."

"So say yes now. Don't let us end. We can FaceTime and text, I can update you on how school is going, and you can tell me about LA. I'll fly out there on my breaks to visit you," I plead.

"You're not getting it. I don't want that," she says. "I need to go to LA on my own. I need to figure out who I am." She rubs her hands along her face. "You need to focus on school and on opening a restaurant. I can't hold you back from that."

"You wouldn't," I whisper, my voice sounding so defeated.

"I would," she argues. "You would be spending all your money on flights when you should be focusing on other things. I can't be the reason your dreams don't come true. I can't let you change yourself for me. You said you wouldn't."

"What if my dreams are different now? That's me changing me, not you," I whisper, but I know she's right. If I were to end up in a relationship with her, I wouldn't put as much energy as I could into the restaurant. I would be editing my plans to fit into hers. I changed my dreams to fit my dad, and I changed my personality to fit Luke. She's making the tough call for both of us.

"Zach, don't give this up for me. Do it for me. Open up the best little Italian place in somewhere like New York City and show everyone how amazing you are."

"What if I don't want to open one in New York?" I ask her, trying to lighten the mood.

"Open it wherever you want, Moretti." She rolls her eyes at me, and I know I'm going to miss that eye roll. "As long as you open it, it doesn't matter, okay?"

"Okay, I can do that." I nod and look back out over the water at the sunset. "Promise me you won't fall in love with any lifeguards-slash-chefs out in LA?"

She laughs and leans her head on my shoulder. "I promise. I'm not going there for love. I'm going for me."

"I know," I say. "I just wanted it stated."

"Well don't go falling in love with any short curly-haired girls." She elbows me, but not hard enough to hurt.

"Deal," I say, pulling her closer to me.

We fall into silence after that, watching the sunset slowly disappear over the Canadian border across the River. It's the most beautiful shades of pink, purple, and yellow mixed together. Sitting here with Sidney should feel like the end of something, but I can't help the hope inside of me about what the future holds for both of us.

She's going to go off to do amazing things in LA, and I'm going to honor my mom in the best way I can think of. Sidney said I was one of the best things to ever happen to her. I don't think she knows she's *the* best thing that has ever happened to me. There's no other experience that could compare to her and the way she makes me feel. And if I truly love her, I have to let her go.

"I'm sorry," I hear her whisper after what feels like an hour.

"I know. But are you sure you don't want to try long distance?" I ask, trying to keep my tone playful.

"I'm sure. I really need to figure out who I am, unattached to anyone."

"I get it, but I had to ask one more time. Promise me one last thing?" I ask, lifting her off my shoulder to look at her.

"What's that?" She asks and tilts her head.

"Don't forget me when you're out in the big city."

"Oh Zach, I'll never be able to forget you." She cups my face and kisses me one last time. And it feels like we are saying everything we didn't get to say in this goodbye kiss. I feel water on my cheek, and I can't tell if they're her tears or mine. But it doesn't matter.

FORTY-THREE

SIDNEY

I wake up and go through the motions of packing. My body is mimicking what I do every year. Packing is always the worst. It means vacation is over, and we all have to return to our real-life responsibilities. For some reason, everyone starts leaving right when we wake up. I don't think I've ever seen my family stay past 9 a.m.

Last night, I walked Zach back up to his car and said goodbye to him one last time. I realized I didn't even get his number, which is probably for the best so I'm not tempted to text him when I get to LA. When he finally pulled away, all my cousins were there waiting for me.

Maeve had a shot in her hand, and Abby had an ice cream bar. I downed the shot followed by the ice cream and collapsed in their arms, crying as they held me. We spent the rest of the night by the fire, and they did their best to comfort me with s'mores and stories.

Now, I feel heavier than I did when I started this trip. It's a different kind of heavy, and I don't know why I'm feeling this heartbroken after only a week. None of my past relationships have had this effect on me, and I'm not sure how to tell if it was only a summer fling high, or if it was real.

I still think breaking things off is the right decision. I need to figure out who I am in this next phase of my life, and I can't do that if I'm always checking my phone to see if he texted me.

My parents are still in the process of hooking the camper to my dad's truck, but other than that, we are all set to leave. Most of the family is gone already, with only a few of us left.

Abby sits in the grass with Sammy, trying to keep him distracted, and this might be my only free moment of time before we are gone for the year.

"Hey Abby, I'm going to go for a quick walk, okay?" I hop off of the picnic table, and Abby gives me a thumbs up. Then I'm running.

It might be a stupid idea. It's only eight, and Zach doesn't have to be at the beach for a few more hours. The possibility of him being there is low, but I would regret it if I didn't try. Try for one last kiss, one last hug, one last look at him before we both leave this place. Selfishly, I don't want our last memory to be last night. Part of me knows if he's there and asks me about long distance again I'll break, and part of me hopes for that.

At this point, I'm letting fate decide because I can't do it by myself. If he isn't there, I won't wait, and I'll go back to camp.

I get halfway down the hill and have to stop to catch my breath. Maybe I should look into gyms when I get to LA and sign up for some classes. I decide to walk the rest of the way, that way I'm not a total panting mess if he's here.

Coming around the corner, my gaze goes straight to his spot at the marina, and my heart drops into my stomach.

It's empty.

He's not here.

Of course, he isn't, why would he be?

This was so stupid.

Stupid doesn't stop my feet from moving though. I head toward the marina and walk down the dock to his empty spot. The water is calm today, and I can see fish and seaweed where his boat should be.

I count to thirty and turn to leave, getting only two steps before stopping again. I peer down at my wrist and see the bracelet I made myself yesterday. It's the same pattern as the one I made for Zach, but the colors are the same shades of red as my sundress.

I untie it and lean down to where the boat ties on the dock are. Tying the bracelet around it, I hope he sees it and knows it's mine. I didn't show him this one, so there's no way he could possibly know, but maybe he will. I don't need this bracelet anyway. Even if he doesn't notice it, I'll know a part of me is always near him for the rest of the summer.

The dock starts creaking. I hear footsteps and a familiar bark. I see Abby and Sammy headed my way, out of the corner of my eye.

"Mom and Dad sent me to get you. We have to leave because we're following Grandma and Grandpa back to help them unpack at home," Abby tells me, and I can hear the sadness in her voice. I can only imagine how I must look crouched in front of Zach's empty space.

I push off my knees and stand up. "I'm ready, let's go."

That's a lie. I'm not ready, but I have no choice except to be. I follow them back up the dock, taking one last glance at the marina with Abby. Taking in the feeling of the Islands one last time to last me the next few years.

FORTY-FOUR

SIDNEY

2 ½ YEARS LATER

"On your left," a rollerblader yells behind me, and I almost jump out of my skin. I've been in LA for a couple years now, and I still haven't adjusted to the hustle of living in a city. I live on a fairly busy street, and there are always people biking, skateboarding, or rollerblading. I even saw someone on a unicycle once.

I punch in the code to my building's front door and slide in, closing the door fast behind me. I always have the irrational fear that someone who doesn't live here will try to slip in behind me, and I don't need to be the reason for anyone's stalker getting in.

I unlock my mailbox, grab the pile of mostly junk mail, and head up to my apartment. It's a cute little place, and I've made it my home over the past couple years. Most of the decorations are nods to things back in New York. The entryway has a large map of the Thousand Islands right above the table for my keys, and I hang my purse on the coat rack next to it. I catch sight of the hat hanging on one of the hooks, and my chest tightens. I haven't been able to get rid of that navy hat no matter how many times I've tried. Maybe today I'll do it, but probably not.

Moving further into my apartment, the kitchen and living room combo has posters for some of my favorite Finger Lakes wineries and local shops. I managed to get a poster for Cyrus's family's bookstore, which always makes me blush if I stare at it after drinking a bottle of wine. I only blush because of the wine, or at least that's what I tell myself.

I flip through the mail and toss each piece into the garbage as I go. I don't need home insurance, I'm not interested in cable, and I don't want coupons for the pet store.

I'm about to throw the last piece of mail away until I realize it only says my name on it. I flip it over and there's no address on the back or on the front. The writing seems familiar, and I can't place it. My stomach twists when I realize that means someone must have hand-delivered it right to my mailbox, slipping it in the slot. I guess I was the only one worried about letting stalkers into the building, thanks a lot neighbors.

I grab my letter opener from the junk drawer and slice through the top of it, pulling out a small postcard. It's a deep maroon with "GRAND OPENING" repeated all down the front in raised gold foil lettering, and it shimmers in the light when I move it back and forth. Flipping it over I see the information for what's opening.

It's a new Italian Bistro opening today, and it's close by. It must be one of those things everyone in the building got, which is why it was hand-delivered. Then again, it had my name on it so that might not be right. I didn't think anyone here knew my name since I keep to myself.

I read the rest of the information about the opening, and my eyes move back up to the restaurant's logo that I glazed over at first, and I suddenly feel like I've been hit by a truck.

I take off my glasses and rub my eyes, thinking maybe I read it wrong. I stare down at the roses and cursive logo and blink a few more times, making sure it's really the same. "Mama Rosa's" stares back at me, unchanged from when I first read it.

My phone suddenly rings from the counter. I drop the postcard, jumping back like I've been burned. My heart pounds, like I ran through a haunted house and barely made it out. I take a second to catch my breath and see Abby is FaceTiming me.

"What?" I snap when the phone connects, and her face fills my screen. I almost denied the call, but she would only keep calling.

"Jesus, sorry? Should I call back?" Abby's eyes widen, and now I feel bad about yelling at her.

"No, sorry. I—" I glance at the postcard, now on the floor. "It's nothing, what's up?"

"Okay, I was only calling to chat." She pauses and glances off-screen. "You're home, right? In your apartment?"

"Yes?" I furrow my eyebrows. She's being weird, and I don't know why. There are too many things happening right now, and I'll snap again if I don't figure out at least one of these things. I prop my phone against the toaster and reach down to grab the postcard, examining it and trying to make sense of it.

"What's that?" she asks and leans forward like she'll be able to get a better look through the phone.

"A piece of mystery mail I got today for some grand opening. I can't figure out why it was sent to me." I show her the "GRAND OPENING" side and stare at the logo.

"I love mysteries. You should go, you probably need dinner anyways," she says.

"Yeah—" I freeze and move the card to glare at her. "I never said it was a restaurant. How did you know that?"

Her face floods red, and her mouth drops open. "It was a guess," she shouts, way too loud.

"Abigail. What do you know about this?" I point the postcard at the phone and give her my best stern Mom impression.

"First tell me what you think it is." She crosses her arms, and she's lucky she's on FaceTime or I would tackle her.

"Fine," I roll my eyes at her. "It's a restaurant opening, and it's for an Italian place, and it's called Mama Rosa's." She's nodding, and I realize I'm thinking through this out loud so I keep going. "You remember Zach?" I ask.

She nods. "Obviously Sidney. Just because you don't talk about that summer doesn't mean we forgot."

"Okay, rude." My whole family was great when I moved out here, not asking me about Zach or if I was seeing anyone else. Abby and Maeve filled everyone in so I wouldn't have to talk about it. I've wanted to bring him up multiple times, anytime something reminds me of him, but I always keep it to myself.

I focused all my new Cali Sidney energy on my job and didn't bother to try to figure out the LA dating scene. Instead, I spent my time becoming friends with my coworkers and joining a local book club.

"Anyways, he wanted to open an Italian place, and his mom was named Rosa, and he wanted to name it after her. But he's in New York, right? This couldn't be his place. This is a strange coincidence, and I am overthinking this, right? Plus, it was hand delivered, and he wouldn't know where I lived." I stop talking and take a deep breath. Abby grins at me like I've cracked the case. "Right, Abby? That's ridiculous?"

She covers her face and furiously shakes her head. "No, it's not ridiculous," she finally says, peeking through her fingers.

"Explain," is all I say since I feel like I might throw up any minute.

"You're not wrong, Sid. It's his place. And your address? I gave it to Cy, he gave it to Zach, Zach sent the invitation. Easy as 1, 2, 3. I'm sorry for giving out your address without your permission."

"I can't tell if I'm mad at you or not." I flip the post-card in my hands. She wasn't wrong when she said I needed dinner. I might as well go check his place out. If he's cooking, he probably won't be wandering around the dining area.

"That's fair, I'm fine with either. But you should go," she says.

"I'll think about it. I have to go." I grab the phone and hang up on her, immediately putting my phone on *do not disturb* so she can't call me back. I need time to think about this and process it. I never thought I'd ever see Zach Moretti again.

FORTY-FIVE

SIDNEY

Standing outside Mama Rosa's, I glance down at the address on the postcard to make sure I haven't shown up to the wrong one. After I got off the phone with Abby, I showered and debated if I should go or not, which turned into me sitting in my towel afterward for thirty more minutes to figure it out.

I opened Instagram and went to Zach's profile. I've done this a few times over the last two years, never following him. He rarely posts, with his last post being a picture of him and Cyrus on his graduation day from culinary school. They both look so happy, and Zach's expression makes me feel confident in the decision I made to break it off with him, although I'm always jealous when I see this picture and it isn't me next to him.

I tuck the postcard into my bag and fix my dress. The same sundress I wore to the market with him that summer. I'm not sure he will recognize me with my longer hair braided over my shoulder and glasses on, so I figured I would wear something that made me feel confident and that he would recognize. I know I probably won't see him.

He might be in a relationship now, because we never promised anything to each other. Hell, he could have a kid by now, anything is possible in two and a half years. I'll never know if I don't go inside.

Taking a deep breath, I pull open the door and walk in. The restaurant smells amazing, and there's soft piano music playing over the speakers. It's dimly lit, and it has an at-home authentic feel, with the brick and vine walls. There's a small bar with around a hundred wine bottles behind it.

The hostess clears her throat, and I jump, not realizing I've been standing there. "Do you have a reservation?" she asks.

"No, I don't. It's only me tonight," I say, adjusting my purse over my shoulder.

"Okay, no problem. We are all booked up for tables tonight, but we do have a seat at the bar open if you would like to sit there." She points to the corner of the bar behind her.

"That's perfect, thank you," I reply and head that way. Of course, there aren't any tables—it's opening day. I can't help but feel proud of him. He managed to make his dream come true. I hope I'll be able to tell him that.

I sit down and look around the rest of the restaurant, waiting for the bartender to head my way, when my gaze stops at the front table next to the window.

Two familiar faces immediately snap their gazes away, and I might have to be bailed out of jail tonight. I hop off the barstool and head their way, pulling out an empty chair in front of them and helping myself to a seat.

"What the fuck is going on?" I hiss, just low enough not to draw attention. I can't believe they would do this.

"Hey Sidney, it's so great to see you," Cyrus chimes, giving my shoulder a small bump.

"No no no, don't act all happy to see me. You two have some explaining to do. So start explaining." I point at Abby who takes a long sip of wine, no doubt avoiding explaining.

"We're here supporting Zach?" she says, but it sounds like more of a question.

"To be fair, I'm actually here supporting Zach," Cyrus interjects. "Mastermind here might have tagged along for the ride after she heard that."

Abby hits him in the arm. "Way to blow my cover. We had a deal!"

"I don't want her to be mad at *me*, she still likes me." He rubs his arm and points at me.

"Hello! 'She' is right here," I wave my hands in front of them.

"Right." Abby faces my way. "I knew Cy was going to be here, and I didn't want you to eat alone if you showed up. I booked a last-minute flight out here, and I also kind of need a place to stay if you don't mind?"

I sit there with my mouth open. "Wait, where were you when we FaceTimed earlier?"

"Cy's hotel room." She gestures to him, and he smirks at me like he hasn't done anything wrong.

"And you're both here alone?" I check behind me, waiting to be surprised by more family.

"Correct, partners and the rest of the Murphy family are all safely back in New York." She nods. "I'm sorry, Sidney. I couldn't tell you."

"Why not?" I snap.

"I didn't want your decision to be swayed. You needed to decide to come here on your own, you know that," she says and reaches across the table for my hand. Her touch is comforting, and her reasoning makes it really hard to be angry at her. Abby and I rarely fight, and if we do, it only lasts a few hours until one of us breaks and apologizes.

"You're paying for dinner." I lean back and grab the wine list from the center of the table.

Her face breaks into a grin. "Absolutely, order whatever you want, please."

"We can try all the desserts, too," Cyrus says, handing me the dessert menu. He points to one halfway down the page.

I follow his finger and notice all the desserts are named after different people, and he is pointing to "Sidney's Tiramisu." A knot forms in my throat, and my vision becomes blurry as tears flood my eyes. I look up at him and open my mouth to say something but nothing comes out. I only point to the menu and look back and forth a few times.

"Yeah, I had a feeling that might happen," he says, pulling a pack of tissues out from his back pocket to hand to me. "If you want to see him, let me know and I can text him. Otherwise, he's not planning on coming out of that kitchen."

That only makes me cry more, and Abby moves to the empty fourth chair to hug me. The fact Zach has been in my city for long enough to open a restaurant and now he won't make an appearance on opening night so I won't be uncomfortable on the off chance I showed up? All the feelings from that summer flood out of the box I had them locked away in, and I have no more strength to hide them anymore.

ZACH

I haven't stopped moving these past few years. With culinary school and learning what it takes to open a restaurant, there hasn't been much time for anything else. I quickly found my footing in school and ended up meeting my business partner, Damon, that first week.

Damon is a few years older than me and was also interested in opening a restaurant. One night when we were drunk and in the back of a dive bar, I told him all about my ideas for Mama Rosa's, and he said he wanted in. The next morning I remember thinking how that conversation would be something we laughed about, but I already had emails from Damon and investors gauging their interest.

A few months later, we were looking at locations and planning out what the restaurant was going to be like. When we narrowed it down to New York City, Los Angeles, or Pittsburgh, I had a long conversation with Damon about how I didn't want to pick somewhere he didn't want to live. In the back of my head, I knew I was never going to go back up to Black Willow Bay.

I wasn't built for a small town anymore. Damon liked Pittsburgh, but that's where my dad was and I didn't want to be in the same city as him. Plus my girl was in a big city across the country, and I had always planned to go find her again. When Damon gave me the go ahead to pick anywhere, I picked LA so fast he barely got his sentence out.

Moving here and setting up the restaurant has been amazing. Now that it's finally here, and it feels like I'm waiting for someone to jump out and tell me it's all been a joke.

I mailed an invitation to my dad a few weeks ago. I would have felt guilty if I hadn't. Then a letter came back from his office telling me he couldn't make it. The letter was clearly a template that I'm sure his assistant filled in and stamped with his signature. If he couldn't manage to tell me himself he wasn't coming, then he didn't deserve any more energy from me. A small part of me still hoped for his approval, but when I got the letter I realized how much I didn't care. I wasn't sad. I was relieved. There would be no repairing our relationship after this, and I was fine with that.

Now, I'm in the kitchen of my restaurant. It's loud, but it's the best kind of loud. I've been here all day getting ready, minus the short trip I made during lunch to Sidney's apartment. It didn't take me long to get into the building, I only needed to smile at the first person to enter, and they held the door open for me. I slipped the invitation into her mailbox, and I ran back to the restaurant. If I had allowed myself to stay any longer, I would have been there all afternoon until she came home.

I don't want to force her to see me, but I haven't gone a day without thinking about her since that last sunset. I hope that summer meant as much to her as it did to me, and I hope Abby and Cy are right when they said this was the best way to do this.

Let Sidney decide to come and see me, then I would know if there was still a chance. If I surprised her, she wouldn't have time to process everything, and I might only end up pushing her further away.

It's taking everything in me not to run through the kitchen doors and look toward the front table. I know Sidney's here because I can hear her laughter every time the kitchen door opens. I keep checking my phone to see if he texted me to come out, which means I've washed my hands too many times to count.

I go back to focusing on running the kitchen, making sure everything is going out on time and being prepared correctly. I'm confident in the staff we've hired, but I can't help but helicopter cook this first night.

Hours later, I finally hear my phone ring with Cy's specific text tone and nearly drop the plate of cannoli in my hands. I take a deep breath and pull the phone out of my back pocket.

CY

come out here whenever you get the chance

CY

I don't apologize for our tipsiness

My heart stops, and I laugh once it starts beating again. Of course, they are tipsy. I would be disappointed if they weren't after being here all night.

I know exactly what their table has gotten, including the five bottles of wine and the entire dessert menu. The idea to name the desserts after people in our lives came one night after Damon and I couldn't figure out how to thank all the people we loved. The only other idea I came up with was painting their names on the wall, which Damon vetoed.

Everything was pretty much wrapped up, and people were mostly only getting dessert and drinks now. It was the perfect time for me to slip out and go say hi.

"Hey Damon, are you good if I head out there?" I hand the plate of cannolis to him. He knows everything about Sidney, and about how I invited her here tonight.

"She's here?" he asks, his dark skin shiny from running around the kitchen all night.

"She's here," I nod. I have to stop myself from jumping up and down like a child.

"Then what are you waiting for?" Damon throws open the kitchen door. "Go get your girl."

I shake my arms out and step through the door. I realize I'm still in my black chef's coat, and it's dirty from being back there, but I'm still presentable. I run my hands through my hair and head toward the front of the restaurant.

It feels like I'm running, but time has slowed down, almost like I'm in a dream and I can't get anywhere. Then I see her.

Her back is to me, but I would recognize that little butterfly tattoo anywhere. Her braid drapes over her shoulder, and she laughs at something her sister said. I'm frozen in place, unable to move forward, watching her, all the memories from that summer flooding back to me like they were yesterday.

Cy's gaze meets mine, and he gives me a small wave, causing Sidney to turn around to see who he's waving at.

She stares directly at me, and I know I must be in a dream when her face lights up like it did all those years ago. I still don't move, worried if I do she'll disappear and be gone from my life again.

I can see her figuring out what to do as she finishes her wine before standing up and heading my way. I glance down and see she's wearing the same rose sundress from our day in town, and my blood rushes to my cock at the memories of me on my knees underneath it.

Suddenly Sidney is standing in front of me and I can already smell her familiar floral scent invading my space, making me calmer. I've spent countless hours in different candle stores trying to find one that smelled like her, but none of them could amount to having her in front of me.

"Hey there, stranger. Fancy meeting you here." She crosses her arms and tilts her head, smirking at me.

"God, I've missed you," I say with a sigh and wrap my arms around her, not worried I might be dirty. I only want to feel her back in my arms where she belongs.

Her arms wrap around me, and I cup the back of her head, burying my nose in her hair and inhaling her scent.

Cy and Abby start cheering from the front of the restaurant, and the entire place erupts into applause, all eyes on us as I hold Sidney in my arms. She drops her arms to my waist and peers up at me, her blue eyes as beautiful as I remember.

"You did it, Zach. I'm so proud of you," she says.

"I did, and so did you. I hear you're doing well," I say and nod back toward the table.

"I am," she pauses. "Cy said you're unattached?" she asks with a raise of her eyebrow.

I nod. "Abby said you're unattached?" I check, already feeling guilty for holding her too long if she isn't.

"I am," she nods and bites her bottom lip. I hold back the cheers in my head.

"Can I kiss you, princess?" I ask. Her grin widens even further as her nickname rolls off my tongue, and it feels so good to be calling her that again.

"If you don't, the crowd will be disappointed." She nods toward the tables around us, everyone still watching us. My heart swells that she wants me to kiss her in front of all these people instead of shoving me away and storming out of here.

I cup her jaw and pull her lips to mine, and I kiss her. I kiss her like it's that summer, I kiss her like we've never left each other, and I kiss her like she's mine.

FORTY-SEVEN

SIDNEY

Zach sits with us for a few more hours, eating the desserts we have left over and helping us finish another bottle of wine. He fills us in on how school was and how the restaurant came to be. I tell the table about how my entry-level marketing position turned into me running my own marketing team. Abby and Cyrus fill us in on their partners and lives.

Zach and I easily fall back into our familiar touches, with his hand either on my knee or the back of my chair all night. The first feel of his calloused fingertips sent goosebumps down my arms and legs, and now I don't know how I went all these years without his touch.

The second Cyrus told me Zach was single, my heart almost stopped. I knew I wanted to try things out with him. Seeing him only confirmed that. He looked like he was seeing a long-lost treasure when he stared at me, and I'm sure I had the same expression.

Now it's the end of the night, and I don't want to leave his side, but I don't want to invite myself over to his place.

Cyrus has already left in his Uber for his hotel, and Abby has a flight out tomorrow morning.

"You're staying at Sidney's tonight, Abby?" Zach asks, locking the front door of the restaurant.

"If she doesn't mind. I really didn't know I would be coming out here," Abby says.

"I don't mind. It's a quick walk that way," I point down the road.

"My place is that way, too. Can I walk you two home?" Zach asks, wrapping his fingers in mine. I'm glad he asked so I didn't have to.

We walk until we reach my apartment, and I point out different shops on the way that I frequent, including my favorite coffee place on the corner.

I punch in my building code and Abby grabs the handle, stopping in the doorway.

"You want to give me your key? I'll leave it under the mat when I leave?" she asks and holds her hand out.

I stop and turn back toward Zach, who beams from ear to ear. "Are you sure?" I ask her.

"Yeah, Sid. You only have one bed, and I'm pretty sure you'd rather share a bed with someone other than me tonight." She laughs and rolls her eyes at me.

"You're not wrong," I say, turning to Zach. "Does that sound good to you?" I check with him, hoping that he won't say no after the little time we've spent together tonight.

"Sounds perfect," he says, winking at me. My face heats, and my stomach twists.

I hand over my keys to Abby and thank her for her meddling. Taking Zach's hand, he leads us back to his apartment, which is only another ten minutes. This reminds me of that day he showed me around town, how I felt like he was a missing piece to me. Holding his hand now feels the same, like we were always meant to find our way back to each other. I can't believe he's been this close to me, and I've never run into him. He admits he's seen me a few times and has hidden. He didn't want me to see him before the restaurant was ready.

Stepping into his place, I think about the first time I saw his apartment in Black Willow Bay and how it had so many random decorations. I can see he brought most of that stuff with him, and there are a few more additions.

I wander around while he cleans up a few things, and I see his place is similar to mine with one bedroom and a small living area. I'm taking in all of his fridge magnets when he comes into the kitchen and wraps his arms around me from behind, dropping his head to rest in the crook of my neck.

"You look so good in this kitchen," he mumbles against my neck, swaying me back and forth.

I rub my hands along his arms, and my hand stops when I feel something around his wrist. I couldn't take my eyes off of him tonight, and I didn't register what he was wearing. I pull his hand out in front of me and see he's wearing two friendship bracelets. One is green and blue, and the other two shades of red.

Tears fill my eyes, and I spin to face him. "You kept these?" I glance from the bracelets to him, holding his arm up in front of him.

"Of course I kept them," he says and brings my hand to his mouth to kiss it. "Princess, I knew you left the red bracelet for me the moment I saw it."

"I wasn't sure," I say through a shaky breath. I don't know why I'm still cautious of this when him keeping and wearing my bracelets clearly means something. I was afraid to love him fully back then, but now I know who I am alone. And frankly? It's boring being alone. I need to show him I feel for him as strongly as he feels for me, and I only know one way to do that. "I think I've loved you ever since that day in town," I say before I can let the words bury themselves in the back of my mind.

"You think?" he asks and steps closer to me, closing the small gap between us. The tips of my breasts brush against his chest.

His green eyes are full of hope and hunger. "No, I know. I'm in love with you, Zachary Moretti. And I'm sorry if that's too much right now, but I can't go another day without letting you know."

He bends down, and I think he's about to kiss me when he wraps his arms under me and hoists me up. My legs come around the small of his back, and my arms wrap around his neck. I don't think I've ever seen him this happy. His eyes filled with joy, and his grin the biggest I've ever seen.

"I've loved you from the moment I saw you, Sidney Murphy." He smiles and crashes his mouth to mine. This kiss is hungrier than our kiss at the restaurant, and he starts carrying me back toward his bedroom.

"I take it that we're doing this thing?" I ask.

"Yeah, princess, we're doing this thing. I've spent almost a thousand sunsets without you, and I don't plan to spend any more alone," he says, stopping to kiss me against the wall, and I can't wait to see where this thing leads us.

EPILOGUE - ZACH
ONE YEAR LATER

Sidney sits at the bar of Mama Rosa's, and I lean against the kitchen entrance taking in the sight of her. One leg is tucked up on the bar stool, chin resting on her knee. She's drinking a fresh cup of coffee, her hair in a messy bun as she looks at her laptop. I've never been more in love with her.

It's Saturday, so she's hanging out at the restaurant with me since I had to come in and get things ready for tonight. Sidney doesn't know it, but I've closed the restaurant for a private event tonight.

"Here you are. Come look at these," she calls me over.

"What arc we looking at, princess?" I place my hands on the bar on either side of her and rest my head in the crook of her neck, one of my favorite spots to be.

"Our engagement picture gallery is ready. They came out really well." She pulls up the gallery and leans her head against mine.

She's right, the pictures are really good. We had our photoshoot about a week ago at the beach during sunset, and we look amazing together, like a painting. "I love them. Can we print them from here?" I ask her, pointing to one where I'm picking her up and her foot is popped.

"Yeah, they would be great if we planned an engagement party," she says, flipping through the rest of the pictures.

"Totally. Print some, and we can hang them up at home." I kiss her cheek and head back into the kitchen, pulling out my phone.

ZACH

she has no idea

ABBY

perfect, let me know when to come by

I open the front door and let Abby in, grabbing the box of decorations from her. The rest of the Murphy cousins follow behind, all carrying various items, including Finn and Jordan with a balloon arch I specifically asked them not to get.

"How long do we have?" Abby asks. Maeve right behind her with a clipboard directing everyone where to put things.

"I sent her to feed the cat, which means she's going to sit with her while she eats. So an hour," I tell her, checking my watch. We've had our calico cat, Willow, for about four months now. Sidney surprised me with her one night after we moved in together. Sometimes I think she loves the cat more than me.

"Perfect, plenty of time to get this set up. The parents are all at the hotel now," Abby says, pulling streamers out of the box in my arms. I've been texting her and Maeve non-stop for the past month planning this surprise. Making sure all the Murphys had somewhere to stay is essentially an event on its own.

Thirty minutes later, the restaurant is decorated with engagement signs, streamers, and balloons. I have the buffet set up toward the back, and the parents are starting to make their way in now. I got a text from Sidney that she left our apartment, which means she's only a few minutes away.

It's a good thing the Murphys are efficient at setting up or else it would ruin the surprise. Abby and Maeve start pushing people away from the front and getting them to quiet down.

I turn the lights off and step outside the restaurant, seeing Sidney come around the corner just in time. She changed because I told her sweats weren't appropriate if she was going to hang out with the dinner crowd. She's stunning in the maroon jumpsuit she changed into, and her hair is braided over her shoulder like the day I got her back.

"Why are you waiting out here?" she asks when she gets close enough not to yell, then notices the dark restaurant. "Why are the lights off?"

"You'll see, princess." I reach out my hand, and she reluctantly takes it with a raise of her eyebrows.

I lead her toward the door and open it, letting her go in first.

"Zach, I can't see anything," she complains as I step in behind her and hit the light switch.

The room floods with light, revealing her family, some of the lifeguards, and some of our friends as they all yell, "Surprise!"

Sidney screams and throws her hands over her mouth, bursting into tears. I wrap her in my arms kissing the top of her head. "Surprise, princess, hope I did okay."

"You got everyone here?" She wipes her eyes and kisses me.

"I did, but I had some help," I point to Abby and Maeve, who are approaching us with two glasses of champagne.

"It was all his idea. We only made sure everyone got here," Abby says, handing me one of the glasses.

"It's so good to see you," Sidney says, hugging Maeve first. "I'm sorry I haven't been able to visit more."

"We get it," Maeve says. "We're glad to be able to finally celebrate with you two."

"I was also thinking maybe we can try to make it to the Islands this year?" I say and wrap my arm around her.

They all gasp and look at me. Sidney hasn't been back since the summer we met, and I worked it out with Damon so my absence wouldn't be a problem. I was waiting for the perfect moment to tell her, and now seems more perfect than ever.

"That would be amazing. Thank you," Sidney says and gives me another kiss.

"Of course, princess. Maybe we can check out some wedding venues when we go," I say, leading her further into the restaurant to say hi to the rest of our guests.

The night goes by quickly, with everyone catching up, drinking, and eating. I watch Sidney all night, and seeing her float around from group to group is amazing. I still can't believe most of these people are going to become my family, or that they're all standing here in my restaurant. Sometimes I think I'm still dreaming, then Sidney pulls me back down to Earth.

She sees me watching her and heads my way, wrapping

her arms around my waist when she gets to me. "I can't wait to marry you, Moretti," she mumbles into my chest.

I wrap my arms around her, and press my lips to her forehead, inhaling her sweet floral scent as I smile against her skin. "I can't wait to spend the rest of my life with you, princess."

THE END

DICKTIONARY

For anyone looking to know when open-door scenes occur. Including the start of some scenes, they can be found in the following chapters:

- Thirteen
- Fourteen
- Twenty-One
- Twenty-Nine
- Thirty-One
- Thirty-Two
- Thirty-Six

ACKNOWLEDGMENTS

To my family, I feel like I'm the quiet one when it comes to all our cousins, so I hope this book didn't shock you too much. You have no idea how much all of you mean to me, and I wouldn't be the person I am today without you. Thank you for always supporting me and being excited for this story. I'm sorry I couldn't fit all of you in here, but I hope you felt represented. I hope you enjoyed reading it and I can't wait to see you all at the Islands soon!

To Grandma Flo, thank you for starting this wild trip over fifty years ago and always bringing the kids back. From turning a trip with seven kids into a yearly event with so many more, you'll never know how grateful I am for you.

To Grandpa Bud, thank you for supporting Flo and towing the camper up each year. The Islands isn't the same without you. You're missed every year you're not there and I wish I could play dominoes with you one last time.

To Grandma Linda and Grandpa David, thank you for taking your family to the Islands. If it wasn't for you my parents would have never met, and this story would have never been written.

To my husband, thank you for always being my cheerleader even if romance isn't your genre. Your support means the world to me and I hope you like at least one romance book now. I can't wait to add the extra epilogue you eventually write!

To my alpha and beta readers, this would have been a

mess without you. Thank you for being honest with me about what worked and what didn't. To those who sat on the phone with me while I rambled on about my characters and scene possibilities, you are my favorite and thank you for listening and being there for me.

To the authors who answered my questions and supported me along the way. I wouldn't have been able to do this as smoothly without all of you. I look forward to continuing to get to know all of you and support your books.

To my editor, thank you for teaching me the differences between so many things. I'm glad I was able to introduce you to the Thousand Islands and salt potatoes. This book wouldn't have gotten that extra finishing touch without you.

To you, the reader, thank you for getting this far and taking a chance on my debut romance. I hope you enjoyed Sidney & Zach's story, and I hope I made you want to visit the Islands (I'll come with you). I know how many books are out there, and it means the world to me that you chose to spend your time reading mine.

And finally, to middle school me who planned a whole book series and only wrote one chapter—we did it!

ABOUT THE AUTHOR

Kayla Martin (she/her) lives in Upstate New York with her husband and Neptune—her tuxedo cat and writing assistant. As an avid reader and audiobook lover, Kayla loves to write swoon-worthy stories that will pull at your heartstrings. Using her big family as inspiration, there is no shortage of hijinks and family meddling involved in each character's story. She believes in writing love stories that help you find joy while also exploring different human experiences about sexuality, mental health, and everything in between.

Connect with Kayla on her website at www.kaylamartinauthor.com to sign up for her newsletter and get early access to news about her latest book! Find Kayla on the following platforms:

www.ingramcontent.com/pod-product-compliance
Lightning Source LLC
Chambersburg PA
CBHW022020310726
48972CB00006B/1733

9798990033214